ALSO BY JESSICA BRODY

Addie Bell's Shortcut to Growing Up

Better You Than Me

I SPEAK BOY

JESSICA BRODY

DELACORTE PRESS

Text copyright © 2021 by Jessica Brody Entertainment, LLC
Jacket art copyright © 2021 by Simini Blocker

Delacorte Press is a registered trademark and the colophon is a trademark of Penguin Random House LLC.

Visit us on the Web! rhcbooks.com

Educators and librarians, for a variety of teaching tools, visit us at RHTeachersLibrarians.com

Library of Congress Cataloging-in-Publication Data
Names: Brody, Jessica, author.
Title: I speak boy / Jessica Brody.
Description: New York : Delacorte Press, [2021] | Audience: Ages 10 and up. | Summary: Twelve-year-old Emmy is struggling to understand boys when she discovers a magic "app" that can read their thoughts, which soon drives a wedge between her and best friend Harper.
Identifiers: LCCN 2020015953 (print) | LCCN 2020015954 (ebook) | ISBN 978-0-593-17368-8 (hardcover) | ISBN 978-0-593-17369-5 (library binding) | ISBN 978-0-593-17370-1 (ebook)
Subjects: CYAC: Best friends—Fiction. | Friendship—Fiction. | Middle schools—Fiction. | Schools—Fiction. | Application software—Fiction. | Cell phones—Fiction. | Single-parent families—Fiction.
Classification: LCC PZ7.B786157 Iam 2021 (print) | LCC PZ7.B786157 (ebook) | DDC [Fic]—dc23

The text of this book is set in 12-point Berling LT.
Interior design by Ken Crossland

Printed in Canada
10 9 8 7 6 5 4 3 2 1
First Edition

FOR CHARLIE (AGAIN),
MY FAVORITE BOY

THE SECRET LANGUAGE OF BOYS

"**HOW TO TELL** if a boy likes you."

I sit up taller, clear my throat, and speak in my most authoritative, official-sounding voice. "'One: You catch him looking at you a lot. Two: He goes out of his way to sit with you. Three: He tries to make you laugh, maybe even making lame jokes.'"

I glance up from my phone to make sure Harper is paying attention. She's sitting next to me on her bed, bent over her sketch pad, green marker in hand, completely absorbed in her latest drawing. She hasn't looked up even once. "Harper," I whine. "Did you hear anything I just said?"

"Mmm-hmm," she says distractedly, which I know is her code for "Sort of."

"It's confirmed. Elliot Phillips totally likes you. It says so right here!" I tap the screen where I have my favorite quiz app open and am reading from a checklist that's supposed to help you decipher the confusing behavior of boys. In my opinion, they don't have *enough* information on this subject. Why aren't there entire libraries filled with this stuff? Why waste time with legal thrillers and true crime stories when *boys* are humanity's greatest unsolved mystery? Or more specifically, the boys at our school. I swear, they're all cryptic aliens from another planet where they speak a completely different language. Sometimes they don't even use actual words. I'm serious. One time, I witnessed Garrett Cole and Jason Sanders have an entire conversation in snorts and grunts. It was utterly baffling. And also really disgusting.

"So," I continue, turning my phone back around. "According to this, it's time to take action. Tonight, I'm making it my mission to get you and Elliot together."

Now Harper does look up. And her face is about as green as the marker in her hand. "What? No. No way. Are you crazy?"

"I'm serious. Harper, you totally like him. And he likes you back. All the signs are there. And . . ." I waggle my eyebrows teasingly. "He's going to be at the carnival. It's the perfect opportunity."

Tonight is Highbury Middle School's first-ever carnival fundraiser. That's why I'm at Harper's house right now. I've assigned myself the job of helping her pick an outfit. She doesn't know this yet, but I've got big plans for tonight. Ever since I heard about the carnival, I've been devising the perfect, foolproof strategy for getting Harper and Elliot together. Now I just have to convince her to go along with it.

"He doesn't like me." Harper shakes her head and returns to her sketch pad. I can't see what she's drawing but knowing Harper, it will be another amazing cartoon. Just like all of her drawings.

"Yes, he does!" I insist, pointing at my phone again. "The proof is all right here. The horoscope app I downloaded last month said your birthdays are a perfect compatibility match. And this quiz confirms it." I scroll back up to the first item on the checklist. "'You catch him looking at you a lot.' Remember the assembly at the start of the semester when we had that boring guest speaker? I caught Elliot looking at you *three* times!"

"Well, the speaker *was* pretty boring. He was probably just dozing off."

I ignore her and scroll down to number 2. "'He goes out of his way to sit with you.' Remember two weeks ago? At the eighth-grade football game? When he practically shoved me off the bench to sit next to you?"

"He got there late, and the rest of the seats were full." Harper caps the green marker and reaches for the red. "And *you* only dragged me to that game so you could 'observe boys in their natural habitat.'" She makes loose air quotes with her fingers.

I harrumph. "I just thought if I went to one game, I could *finally* understand what those football players talk about at lunch."

"Which you still can't."

"'Heisman' doesn't even sound like a real word!" I complain. "It sounds like something you do when someone is choking."

"That's 'Heimlich.'"

"Whatever," I mutter. "It's a stupid game, and—" I stop when I suddenly realize what Harper has just done. She's sneakily changed the subject by getting me all riled up about football. "'Number *three*,'" I say pointedly, returning my attention to my phone. "'He tries to make you laugh, maybe even making lame jokes.' Remember what he said Monday at lunch? 'Why did the scarecrow get an award?'"

"'Because he was outstanding in his field!'" Harper cracks up at the memory of Elliot's joke. She even snorts a little.

"See?" I say. "You think it's funny! You two are totally meant for each other."

"It *was* funny."

I shake my head. "No. It most certainly was *not* funny. I'm sorry, Harper. That joke belongs firmly in the *lame* department."

"Come on, it's a total dad joke. You know dad jokes are always funny."

I grow quiet as a chill settles over the room. Harper realizes what she's just said and claps her hand over her mouth. "Oh gosh, Emmy. I'm so sorry. That was totally rude. I didn't mean—"

"It's okay," I rush to tell her, trying to wave away the awkwardness that has filled the space between us. It's rarely awkward between Harper and me, except when she accidentally says stuff like that. I guess it's hard for someone with a dad to remember that not everyone has one. At least, not one who stuck around. But the best thing about me and Harper is that it never stays awkward between us for long. And even when we do fight—which is hardly ever—we always make up within a day.

"Emmy . . ." She looks like she's going to apologize again, so I cut in.

"It's fine! Don't worry about it." But even as I tell her this, a part of me is just the *slightest* bit worried. Is it possible that I don't get lame "dad jokes" because I didn't have a dad around to tell them? I mean, it's been eight years. I'm totally over it. That box is *closed*. But it's questions like this that niggle at me. That slowly pry open the lid of the box and make me wonder what's inside.

I brush off the feeling with a shake of my head and refocus on my phone. "'Number Four. He goes out of his way to compliment you.'"

"He does *not* do that," Harper says as she returns to her drawing.

"Um, hello?" I switch to the SnipPic app on my phone, click on Harper's feed, and show her the screen. "He's liked almost every single photo you've posted in the past month!"

"That's not the same thing as a compliment," Harper argues.

I grunt in frustration. "It's called a 'like' for a reason. A like *is* a compliment." Why does she have to be so difficult? Why can't she just see what I see? "Harper, there are ten things on this list, and I've been able to check *all* of them. It's time to do something about it. I've been thinking about it a lot, and I have a plan."

Harper's eyes flash to me and I immediately see the panic written all over her face. "No. No plans. No schemes. No 'projects.' We've been over this. Remember in fifth grade your big plan to set up your babysitter with the pizza delivery man? He stepped on one of the fireworks and it singed his eyebrows off."

I lower my phone and sit up straighter. I will not let Harper derail me with reminders of the past. Besides, I've learned a *lot* since fifth grade. And I'm pretty sure no one is going to lose their eyebrows tonight.

"This plan will work," I assure her, and then, when I'm certain I have her attention, I continue. "Okay, so you know our first middle school dance is coming up in a few weeks. Wouldn't it be amazing if you and Elliot could go *together*? Like, as a couple?"

"No." Harper's voice is firm. "Absolutely not."

My face falls. "You mean you don't want to go to the dance with Elliot?"

"I mean I don't want to use one of your elaborate schemes to make it happen. If Elliot and I are meant to be, it'll happen on its own."

I sigh. I can tell it's time for one of my pep talks. "Harper," I begin earnestly, like I'm giving a speech to the entire nation. "This is the twenty-first century. We have cars that park themselves and apps that can do your math homework for you. Right now, I'm in the middle of an online Monopoly game with someone who lives in *France*. You can't rely on destiny anymore. You have to *make* things happen for yourself."

"Or have your best friend do it for you?" Harper asks with a smirk. My pep talks never fail to make her smile.

"Exactly! Think of me as your . . ." I reel my hands around, searching for the perfect title. "*Love Coordinator.*"

Harper snorts. "'Love Coordinator'?"

I give her a proud salute. "Reporting for duty."

She can't help laughing at that, and I feel giddy. Harper has the best laugh in the world.

She plucks a black marker from her case and resumes drawing. "I don't know, Emmy. What if you're wrong? What if he *doesn't* like me? What if the whole thing backfires and I look totally stupid?"

I sigh again. This is so Harper—she can be overly cautious sometimes. Okay, that's putting it nicely. She's a total coward. Me, on the other hand, I like to take risks. My motto is No Risk, No Reward. Harper's motto is Be a Turtle and Keep Your Head in Your Shell and Only Come Out When It's Safe and Always Move at the Slowest Pace Possible.

Okay, not really, because what a lame motto that would be. But that's pretty much how she lives her life. Which is why she's lucky she has me as her best friend. It's the best friend's job to recognize the other person's flaws and help her move past them. And Harper has liked Elliot since the second week of seventh grade. He's the reward. And it's time for her to take the risk.

"You're not going to look stupid. You need to trust me." I scoot to the edge of the bed and hook up my phone to the speaker on Harper's nightstand. I put on one of our go-to "get pumped!" songs and then head to Harper's closet.

As Berrin James, our favorite singer, belts out the chorus to "Every Heartbeat," I riffle through Harper's clothes before plucking a rust-colored corduroy skirt from its hanger and laying it neatly on the bed.

"Okay, I think this with your black-and-white-striped scoop-neck shirt and that denim jacket with the little stars on it would be perfect. Super cute but not trying too hard, you know? Elliot will love it."

"Em."

I look up to see Harper has closed her sketchbook and placed it on her nightstand. Her eyes are now locked on me and she's got this kind of anxious expression on her face. "Yeah?"

"Why are you doing this?" she asks after a long moment.

I turn back to her closet and locate the denim jacket to go with the skirt. "What do you mean?"

"I mean, *'Therefore, fair Hermia, question your desires. Know of your youth. Examine well your blood—'*"

I scrunch up my face. "Huh?"

Harper laughs at my baffled expression. "Haven't you done the homework for Language Arts yet? *A Midsummer Night's Dream*, act one?"

I groan. "Don't remind me."

"It means, think about what you really want and why."

I throw my hands up. "Then why doesn't Shakespeare just say that? Why does he have to be all cryptic about it? Oh, right, because he's a *boy*." I toss the jacket onto the bed. "I'm so failing Language Arts this semester."

"No, you're not," Harper assures me. "But you still haven't answered my question. Why are you going through all this trouble to get me and Elliot together?"

"Because the horoscope app said—"

"No," Harper cuts me off. "Not the app. Why does this matter to *you*?"

I spread the sleeves of the jacket out on the bed and run my fingertips over one of the little white stars. "Because it's *you*," I say, emphasizing the same word. "You're my best friend."

But for some reason Harper doesn't look convinced by my answer.

"Think about it this way," I say, returning to the closet to fetch Harper's black fringe booties. "What's the one thing that I want more than anything in the world?"

"To launch the most downloaded app in history," she says automatically. She doesn't even have to think about it.

"Exactly. And wouldn't you do *anything* to help me accomplish that?"

Harper bites her lip. "I guess so."

"You totally would! Why? Because we're BFFs and that's what BFFs do. We help each other achieve our goals."

"But that's different," Harper argues. "My lifelong goal is not to go to a middle school dance with Elliot Phillips."

I wave this away. "You know what I mean. I want you to be happy. And you've had a crush on him for the past month. It's time to do something about it. It's time to launch that app."

Harper scrunches up her face. "Ew! That's gross!" Then her disgust turns to confusion. "Wait, *is* that gross?"

I tilt my head. "I'm not sure. Maybe?"

We both break into fits of giggles and fall onto our backs on the bed. The song comes to an end and another Berrin James classic comes on over the speaker. When we finally catch our breaths and the room is quiet again, Harper clasps my hand in hers and gives it a squeeze. "When you do launch your app, I get to design all the graphics, right?"

"Of course!" I say with a smile. "I wouldn't hire anyone else in the world."

"Sweet." We stare up at Harper's ceiling, where a giant poster of Berrin stares back down at us, his dark eyes all smoldering, his smile all mysterious, like he has a secret he's keeping from the entire world.

When I peer over at Harper, her brow is crinkled the way it always is when she's thinking hard about something.

"Do you really think he likes me?" she asks in a tentative voice.

I squeeze her hand. "Absolutely."

"He *is* cute," she says, and I can tell she's starting to get excited about the idea. Harper is usually hesitant about my plans at first, but she always comes around eventually. It's just the way Harper is.

She draws in a deep breath. "Okay. What's the plan?"

I stand up and do a celebratory jump-kick on the bed. "Woo-hoo! Hi-ya! Omigosh, it's going to be ah-mazing! You'll see! You and Elliot are so totally soul mates! You're going to kiss and fall in love and get married!"

Harper jumps to her feet and grabs for a pillow, wielding it at my head. "Stop! We are not!"

I dodge the pillow and keep jumping. "And have babies and drive a minivan and grow old together and play dominos in the park!"

Harper makes another swipe with the pillow. "Shut up!"

"Just don't forget to thank me at your wedding!" I stop jumping and breathlessly press my hand against my heart, turning my voice all sweet and syrupy. "'If it weren't for my very best friend in the whole world, Elliot and I never would have fallen in love.'"

Something lights up in Harper's eyes and she hops off the bed and reaches for her sketch pad. "I almost forgot! This is for you." She grabs a marker and quickly scribbles her signature at the bottom of the drawing. Then she rips out the page and hands it to me. I turn the paper over, and my mouth drops open. As predicted, it's amazing. Beyond amazing.

Harper has drawn a cartoon version of me as Cupid, with wings on my back, a bow and heart-tipped arrow in my hand, and a mischievous smirk on my face. All around me are floating red heart bubbles and at the bottom of the page, right next to her signature, Harper has written, "Emerie Woods: Love Coordinator."

"Do you like it?" she asks nervously.

My smile grows to the size of the sun. "I think it's your best yet."

THERE'S AN APP FOR THAT

AS HARPER'S MOM backs out of the driveway, I triple-check that everything is in place and ready.

Tonight's entire plan is dependent on my phone. Good thing I was able to convince Mom to buy me the most upgraded, fastest, fanciest model on the market at the start of this year. But trust me, it wasn't easy. There was a *lot* of groveling involved, in which I swore I wouldn't ask for another phone for five years.

"Are you sure this is going to work?" Harper whispers next to me in the backseat of Ms. Song's car. It's probably the third time she's asked this since I explained my five-phase plan for tonight.

"Don't worry," I tell her in my most confident tone. "It'll work."

The plan is all about getting Harper and Elliot alone together at the carnival. Because I'm convinced if they can just have a moment to themselves, with no one else around and no distractions, *something* will happen. Elliot will confess his feelings. Or ask Harper to be his girlfriend. Or maybe even *kiss* her!

"I don't know," Harper says, sounding way too skeptical. "It all sounds a little . . . *complicated.*"

My shoulders sag in disappointment as I drop the phone into my lap. I kind of expected her to clap and tell me how genius and inspired the plan was. After all, I spent a lot of work on it, researching and plotting and downloading the right apps.

"Trust me, I know what I'm doing." As proof, I pull out the folded-up drawing of me as the Love Coordinator and show it to her.

"What are you girls talking about back there?" Ms. Song asks, darting glances at us in the rearview mirror.

"Nothing!" Harper calls back innocently as I return the drawing to my pocket. We share a knowing look and immediately break into giggles. Harper is definitely excited, even if she doesn't want to admit it. And how could she not be? Elliot Phillips is super cute and smart and he's nice to everyone. Even the teachers love him. He's a total catch!

"Emmy, does your mom know where you are?" Ms. Song asks as she turns onto the main road.

"Yes," I say confidently. "I put it on her calendar app, but I'll remind her again right now just in case." I quickly type out a text message to Mom.

"Good. Because I prefer *not* to see police cars in my driveway again." Ms. Song flashes me a smile in the rearview mirror to let me know she's joking. Well, sort of.

"Me too," I say with a groan, and we all share a laugh at the memory of what happened two weeks ago. I told my mom *three* times that I was hanging out at Harper's after school. But my mom? Well, she can get a little . . . *distracted*. Long story short, she forgot, and when I didn't come home by six o'clock, she freaked out and called the police.

My phone chirps in my lap and I glance down to see a reply.

> **Mom:** Thanks for the reminder! I sent the
> boys over to the neighbors' to watch a movie
> so I can get some work done. The Nagmans
> are killing me! Have fun!

As soon as I read the text, I get a familiar whirling feeling in my stomach. Harper calls it my Tummy Tornado because the only way I can describe it is like a storm swirling inside me whenever I'm nervous about something. Which is a lot of the time.

"Uh-oh," I say, still staring at the screen.

"What's wrong?" Harper asks.

"My mom sent the twins to Grant's house to watch a movie."

"So?" Harper asks. "Just because *you* can't stand Grant doesn't mean—"

"No," I interrupt. "I mean, *yes*, I can't stand him, but that's not why I'm worried. If the twins are next door, it means my mom will be all alone and she'll forget to eat dinner again."

"Should I bring her something?" Ms. Song asks, always so eager to help.

Sometimes I wish Mom's only job was being a mom, like Ms. Song. But it's not. My mom runs her own interior design company, which basically means she makes the inside of houses look good. Lately, her big new client, the Wagman family (or the "Nagmans," as we call them), has been giving her a lot of trouble. No matter what Mom does, they're never happy. I guess it's a good thing Mom loves her job so much. But sometimes I worry that she might love it a little *too* much, because whenever she's working on a big project for a difficult client, like the Nagmans, she kind of disappears.

"I have some leftover lasagna from dinner last night," Ms. Song says. "I could drive it over to your house after I drop you off at the carnival."

"Nah, I got it," I say, already scrolling through my phone to where I keep all the food-related apps. I tap on the Ding Dong Delivery icon and, after a few clicks and a facial recognition scan, presto! A feast of hummus, chicken kebabs, and a Greek salad is on its way to my house.

"It's done," I say as the order confirmation pops up. "My mom is fed."

Ms. Song flashes me another warm smile. "You're a good daughter, Em."

I shrug and turn to face out the window. "She does her best. Sometimes she just needs a little help."

Ms. Song turns left onto Highbury Parkway and the car picks up speed. Harper lives on the far other side of town from school and has to either take the bus or drive. I, on the other hand, live within walking distance.

Which I guess is nice, except when it's cold or raining. But Harper insists it's still better than the bus, which apparently is torture.

My phone chirps again, and I look down to see a notification from my ongoing Monopoly game with Aurélie, my French game-pal. It's my turn. Aurélie must not be able to sleep, because it's the middle of the night in France right now.

Harper glances over at my screen as I roll my digital dice and land on the Electric Company. I hover my finger over the DISMISS button, but Harper stops me.

"No, buy it."

I roll my eyes at her. "You're the only person on earth who buys the Utilities."

She grins at me. "They're my secret weapon."

I click on DISMISS and a moment later a message pops up in the chat box.

Bon choix.

Harper struggles to read the French text in a horrible American accent. "'Bone choycks'? What does that mean?"

I take a screenshot of the chat box and upload it to one of my favorite apps, called iSpeak Everything. It's so cool. You can speak or type or upload photos of text in any language in the world and it will translate it to English. And the other way around. This app is the only reason I'm able to play Monopoly with someone who lives halfway across the world.

"She said, 'Good choice,'" I tell Harper as the English translation appears on the screen. "See? You're the only one who buys the Utilities."

I press the little microphone button in the app and say, "My best friend wanted me to buy it! Can you believe it?" A wheel spins on the screen before the French translation appears and I cut and paste it back into the Monopoly game.

This is why apps are the best. I have an app for absolutely everything: keeping track of my homework assignments, organizing my closet and bookshelf, editing photos, logging how much water I drink each day, storing all my passwords, identifying birdcalls (okay, to be perfectly honest, I haven't exactly *used* that one yet, but it still seems like a good idea to have just in case you're in an emergency situation and everything depends on being able to identify a bird by the sound it makes). I even have an app for keeping track of all my apps!

My phone dings again, and Harper and I both look down. Aurélie has sent the winking-face-with-tongue emoji in response. We burst out laughing. Some things you just don't need to translate.

Ms. Song steers the car off the parkway and into the driveway for Highbury Middle School. I squeal and grab Harper's hand when I see the football field. It's been completely transformed. There are games and food carts and red-and-white-striped tents! It looks like a *real* carnival.

Ms. Song pulls up to the curb and we hop out of the car. A jolt of giddiness shoots through me as the scent of hot dogs roasting and funnel cakes frying hits my nostrils. This is so cool.

Highbury Middle School has never had a carnival fundraiser before, but this year Brianna Brown's mom is head of the PTA and she organized the whole thing. That's another thing my mom will never do. She barely has time to feed herself; I can't see her organizing any school fundraisers anytime soon. I guess it helps when you have two parents in the picture instead of just one.

"Have fun!" Ms. Song calls from the open window. "Text me when you want to be picked up."

"Okay!" Harper calls back as we wave goodbye. We walk under the giant archway that marks the entrance of the carnival and, in the flashing lights of the sign, I catch sight of Harper's outfit. She looks incredible. She's wearing the clothes I picked out for her, and I've braided her long black hair into a side braid and even woven in shimmery pieces of silver thread that make her hair look like it's sparkling. Harper got her hair from her dad, who was born in Korea, and her hazel eyes and fair complexion from her mom, who was born right here in Highbury.

And even though tonight is not about me, I still spent some time selecting my outfit. I'm wearing my favorite pair of frayed skinny jeans with the hole in one knee, a button-down shirt with a long burgundy cardigan, and my black strappy sandals, which are actually a key detail in tonight's plan.

Then, to top it all off, I spritzed both of us with Harper's favorite body spray. It's called Starry Skies, and it smells amazing.

"Are you ready?" I ask Harper, bouncing slightly on my toes as we approach the red-and-white-striped ticket booth.

Harper gives me a thumbs-up. "Ready." But I can tell she's super nervous. She's all jittery and fidgety.

"How about we go over the plan one more time," I suggest. "Just to be safe."

Harper releases a shaky breath. "Good idea."

"Phase One?" I prompt as a group of eighth-grade girls weaves around us to get in line.

"Enter the carnival and locate Elliot." Harper can't even say his name without a small smile sneaking onto her face.

I nod. "Good. Phase Two?"

"Find a quiet, secluded place to hang out."

"And that's where we'll launch into Phase Three. Which is . . . ?"

"Lure him in with the riddle," Harper recites dutifully.

I show Harper the app I downloaded yesterday. It's called The Riddler and I know that it's Elliot's favorite app because I've seen him playing it every day between classes, even though we're not supposed to use our phones at school.

"Once we post the selfie of us totally stumped on one of the riddles, Elliot won't be able to resist coming to help!" I turn off the screen and pocket the phone in my cardigan. "Which leads us to . . ."

She draws in a deep breath, like she's trying to psych herself up for what's coming next. "Phase Four: You fake a wardrobe malfunction and excuse yourself, and Elliot and I will be . . ." She releases the breath. "Alone."

I can't help but beam as she says this last part. It really is the perfect plan. I should win an award or something. *Are* there awards for getting your best friend together with her crush? There should be! It could be called the Love Coordinator Awards, and the statue would be a little golden Cupid holding a bow and arrow.

"And then?" I say with a flirty wiggle of my eyebrows.

"Emmy!" Harper screeches. "Stop with the eyebrows! I don't know what will happen. I can't predict the future."

"I can," I insist. "Phase Five! All systems go! Rocket launch!" I make kissing sounds at Harper until she plants a palm on my face and pushes me away.

"We'll see," she says as she joins the line at the ticket booth. But even in the dim glow of the carnival lights, I can see the hint of a blush on her cheeks.

After completing only half a lap around the football field, I can tell you two things: (1) This carnival is awesome. There are games and yummy-smelling snacks and even a booth where you can throw pies at teachers' faces! And (2) It reminds me of the middle school cafeteria. It's basically all the same groups having all the same conversations, only in a new setting.

For instance, Alexis Dawson, Darcy Cohen, and Isla Lang from the dance team are all in line at the lemonade stand, talking about how many pirouettes they can do in a row. Garrett Cole is at the beanbag toss, showing off to a pack of other seventh-grade football players as he successfully lands beanbag after beanbag in the hole. Brianna Brown is waiting for the photo booth with her friends from the girls' basketball team, talking about their free-throw percentages. And Kyle Bates and his friends are stuffing their faces with funnel cakes while rehashing the latest video from some YouTube channel they all watch called "Dude-Possible." It's been all the rage among the boys in our class lately. I've tried watching it, but it makes absolutely no sense. It's just a bunch of dudes who hang out and blow stuff up.

As we make our way through the carnival, I keep my eyes peeled for Elliot's spiky, dark-blond hair, which, in my opinion, has way too much gel in it. "Do you see him?" I ask Harper, leaning to peer around a clown walking by on stilts.

Harper shakes her head. "Not yet."

We're slipping past the backside of the fake-tattoo booth when I hear someone whisper, "She's not just hot, she's *beyond* hot."

My ears instantly prick up and I angle my body toward the conversation. Four seventh-grade boys are standing next to the cotton candy cart. I recognize the one who spoke as Leo Burns, who has a locker near mine.

"The hottest," agrees a redheaded boy named Victor. "Have you seen those glittery pants?"

"Yes!" Leo says. "They're all I can think about!"

My chest flutters with excitement as I casually glance

around the carnival, trying to find the owner of these glittery pants. If I can figure out who Leo is crushing on, maybe I can work my Love Coordinator magic on *two* couples tonight!

"What? I haven't seen those pants!" whines a boy named Micah Lowenstein.

"They're gold and they have little stars on the butt," Leo explains, practically swooning right into the cotton candy cart.

I keep searching the football field. These pants sound pretty cool. A little much for a school carnival but maybe it's like a circus cosplay thing or something. But for the life of me, I can't find a single person wearing glittery gold pants with stars on the butt.

"I definitely haven't seen those," Micah says. "Where are they?"

Yes, I repeat in my mind. *Where are they?*

"You have to get to level twelve," Leo says. "She starts wearing them when she goes into the dungeon to find the dragon slayer."

Level 12? Dungeon? Dragon slayer?

"Dang it!" Micah says, slamming his fist into his palm. "I'm still stuck in that stupid goblin swamp on level eleven."

The flutter in my chest instantly snuffs out. Are they talking about a video game? The hot girl in the glittery pants isn't even *real?* Why on earth would they waste time talking about imaginary girls when there are *real* girls all around them?

"Dude, trade your Skeleton Stone for the Serenity

Sword," Victor says with authority. "It's the only way to defeat the Goblin King and win the Inferno Potion."

"But the Skeleton Stone is worth more than twenty Zoinks!" Micah protests.

Okay, now they're not even making sense anymore. *Ugh.*

Desperate to get away from this pointless conversation, I tug on Harper's arm and am about to head in the direction of the ring toss game when I feel a strange sensation come over me. It starts in my chest but quickly spreads to my arms and legs. It's almost like a shiver except it's warm and tingly. I glance over my shoulder and that's when my gaze lands on something dark and shimmery in the distance.

I begin to walk toward it, and the closer I get, the more that strange tickling sensation grows. Like the shimmery dark object is tugging at me, drawing me in.

"What is that?" Harper asks, appearing beside me.

"It looks like some kind of lake," I say, squinting.

"In the middle of a football field?"

As we get closer, I see that it *is* a lake. A fake one, anyway. Someone has filled a large kiddie pool with water and set up a bunch of cool blue lights, fake boulders, and shrubs around it to make it look real. There's even mist swirling off the top!

"'The Enchanted Lagoon,'" I read aloud from the little sign posted nearby. "'Where all your wishes come true.'"

"Cool," says Harper.

"It's perfect!" I shriek.

Harper shoots me a puzzled look. "For what?"

"Phase Two! Find a quiet, secluded place to hang out." I glance around the lagoon, which is tucked, almost out of sight, behind the fun house. No one seems to have even noticed it's back here but us. "Quiet," I say, counting on my fingers. "Secluded. *And* romantic! I mean, look at that mist! We couldn't have asked for a better location." I gesture to the sign. "And it's where all your wishes come true!"

I turn back to Harper, but she's not even listening to me. She's staring at something in the distance.

"Harper?" I say, but instead of answering, she grabs my hand and squeezes it so hard, I let out a tiny yelp.

I follow her eyeline until I see what has caught her attention. And suddenly I understand the urgency. Because standing in line at the popcorn cart, in all his gelled-hair glory, is Elliot Phillips.

LOVE COORDINATOR, REPORTING FOR DUTY

"TILT YOUR HEAD a little more to the left," I tell Harper as we squeeze closer together on one of the fake boulders surrounding the kiddie pool. "And hold up my phone a tad higher so that the riddle app is visible. Good."

I angle the camera on Harper's phone and extend my arm out to capture both us and the misty lagoon in the background. Harper and I have taken about a million selfies together, so we're pretty used to the routine. But this one has to be *perfect*.

"Can you look a little more stumped?" I ask.

She narrows her eyes into the camera. "Like this?"

I giggle. "Now you just look constipated. You need to look more *confused*."

"Maybe I'm confused by why I'm constipated!" Harper jokes, because that's what she does when she's nervous. But I still hear the rattle in her voice.

"You need to be confused about the *riddle*. Like this." I twist my lips to the side and make my best "stumped" face into the camera. Harper copies me and I line up the shot. "Yes! Good! Hold it right there."

"Wouldn't it be easier if we just, you know, *talked* to Elliot?" she mumbles through her twisted lips.

"This will work better," I assure her, and start snapping photos, making sure we have lots of choices. As soon as I'm finished, Harper collapses against me as if she's just run a marathon.

"Love coordinating is exhausting!" she says dramatically.

"We're almost there." I swipe through the photo options and scrutinize each one. Harper's expression still looks forced but it'll work. I select the one where the Riddler app is most visible, slap a filter on it, and post it to Harper's SnipPic account with a caption that reads: Riddles are HARD! Can anyone help us?

It doesn't take long for Phase 3 to work its magic. A moment later, we both squeal when Harper's phone dings with the notification that Elliot Phillips has liked her photo. And not two minutes after that, we hear footsteps approaching and look up to see Harper's crush walking straight toward us.

I quickly turn her around and pretend to be all mesmerized by the Enchanted Lagoon.

"Wow. I didn't even know this was here," Elliot says, sidling up next to us. He bends forward to read the sign. "'Where all your wishes come true.'"

"Oh, hey, Elliot," I say, trying to keep my voice casual. "What are you doing back here?"

"I heard you needed help with a riddle," he says with a smirk.

"Maybe you should go work the psychic booth," I tease, flashing him the same smirk.

"Hi, Harper," Elliot says, turning his dimples on my silent best friend.

I nudge her and she chirps out a nervous little "Hi."

"So, you like riddles?" I ask.

"Yeah, I'm pretty obsessed. I actually have the same app."

"No way!" I turn to Harper with an expression of fake shock. "Can you believe that?"

She shakes her head, looking a lot like my grandmother's Chihuahua during a thunderstorm. I try to telepathically send her calming vibes, but she's still as rigid as a block of ice.

Elliot sits down on the boulder next to us and pulls out his phone. "Riddles are kind of my thing. Which one are you stumped on?"

"Uh," I say awkwardly, panic starting to seep in. In all of my elaborate planning, I forgot to *look* at the actual riddles in the app. "The one about the . . . um . . . um . . ."

"Zombies," Harper says quietly, and I glance over again, this time with *real* shock. Has she actually *done* these riddles?

Elliot's eyes instantly light up. "Oh, I did that one yesterday! It's pretty tough, but I can give you some hints." He swipes through the app and starts to point at the little illustrations on the screen. "You see, the trick is, you've got to get the old man across the bridge first. . . ."

But I'm barely listening to what he's saying, because my mind has already moved into Phase 4: Fake a wardrobe malfunction to get them alone.

Making sure Elliot's attention is still distracted by the riddle, I discreetly reach down toward my heel and unbuckle the strap of my left sandal.

"Then, after you get the old man across, you have to focus on the janitor, who—"

"Oh no!" I shout in my most dramatic voice, startling both Elliot and Harper. I gesture helplessly at my sandal. "My shoe strap broke! I better go see if I can find some duct tape or something to fix it."

I'm just about to pop up to my feet and scuttle away, leaving Elliot and Harper alone in this romantic blue-lit lagoon where all your wishes come true, when someone else jumps to their feet.

"I'll get it for you!"

I stare up in disbelief. Harper is standing over me, her eyes wide and her face flushed like she just watched a horror movie. I wonder if, in her nervousness, she got confused about the details of the plan.

"That's okay," I say quickly as I stand up and wobble on my unstrapped sandal. I shoot Harper a pointed look. "*You* stay here. *I'll* go get the duct tape."

"No, I'll go," Harper insists. "You shouldn't be walking in a broken shoe."

What is she doing? Does she not understand the whole purpose of Phase 4?

Elliot can clearly sense some kind of tension in the air because he stands up too and glances nervously between me and Harper. "Um, I can go look for duct tape?" he offers.

"No!" Harper and I both shout at once, causing Elliot to startle and sit back down on the rock.

I make another attempt to convince Harper with my eyes. "Harper," I say gravely. "I'm going to fix my sandal and *you* are going to stay here with—"

But she doesn't even let me finish. She just bolts without another word. I watch in total disbelief as she disappears back into the carnival, running way too fast for me to catch her with my "broken" shoe.

WHAT. WAS. *THAT*?

"Is everything okay?" Elliot asks, but I ignore him and pull out my phone, firing off texts to Harper.

> **Me:** Where are you?
> **Me:** What just happened?
> **Me:** Are you coming back?

Until finally a reply comes that makes my heart sink to the pit of my stomach.

> **Harper:** Sorry. Can't do it. ☹

Lowering my phone, I try to stomp my foot in frustration, but my sandal strap is still unclasped, and I nearly topple over. I can't believe it! She chickened out on me! After all that work and effort and planning, she pulled a total Harper, retreating back into her turtle shell the minute things got scary.

How is she ever going to get together with Elliot if she's not brave enough to be alone with him? A Love Coordinator can only do her job if the participants co-operate!

"Did you two have a fight or something?" Elliot asks, and I nearly startle at the sound of his voice. For a moment, I forgot he was even there. "I can never tell with girls. It's like they fight in secret code or something. I have a younger sister, and I swear she's a whole other species."

I exhale loudly. "No, we didn't have a fight. Harper is just . . ." I pause, trying to figure out how to finish that sentence without betraying my best friend. "She just gets overwhelmed easily."

"I'm sorry!" Elliot says, jumping back to his feet. His eyes are so filled with genuine concern, my heart breaks for him. He's *so* obviously in love with her! "Did *I* overwhelm her? Was it the riddle?"

"No," I rush to assure him. "You didn't overwhelm her. It's just . . ." But once again, I don't know how to finish the sentence. Every possible explanation for Harper's behavior feels off-limits, and I'm dancing around the truth like a bouncy marionette. I wish I could just *tell* him and get it over with.

Harper likes you too! She's just too scared to do anything about it!

Of course, I can't say that, though. I would never say that. Harper is my best friend. I would never betray her trust like that.

But . . .

The word sticks in my head like a piece of gum to the bottom of a desk. An idea is forming in my mind. A backup plan. A Plan B.

I can't directly *tell* Elliot how Harper feels about him, but what if I could get him to *guess?*

If I just gently led him in the right direction with some clever, well-placed hints—like a riddle!—and he came up with the truth all on his own, that would be okay, right? It wouldn't be a betrayal of Harper's trust, but I would still be helping my best friend. I would be helping *both* of them. Because Elliot is still looking at me with those pathetic, lovesick puppy eyes, clearly heart-broken at the thought of upsetting Harper.

"It's what?" he asks, staring expectantly at me.

"Huh?"

"You said 'You didn't overwhelm her. It's just . . . ,' and then you went quiet for almost a minute."

"Oh! Right. Yes." I clear my throat and stand up straighter. I will have to be very careful of what I say. I will have to choose every word precisely. My meaning has to be *implied* but not actually said.

I take a deep breath. "It's just, well, okay, here's the truth. Harper and I didn't actually need help with a riddle."

Elliot's brow furrows. "What?"

"That's not why we posted that picture to SnipPic."

"So you already knew how to solve the riddle?"

I shake my head. "No. We never even looked at the riddle."

"Then why did you have it up on the Riddler app?"

I lean in a little closer to him, trying to catch his eye as I say, "We just wanted you to *think* that we were trying to solve the riddle."

There. That should do the trick. He has to catch my meaning from that.

Elliot gnaws on his bottom lip, looking totally pensive, like he's retracing the steps of the night in his mind. "So was it another riddle you were trying to solve? Was it the one about all the doors?"

My shoulders drop. Really? He still thinks this is about riddles?

I squeeze my phone in my hand, take another deep breath, and try again. "No. We weren't trying to solve *any* riddles. We posted that picture because we know that *you* like riddles. And I thought if we posted a picture of us trying to solve a riddle, then maybe you would . . ." I gesture to the secluded lagoon. "You know."

Elliot stares over my shoulder at the misty blue water. He has this thoughtful, far-off look in his eyes that I *hope* means he's slowly putting the pieces together. I'm not sure how many more hints I can drop.

Then, miraculously, his eyebrows suddenly shoot up and his eyes widen, and he says, "Wait a minute, you posted that picture for *me* to see?"

Finally! I think, silently congratulating myself on a Plan B well executed. But I'm careful not to let any of my excitement show. I need to continue to play it cool. He needs to figure this all out on his own. So I just shrug and casually lower my gaze.

"Because you wanted me to come find you here?" Elliot confirms.

Ding! Ding! Ding! Step right up, ladies and gentlemen. We have a winner!

I lower my head and bite my lip to keep the triumphant smile from taking over my entire face. "I just thought, you know, secluded location, away from the rest of the carnival, Enchanted Lagoon, it's the perfect location for—"

"Totally!" he says, and there's this nervous excitement to his voice. "That's why you pretended to have a broken shoe, right? So you could send Harper away?"

Wait . . . WHAT?

My head snaps up. Elliot is looking at me with sparkling eyes and a knowing smile like he's just solved the riddle of the century.

"Actually—" I start to say, but he cuts me off again.

"I'm so relieved. I thought maybe you hadn't noticed my hints."

"Hints?" I repeat anxiously. My mind is spinning. The Tummy Tornado is in full cyclone mode.

"Yeah," he says with a bashful look. "You know, how I always try to sit next to you. Like at the football game two weeks ago? And how I try to make you laugh. Although, sorry, that scarecrow joke was super lame. And I swore you knew when you caught me looking at you at the assembly during the first week of school."

I want to scream. I want to shout, *No! You've got it all wrong. You're confused. You weren't looking at me! You were looking at* Harper*! You sat next to* Harper *at that football game. You told* Harper *the lame scarecrow joke!* But I can't seem to find any words. My mouth has gone dry. My tongue has turned to stone. All I can utter is a horrified *"Me?"*

"Of course," Elliot says with another shy smile. "Why do you think I've been liking all of the pictures Harper tags you in? I didn't want to like *your* posts because I thought that would be too obvious and I didn't want to seem desperate."

This isn't happening. I feel sick. I think I'm going to throw up in this Enchanted Lagoon. They're going to have to change the name on the sign to "The Vomit Lagoon." I stare down at my feet, trying to figure out what to do. What to say. I was so certain Elliot liked *Harper.* He couldn't have liked me this whole time! He's joking. He has to be. This is some kind of prank.

But then, out of the corner of my eye, I see movement. Something is coming toward me. Something pink and puckered and—OH MY GOSH! They're lips! Elliot's lips are heading straight toward mine! Why are his lips doing that?

"You're right," he whispers dreamily. "This is the perfect location."

My vision finally comes flooding into focus, and Elliot is right there, less than an inch away. His eyes are closed, like he's about to . . .

NOOOOOO!!!!!

I scurry backward, away from his still-puckered lips, but my left heel snags on something and I hear a horrendous ripping sound. It takes me a moment to realize that the thing I've tripped over is my unlatched sandal strap, but by then it's too late. I'm already stumbling, staggering, teetering, arms windmilling as I balance precariously on the edge of the lagoon.

I clutch my phone like it's the lifeline that will save me from this horrific, humiliating doom. But it doesn't save me. Nothing saves me. By the time Elliot opens his eyes and registers what's happening, gravity has taken over. He reaches out to grab me but I'm already falling. Falling, falling, falling. I let out a piercing scream right before hitting the water with an almighty splash.

NO SIGN OF LIFE

QUESTION: HAVE YOU ever fallen into a kiddie pool in the middle of a school carnival? It's about as embarrassing as it sounds. My clothes are drenched. My hair is sopping wet. And the Enchanted Lagoon is no longer the quiet, secluded location it once was. People are arriving by the second to find out what all the splashing and screaming is about.

I scramble to my feet, desperate to get out of this water—which actually kind of smells now that I'm up close and personal with it. Elliot reaches out his hand to help me, but I just scowl back at it. I don't need *his* hand. His hand and his kissy lips and overly gelled hair can stay right where they are, thank you very much.

When I finally manage to step out of the kiddie pool and back on dry land, the first face I see is ironically the last face I hoped to see.

Harper is standing frozen in the center of the gathering crowd. Her gaze is cloudy and unfocused. Her lips are trembling like she might cry. And in one, heart-wrenching, earth-shattering, tornado-launching second, I know that she knows.

She saw and heard *everything.* I can see it in her eyes and her tense posture and in the paleness of her cheeks. I can sense it in the air. When you've been friends with someone for as long as Harper and I have, you just *know* things. She must have changed her mind and come back to the lagoon right as Elliot was . . .

I feel sick again.

I run to her, ignoring the stares and snickers, my clothes and hair dripping water all over the grass. "Harper, I'm sorry. I didn't know—I didn't think . . ."

But my voice trails off when I realize she's not looking at me. She won't even meet my eye. Her gaze is trained downward, at something behind me.

"Your phone," she says, and her voice sounds like it's coming from miles away, not from mere inches in front of me.

"My what—" I turn around and suddenly it feels like I'm falling all over again. My stomach plummets to my knees. My breath catches in my chest. My heart stops.

Because there, beneath the misty blue water, sunken like a brick, is my super-expensive, fanciest-model-on-the-market, costs-more-than-some-people's-rent phone.

"Oh my gosh!" I run back to the lagoon and plunge into the water, struggling to make my way toward the dark object lying on the bottom of the kiddie pool. But the moment I pull my phone out of the water, I know it's not good.

The screen is completely dark. I jab at it anxiously with wet fingers, but nothing happens. I slam down on the reset button and wait, feeling like a lifeguard trying to give CPR to a waterlogged swimmer. But there's absolutely no sign of life.

"What happened?" comes a worried voice. I look up to see Brianna Brown's mom, the head of the PTA, rushing toward the lagoon. "Emmy, are you okay?"

I nod even though it's a huge lie. Nothing about any of this is okay. I broke my phone *and* my best friend's heart all in one night.

"Come on, let's get you dry."

I slowly step out of the pool for a second time and Ms. Brown wraps an arm around my shoulders.

I have to say, for a moment, it feels nice. Comforting, even. The way mom hands are supposed to feel. Then I remember that look on Harper's face and I turn back to where she was standing just a moment ago. But all I see is a blur of movement and her shadow vanishing into the carnival.

Ms. Brown guides me up to the school and into one of the girls' bathrooms, where she makes me stand under the hand dryer for five minutes. When my clothes are somewhat dry, I break away and run back to the football field to find Harper. I have to talk to her. I have to make sure she's all right.

My damp hair attracts plenty of strange looks from people at the carnival, but I ignore them, casting my gaze around for Harper, until I finally spot her standing alone next to the face-painting booth.

"Harper," I say breathlessly as I run up to her. "I'm so sorry. I swore I thought he liked you. I was so certain. I had no idea that—"

"Stop," Harper says, and there's an edge to her voice that makes me flinch. A few of the face painters glance our way. Harper breathes out a sigh, and when she speaks again, the sharpness is gone. "It's fine. I'm fine. It's not your fault, Emmy."

But even as she says this, I can tell she doesn't fully believe it.

I don't fully believe it. Of course this is my fault.

"I texted my mom," she says quietly. "To pick us up."

I nod. "Okay. But do you want to talk about—"

"No," she says in a firm voice, and I know not to push the issue. I can tell she's already back in her shell. And there's nothing I can say to bring her out again.

Less than a half hour later, Harper and I are back in Ms. Song's car, riding in silence. But it's not just my damp clothes that feel strange and uncomfortable. Everything about this car ride feels off. I can't believe that less than a few hours ago we were right here, in these same seats, bouncy and giddy and ready to embark on an exciting night that I was certain was going to change our lives.

Well, maybe the last part was right. I do feel like something has changed. Harper hasn't spoken since we left the carnival. She just stares out the window.

This is so like Harper. She'd always rather draw than talk. But it never bothered me before because I could always read her. I somehow always knew what she was thinking and could say the right thing to make her feel better. It's like she was the pictures and I was the words and together we made a complete story.

But now, for the first time in our five-year friendship, I can't read her. I don't know what she's thinking. I mean, obviously she's upset, but is she upset at me? At Elliot? At the horoscope app that started this whole thing?

"How about some music?" I suggest, because it's the only thing I can think of that might lighten the mood and cheer up my friend.

Harper shrugs but doesn't turn away from the window.

"Good idea!" Ms. Song says brightly. I can tell she knows something is up. The way moms always seem to know. She keeps peeking at us in the rearview mirror.

Because my phone still won't turn on (and I'm trying really hard not to think about that right now), I grab Harper's phone from the seat between us and scroll through her music. I know exactly what to put on. Berrin James has been pumping us up and cheering us up for years, and I keep my fingers crossed that he won't fail us tonight. I find his latest song that just released yesterday and, making sure Harper's phone is connected to the car's stereo, turn up the volume and push play.

A soft piano riff fills the car. Then, a few seconds later, the drums kick in and Berrin's deep, silky voice sings, *"You said, 'Meet me on the corner of Magnolia Street and Yesterday.' Back when we were thieves in the night, before Tomorrow stole you away."*

I've already listened to this song at least twenty-five times since it dropped last night. I think it might be my favorite of his yet.

"Pink-scribbled hearts on the sidewalk, all cracked and faded to dust. Gold-painted stars on the ceiling, but it was never enough."

Berrin finishes the first verse, the drums ramp up, and the powerful guitar comes in, indicating the start of the chorus. I tip my head back and sing along at the top of my lungs, the way Harper and I always do.

"And now I've walked every block and I've roamed every road. I've wandered in circles—"

The music comes to an abrupt halt and I look over to see Harper holding the phone, her finger on the pause button.

"What's wrong?" I ask. "I thought you said you loved his new song."

"I do," Harper says, and then shoots me a sharp look. "I just don't want to listen to a depressing *breakup* song right now."

"Yeah, but it's about Kelsey Kapur, and you know they always get back together."

Harper looks at me like she doesn't recognize my face. "It is *not* about Kelsey Kapur," she says, and her voice is just the slightest bit too sharp. "It's about Julianna Allen, the most devastating breakup of Berrin's life."

I know I have to tread lightly here because Harper is in a fragile state and I can tell she's getting a little too worked up about this, but she's completely wrong.

"No," I say carefully. "It's about Kelsey. The biggest clue is when he says 'thieves in the night.' Because he stole her from Maddox King and a lot of people think that's why his band Summer Crush broke up and why Berrin went out on his own."

"No, Emmy." Harper crosses her arms adamantly over her chest. Her body language is way too strong for a conversation about a song. "The biggest clue is in the bridge, when he sings, 'I looked back and you were *gone*.' He's talking about Julianna getting married to someone else and how he lost his shot with her forever."

"Or maybe, because he's always getting back together with Kelsey, he's saying gone for *now*, but not gone for good."

"For *good*," Harper says, and there's a firmness to her tone that startles me. I shrink into my seat and keep my mouth shut. For the first time in my life, I don't want to talk about Berrin James. It doesn't even feel like we *are* talking about Berrin James anymore. And we've never disagreed on the meaning of his lyrics before.

When Ms. Song pulls up in front of my house a few minutes later, I want to scream, *No! Don't take me home yet! We have to talk about this! We have to work it out! We never fight for long. We always make up right away.*

But that's the problem. This doesn't even feel like a fight. It feels like something else. Some new, uncharted territory. We've ventured into a dark wood and I can't see the path in front of me. And when I look back, Harper is gone.

Just like the lyrics.

I glance at Harper one last time, hoping she'll change her mind and say, "This was silly. I'm being silly. Everything is completely fine. Nothing has changed."

But she doesn't. She won't even meet my eye.

Clutching my dead phone in my hand, I climb out of the car and, in the most upbeat voice I can muster, say, "I'll text you later!" It's not until I reach my front door and let myself inside that I realize I can't even do that.

I stare down and my reflection stares back at me from the dark, water-damaged screen, all sad and desperate and warped. Our friendship suddenly feels a lot like this broken phone. Just moments ago, it was sparkling and illuminating with life. Now there's nothing. And all I can do is hope that both of them will eventually turn back on again.

IN (STINKY) RICE WE TRUST

I ENTER THE house to the sound of yelling in a strange, alien-like language, which can mean only one thing: my brothers are home.

"Stack-o-pack! Gack-i-vack-e mack-e thack-e rack-e-mack-o-tack-e!"

"Nack-o! I hack-a-dack i-tack fack-i-rack-sack-tack!"

I find them in the living room, clearly in the middle of a fight over what to watch on TV. Isaac is standing on the couch, holding the remote high over his head, while Ben tries to grab it from his hand. Evidently, this has been going on for a while, because throw pillows are on the ground and the couch cushions are askew.

"Wack-e-rack-e nack-o-tack wack-a-tack-chack-i-nack-gack thack-a-tack shack-o-wack!" Ben says, making a jump for the remote. Isaac leaps from the couch to the coffee table to get away.

"Mom!" I call at the top of my lungs. "They're doing it again!"

A moment later, my mom walks out of her office with a wireless headset on her head and a cup of coffee in her hand. "No, I told you. I sent that lamp back on the fourth. Today is the nineteenth and my clients haven't seen a refund to their credit card statement yet." She mutes the call long enough to bellow into the living room, "Isaac. Ben. We've been over this. If you can't say something we can all understand, don't say anything at all." Then she's talking into the headset again. "The order confirmation number? Yeah, hold on, let me get it." She disappears back into her office, and the second she's gone, the boys launch into their fight again.

"Back-u-tack-tack-hack-e-a-dack!" Ben snaps at Isaac, which I suppose is an insult, because Isaac looks mortally wounded before anger flashes in his eyes and he shouts back, "Lack-o-sack-e-rack!"

Mom and I have tried to make sense of their alien language so many times. I even recorded them speaking it once so I could try to break it down and search for words on the internet. It's obviously a real language, because they seem to understand each other, but it's a code that Mom and I just can't crack. Neither can the boys' teachers at school. Nor the principal, whose office they've been sent to at least three times in the past month. I've basically just given up.

Ben makes another grab for the remote, but Isaac bounds off the coffee table and starts running around the room.

"Mom!" I call again. I don't have the energy to deal with my eight-year-old brothers and their secret language right now. I have to figure out how to fix my phone so I can text Harper.

Mom pops her head out of her office. "Emmy, I'm kind of in the middle of something."

I point at the war zone that used to be our living room. "I have to look for something on YouTube and Isaac won't give up the remote."

Mom looks at me like *I'm* the one speaking in a non-sensical language. "Why don't you just watch YouTube on your phone?"

"Because . . . ," I start to say but immediately stop myself. There's no way I can tell Mom the truth about what happened to my phone. She'll kill me. Or at the very least, she'll lecture me to death. I'll get all of the greatest hits of Mom's lectures, like: "This is why twelve-year-olds shouldn't have state-of-the-art phones power-ful enough to launch spacecraft." And "When I was your age, we didn't have cell phones and had to write things down on paper and navigate places with our brains." And of course, there's the popular "Your generation is way too dependent on these things."

I've heard them all a million times. And I can't stand to hear another one right now. "Because the battery is dead," I say quickly. I hate lying to Mom, but she's clearly as stressed out as I am right now, and I convince myself that she would appreciate not having one more thing on her plate tonight. Plus, if I can just fix the phone myself, she never has to know that it was broken.

And if I can't . . .

No, I won't even allow myself to go there.

"I'll have to call you back," Mom says into the head-set before taking off after the twins. I can hear screaming at the top of the stairs, which is evidently where World War Remote has ended up. There's a commotion, the stomping of feet, and more whack-a-tack babbles, but finally Mom comes down the stairs victorious. Her hair is a bit disheveled, her face looks a little more tired, but she has the remote in her possession.

"Keep the volume down," she warns as she hands it over. "I have a big meeting with the Nagmans tomorrow, and I still have a lot of work to do."

"Thank you," I say with overwhelming gratitude as I hurry into the living room and plop down on the couch. Sometimes it feels like it's us against them in this house. Girls against boys. It's nights like these that I wonder if Mom really does miss Dad, despite her insistences that she doesn't.

For the next half hour, I watch video after video of people doing all sorts of strange things to their water-damaged phones: shaking them, blow drying them, vacuuming them, strapping them to the hood of their car and then driving on the freeway (Seriously? Who honestly thinks that will work?) until I finally find a video of someone who claims that soaking a phone in a bowl of rice overnight will absorb all the water and fix the problem. I figure it's as good a solution as any.

I turn off the TV and rummage around in the pantry until I find an unopened bag of brown rice gathering dust on a high shelf. Not surprisingly, the expiration date on it is five years ago. Mom isn't much of a cook. She tries sometimes and it usually ends with us eating out or ordering in.

I grab a bowl and the expired rice and carry everything upstairs. After setting my phone carefully down in the bottom of the bowl, I open the bag of rice, instantly gagging at the stench that attacks me. It smells like a boys' locker room . . . *after* gym class. This rice has definitely gone bad. Probably even moldy. Can rice even grow mold? I would ask Google but I kind of need my phone for that.

Unfortunately, though, this rice is all I have.

Burying my nose in the sleeve of my still-damp cardigan, I pour the rice into the bowl until the phone is completely covered. As I stare at the mountain of stinky rice sitting on my desk, my first thought is *What if it doesn't work?*

The only reason Mom agreed to buy me this fancy-pants phone in the first place was because I promised— no, *swore*—that I wouldn't ask for another phone for five years. What if she holds me to that? I can't live without a phone for five years! How will I watch YouTube? Or post to SnipPic? Or edit photos? Or pick out clothes to wear? Or check the latest Berrin James news? Or order food when Mom works late? Or identify the stars in the sky (okay, I admit, I don't actually use that app all too much, but it's nice to know it's there when I need it.)? How will I listen to music? Or watch TV? Or play Monopoly with my French game-pal?

And worst of all, how will I text Harper?

I shut my eyes tight against the spiral of panicky thoughts that are swirling in my mind. I need to calm down. I need to take deep breaths and trust in the universe.

And the rice.

Plink!

My eyes snap open at the sound of something hitting my window. I turn to see my next-door neighbor Grant standing in his bedroom with a number 2 pencil poised in his hand, and groan. Just when I thought my night couldn't get any worse.

Plink!

The second pencil bounces off the glass and falls into the small lawn that divides our two houses. Reluctantly, I walk over to the window and slide it open.

"What do you want?" I mutter. I know I sound totally rude, but I'm sorry, I'm not in the mood to be nice. Especially not to nosy, know-it-all neighbor boys who do nothing but insult me and tell me how I'm living my life all wrong.

Grant leans on the windowsill with the casual air of someone about to give a long-winded speech and I notice he's wearing his painting smock. Behind him, I can just make out his easel set up near the bed.

He opens his mouth to say something but seems to lose his train of thought as his nose scrunches in disgust. "What is that smell?"

I hold up the rice bowl. "This."

Grant squints. "Is that a science experiment or something?"

I shrug. "Sort of. I was at a carnival and I dropped my

phone into an Enchanted Lagoon and now it's dead. I'm trying to bring it back to life."

"That's it?" he asks, and I immediately bristle at his mocking tone. "By the look on your face earlier, I thought someone had *died.*"

"No, Grant. No one died." I glance at my bowl of rice and let out a forlorn sigh. "Except my phone."

Grant makes that obnoxious *tsk* sound with his teeth (that I swear he practices in the mirror every day to get just right). "It's only a phone, Emmy."

I set the bowl back down on my desk with an angry *clank* that shifts the mountain of rice, sending another gust of stinky feet smell into the air. "Well, it was a really expensive phone," I say, hoping that will settle the argument.

But of course, it doesn't. Because this is Grant we're talking about. Nothing settles an argument with Grant unless Grant is the one who said it. He shrugs. "I'm just saying, there are people in the world who don't have a place to sleep at night." He holds out his hands, palm side up, and shifts them up and down, like he's miming a balancing scale. "Sometimes it's helpful to keep things in perspective."

This is exactly why I didn't want to open the window. The last thing I need right now is Grant Knight lecturing me on how to be a better person. I grit my teeth. "Thanks! I'll be sure to keep that in mind."

I shut the window and stomp around my room, trying to shake off the encounter. Talking to Grant always makes me feel anxious and off balance, like I'm walking on two left feet.

When I glance back through the window, Grant has returned to his easel, his paintbrush moving quickly but confidently across the small canvas. The painting doesn't look like much yet, but knowing Grant, it'll be another "masterpiece." I'm not an art critic or anything but I've heard Mom throw around the term "child prodigy" more than once when talking about Grant. I wonder if that's why his parents started homeschooling him in the third grade. Because he was too smart for regular school.

"He certainly thinks he is, anyway," I mutter aloud as I reach for the curtains.

But just before I pull them closed, I remember another piece of artwork.

Harper's.

With a gasp, I reach into the pocket of my cardigan and pull out the folded-up drawing. I had put it in my pocket earlier for safekeeping. So much for that. It's now soggy and sticky in my hand.

Careful not to rip the fragile paper, I unfold it and tears instantly spring to my eyes when I see Harper's drawing of me. Or rather, what's left of it after my little night swim in the Enchanted Lagoon.

The only thing still intact is Harper's signature on the bottom left corner. The rest of it looks like a kindergartner's watercolor project gone bad. The cartoon drawing of me as Cupid has been completely destroyed. I'm now just a smear of color and distorted shapes. And the little heart-shaped balloon floating near the top of the page looks like someone shot one of Cupid's arrows through it, leaving behind a messy, broken heart that's barely recognizable anymore.

I squint at the bottom of the page, struggling to make out the remnants of the words that Harper scribbled next to her signature.

Emerie Woods: Love Coordinator

And suddenly, I'm overtaken by sobs. I collapse on my bed, tears falling onto the page, smudging the colors even more. But I don't care. The picture is already ruined. And it's my fault. I'm not a Love Coordinator. I'm a Love Destroyer. I read the signs all wrong. I interpreted everything wrong.

This is *all* my fault.

No, I think bitterly. That's not true. It's not *entirely* my fault. It's also Elliot's fault. He was the one sending out the cryptic signs to begin with. If boys would just tell you what they're thinking instead of making us guess all the time, this disaster of a night never would have happened. Harper wouldn't be upset. I wouldn't be wearing clothes that still smell like an old kiddie pool, feeling the guiltiest I've ever felt in my life. And I would have a phone that worked.

With a sniffle, I flip onto my side and stare at the bowl sitting on my desk. Somewhere buried under that mountain of brown rice is my phone. Broken, waterlogged, destroyed by the Enchanted Lagoon, where all your wishes come true.

"I wish," I mutter in a hopeless voice, "that boys weren't such a mystery."

And then, somewhere between wishing and crying, I fall asleep, still wrapped in my damp clothes, with the smell of stinky rice wafting through the air.

BOYS SAY THE MEANEST THINGS

THE MOMENT I wake up and see daylight streaming through my window, I leap from my bed and race over to my desk. Plunging my fingers into the bowl of rice, I pull out my phone and, after brushing off a few smelly grains stuck to the side, hold it tightly between my fingers, saying a silent prayer to the technology gods.

Please work.

Then, ever so carefully, with the precision of a brain surgeon, I hold down the power button and wait.

And wait.

And wait.

The phone . . .

Does nothing. The screen stays black. It doesn't chirp or vibrate. It just lies dead and limp and cold in my hands. My heart plummets. The next five years of my life flash before my eyes and they're grim. Grim and dark and phoneless.

And then there's light.

Light?

Light!

The screen is lighting up. It's coming alive. There's a flash of color and there it is! My home screen! My apps! It works!

I let out a whoop loud enough to wake the neighbors and jump off the bed, dancing and twirling around my bedroom with my phone held high over my head.

And apparently, my whoop *was* loud enough to wake the neighbors because when I glance toward the window, I notice Grant is staring at me, dressed in his pajamas, with the oddest expression on his face. He tilts his head in a silent question. I show him my lit-up phone and give him a thumbs-up. He flashes me a smile, which I can tell is totally fake.

Pshhh. He doesn't care about my fixed phone. If it were up to him, nobody in the world would have phones and we'd all be driving around in horse-drawn buggies, talking to each other through tin cans on strings.

Well, I don't care what Grant Knight thinks. I've just witnessed a miracle! A real-life miracle. My phone has been brought back from the dead. I can't stop looking at it and touching it and petting it.

Obviously, the very first thing I do (after I'm finished celebrating) is text Harper. I flood her phone with more apologies about last night and funny GIFs and emoji-filled exclamations about my phone working again. Then I quickly type out:

Me: Meet at my locker before first block like always?

I push SEND and hold my breath. Somehow so much seems to depend on her answer to this little question. When I see the three dots appear, indicating that Harper is texting back, I feel a tidal wave of relief wash over me. Everything is going to be fine. My phone is working. Harper had some time overnight to think and recover. We're back on track.

The phone chirps in my hand and I eagerly glance down.

Harper: Ok.

I frown at the screen. *Ok?* That's all she has to say? No exclamation marks? No emojis? No GIFs? Just "Ok"?

I feel the Tummy Tornado start up again, but I tell myself to take deep breaths and calm down. It's Monday morning. She's probably super busy getting ready for school and didn't have time for GIFs and emojis. I'll see her at my locker and everything will be back to normal.

I'm still staring at my phone when I arrive at Highbury Middle School after walking the seven blocks from home. I just can't believe it's working again. I tested the speaker and the microphone and all the buttons and everything seems fine.

Merging into the hordes of kids getting off the buses, I shuffle toward the front entrance. All around me there's noise and chatter and the sounds of last-minute videos being watched and texts being sent.

"Phones off and put away!" comes the deep, booming voice of Mr. Langley, who's standing guard over the school. Harper and I call him the Gargoyle because of the way his thin strands of hair sometimes stick straight up like horns and because he's always perched on the front steps every morning, watching over us with his beady little gargoyle eyes. "You know the rules."

All around me, kids are groaning and putting away their phones. I'm just about to turn off my own when something on the screen catches my eye and my feet drag to a halt.

I know the layout of this phone better than I know my own house. I've spent hours meticulously organizing it, grouping apps by categories and positioning them on pages based on frequency of use. I could be wearing a blindfold and still find anything on this phone. Which is how I know that the app sitting in the middle of page three is all wrong.

That space is supposed to be reserved for iSpeak Everything, the app I use to translate my conversations with my French game-pal. I know because it's located right next to all my other language-related apps. Like Dictionary and Thesaurus and that app that teaches you how to speak foreign languages using pictures of fruit.

But the app staring back at me is definitely *not* iSpeak Everything. It kind of *looks* like iSpeak Everything. The icon is the same dark blue color, but instead of a picture of a globe in the center, like there used to be, there's a white silhouette. It looks like the same symbol you see on the door to the boys' bathroom at school: a round head sitting above a square body with long tube-y arms and legs.

I squint at the text under the icon and my brow furrows deeper.

What the heck?

As students stream around me, scurrying toward the building, I reread the letters again, certain I must have misunderstood them. But they don't change.

In crisp white text, where it used to say iSpeak Everything, it now says:

```
iSpeak Boy
```

The first warning bell rings, reminding me that I have exactly five minutes to get to first block. But I ignore it. I'm too mesmerized by this mysterious app on my phone. Did iSpeak Everything release a new update that changed the name?

I feel that strange sensation come over me again. The same one I felt at the carnival last night. It's tingly like a shiver but it also feels like something is pulling at me. My finger seems to move all on its own, inching toward the screen, toward that little blue icon. I just have this overwhelming urge to touch it.

Click.

The moment my finger makes contact with the screen, I'm suddenly shoved from behind. I stumble forward. My phone goes flying out of my hands. I manage to catch it just as a boy named Matt Clemens pushes past me.

"Hey!" I shout after him.

But he just turns and calls over his shoulder, "Don't fall into any more kiddie pools!" before laughing and scurrying toward the front door of the school.

My phone lets out a chirp, notifying me of a new alert. It's probably a text message form Harper, asking why I'm not at my locker like we planned. I brush off my annoyance with Matt and hurry toward the steps, prepared to type out a hasty response as I go, but once again, my feet slow to a stop as I peer down at my phone.

The mysterious new app is now open and two little bubbles have appeared—one blue and one green. They're positioned on opposite sides of the screen, like a text message conversation. Except it's *not* a text message conversation. It's something else. Something very, *very* strange.

Matt Clemens

Don't fall into any more kiddie pools!

Translation

She looked at me! A girl looked at me! I think I might throw up.

What is this?

"Dude!" says a voice from behind me, and I look up to see Tyler Watkins and his friends striding toward the entrance, playfully pushing each other and cracking jokes. "Logan, what's up with those pants? They make you look like a giraffe!"

The rest of the boys in the group all crack up. Logan Lansing, who is unusually tall for his age, looks momentarily embarrassed as he glances down at his jeans. They're a bit tattered and scuffed but I definitely don't think they make him look like a giraffe. He jabs Eric Garcia with his elbow. "You mean like the stuffed giraffe Eric still sleeps with?"

All the boys turn and direct their laughter at Eric. "I do not!" he insists, pushing Logan so he stumbles off the sidewalk onto the grass.

"Oh, that's right!" says a tough boy named Ryan Cho, who is known for being mean to everyone, even the teachers. "It's a stuffed zebra."

The boys continue to cackle as they bound up the steps toward the front door. I watch on in complete disbelief. Why are boys so mean to each other? If girls were that mean to their own friends, we wouldn't have friends!

My phone lets out a series of chirps, one after another. It sounds like a room full of birds all trying to talk over each other. *Tweet! Tweet! Tweet! Tweet!*

My gaze snaps back down to my phone as more bubbles start to pop up on the screen. Blue, green, blue, green, blue, green, blue, green.

Tyler Watkins

What's up with those pants? They make you look like a giraffe!

How is it possible that Logan and I are the same age and he's so much taller than me? Will I be this short forever?

Logan Lansing

You mean like the stuffed giraffe Eric still sleeps with?

Translation

Quick! Change the subject before they notice the giant hole in the crotch that my mom *still* hasn't fixed.

Eric Garcia

I do not!

Translation

Don't cry. Don't cry. Don't cry.

Ryan Cho

Oh, that's right! It's a stuffed zebra.

Translation

I still can't believe Mom threw away Sir Stripes-a-Lot. I can't sleep without him!

I feel a strange panicky feeling in my chest. It's like tiny explosions are going off, leaving me slightly queasy and *very* confused. What am I looking at? What's going on? Is this for real?

I scroll back up to the top, desperate to try to make some scrap of sense out of this. But before I have a chance to reread anything, a dark shadow falls over my phone, blocking my view of the screen. My stomach fills with dread. My heart starts to pound. I don't have to look up to know who it is. The shadow is in the exact shape of Assistant Principal Langley.

THE GARGOYLE OF HIGHBURY MIDDLE SCHOOL

"**THE WARNING BELL** has rung, Ms. Woods. What does that mean?"

I gaze up into the cold, stony eyes of Mr. Langley and cringe. "It means phones are off and put away."

"It means phones are off and put away," he repeats with a satisfied nod. "So what is *your* phone doing on and out?"

At that exact moment, my phone lets out another loud chirp, as though it's tattling on me. With shaky hands, I put it on silent mode, turn off the screen, and stuff it into the pocket of my jeans. "Sorry," I say as sweetly as I can.

"I've had my eye on you, Ms. Woods," Mr. Langley says menacingly. "You seem to have an especially blatant disrespect of the Proper Phone Use Policy."

"Sorry," I mutter again, but to be honest, I'm barely listening. I'm too busy thinking about my phone. It's now vibrating like crazy against my hip. What is the deal with that app? It almost seemed like it was . . .

No. I won't even go there. Because it's impossible. I know what apps are capable of doing and it's not *that*.

"You know," the Gargoyle is now saying. "I've been teaching for thirty-seven years. That's three times longer than you've been alive. But this generation, *your* generation"—he points at me and scowls as though I'm the nationally elected representative for my generation— "I've never seen anything like it. You worry me. All of you. With the phones and the apps and the selfies and the GIFs. How are you not *exhausted* already? How do you even have space in those tiny little brains of yours for higher learning? How are you going to get jobs in the real world if you can't communicate with each other face to face?"

Mr. Langley continues to blather on about the downfall of the planet and how it's all my fault. Meanwhile, I'm starting to panic. The final bell is about to ring. I'm going to be late to class. And my phone is still vibrating in my pocket. I'm desperate to look at the screen and try to figure out what the heck is going on.

I tune back into Mr. Langley long enough to hear him say, ". . . in college we had to handwrite all of our essays—in *cursive*!—and now they're not even teaching cursive in schools anymore—"

"Thanks for the pep talk," I say with a bright smile. "I'm super inspired, but I'm going to be late to first block." Then, before he can start up again, I take off toward the door.

"Keep that phone off!" Mr. Langley calls after me.

"I will!" I shout, even though it's a big fat lie. No one at Highbury actually follows the rules when it comes to phones. The administration calls it the Proper Phone Use Policy. We all call it the P-PUP and we only honor it when there's an actual teacher around to see.

The moment I'm inside the building, I head straight toward the nearest bathroom. It's the only safe place in the school to look at your phone without getting caught. But, as I weave through the crowded main hallway, my phone continues to buzz uncontrollably in my pocket. Like a fly being electrocuted over and over again.

"Did you guys see the latest episode of 'Dude-Possible'?" Jackson Harris is asking his friends as they fall into step ahead of me in the hallway.

Bzzzz, goes my phone.

"YES!" cries Cole Campbell, bouncing up and down on his toes. "When Dude-John blew up his girlfriend's perfume bottle? I almost died laughing."

Bzzzz, goes my phone again.

"Most. Epic. Episode. EVER!" agrees Lewis Wright. "Definitely my favorite."

Bzzzz.

"Don't say anything else!" Kyle Bates shouts. "I haven't watched it yet. My brother got *another* award at school last night and the whole family had to go watch him receive it." He rolls his eyes. "I mean, seriously, stop being so smart so I can have a life!"

Bzzzz.

They all crack up. Mitchell Valentine stops walking and turns around. "Ewww! What is that smell?" He wrinkles his nose, and for a moment I panic, thinking he's talking to me. But instead, he turns to Cole with a disgusted look on his face and says, "Dude, did you rip one?"

Thankfully, the girls' bathroom is right in front of me. I hold my breath to avoid the smell and make a mad dash to it, slipping inside just as the final bell rings and my phone lets out one last *bzzzz*. It isn't until I'm safely behind the door of the last stall that I finally dare to take my phone out of my pocket.

The strange app is still open, and a slew of new blue and green bubbles have popped up onto the screen.

Jackson Harris

Did you guys see the latest episode of Dude-Possible?

Translation

If I get them talking about the show, no one will find out I spent the night watching Berrin James videos instead.

Cole Campbell

YES! When Dude-John blew up his girlfriend's perfume bottle? I almost died laughing!

Translation

I love the smell of girls' perfume. There's a girl with a locker near mine who wears the most amazing perfume. It smells like heaven.

Lewis Wright

Most. Epic. Episode. EVER! Definitely my favorite.

Translation

I can't believe my mom still won't let me watch it! She's so annoying!

Kyle Bates

Don't say anything else! I haven't watched it yet. My brother got *another* award at school last night and the whole family had to go watch him receive it. I mean, seriously, stop being so smart so I can have a life!

Translation

I will never be as smart as my brother. Why did my parents even bother to have me if they already had the perfect son?

Mitchell Valentine

Ewww! What is that smell? Dude, did you rip one?

Translation

Whoops. I just farted.

My heart is pounding so hard in my chest. My mouth is as dry as sand. My hands are gripping the phone so tightly, I fear I might break it again.

This can't be for real. It just can't. It has to be some kind of joke. A hoax. There's a hidden camera watching me somewhere and the video is going to go viral on YouTube and get a gazillion views and I'm going to be invited onto talk shows where stiff-lipped hosts in expensive suits ask me questions like "And you never thought that it might be a prank?" And I'll say, "Well, Patricia, I did have an inkling. . . ."

And yet, I can't tear my eyes away from the screen. I can't stop reading. That is, until I scroll up to the next message.

Assistant Principal Langley

The warning bell has rung, Ms. Woods. What does that mean? It means phones are off and put away.

Translation

It means only six more hours until I can get the heck out of here, go home, and soak in a luxurious bubble bath.

Ewww! Yuck! Gross! Ick! Noooooo!!!!!
The Gargoyle in a bubble bath? That is a mental picture I will *never* get out of my head for as long as I live. Gagging, I fumble for the power button and plunge down hard, not daring to release my finger until the screen is dark.

MYSTERY AT THE GUIDANCE COUNSELOR'S OFFICE

AS SOON AS the bell rings at the end of Social Studies, I head straight to Brianna Brown's locker. Thankfully, she's there, talking to her basketball team friends. I pull her aside and, ignoring the freaked-out look on her face, immediately launch into the question that has been racing through my brain ever since I left the girls' bathroom.

"Do you know anything about the Enchanted Lagoon?"

She glances over her shoulder, like she's looking for someone to rescue her from this weirdo who's kidnapped her from her friends. "Huh?"

"At the carnival last night," I clarify. "There was something called the Enchanted Lagoon. My phone fell into it."

"Didn't *you* fall into it?" she asks, doing a terrible job of hiding her smile.

I roll my eyes. "Yes, but that's not the point. Your mom was in charge of the carnival, right? Did she tell you anything about the lagoon? Anything weird or strange or, I don't know, maybe *mysterious*?"

"It was just a kiddie pool," Brianna says, like I'm too dense to have figured that out on my own.

"I know. I just—" I sigh. I can't tell her what I'm really thinking. That something strange happened to my phone when I fell into that water. Something to do with that sign next to the pool that read, "Where all your wishes come true."

A shiver passes over me.

Brianna shrugs. "All I know is she picked up the kiddie pool from some garage sale and it broke." Her mouth twists as she attempts to hide another smile. "After *someone* fell into it."

Great. So not only am I the girl who fell into the kiddie pool at the carnival, I'm also the girl who broke it. "Thanks," I mutter to Brianna as she walks back to her friends. Although I don't know why I'm thanking her. She was no help at all.

I have to talk to Harper. She'll help me figure this whole thing out. I'll show her the weird app and then she can tell me what she thinks. Or maybe she'll just tell me I'm losing my mind. Which very well might be the case.

Unfortunately, though, today is an Even Day. We only have blocks 2, 4, 6, and 8, which means I don't have any classes with Harper. We only have one class together this semester: Block 1, Computer Science. It's a cool elective where you get to learn how to build websites and apps. But we almost didn't even have that together. Thankfully, Harper decided to transfer in at the last minute.

On Even Days—because our classes and lockers are so far apart—I usually only see Harper before school, after school, and at lunch. And since I missed her at my locker this morning, I have to wait until the middle of the day to talk to her.

Finally, when the bell signaling the end of fourth block rings, I leap from my chair and race out of the classroom.

It's pizza day in the cafeteria, and I pay for my food and grab two seats at our usual table in the back, positioning my tray in front of the second seat to save it for Harper. As I take small bites of my pizza, I keep my eyes glued to the cafeteria door, waiting for Harper to make her entrance so that I can wave her over.

Students are pouring in by the bucketload, sliding into seats and blabbing about their day. It isn't until my teeth sink into crust that I realize I've already finished my first slice of pizza and Harper still isn't here. That's strange. Her fourth-block classroom is closer to the cafeteria than mine. What's taking her so long?

I swivel my gaze around the room, just to make sure I didn't miss her. But I don't see her anywhere.

"Excuse me," I say, tapping the shoulder of the dark-haired boy sitting behind me at the next table. "Have you seen Harper Song today?"

I don't even realize who the boy is until he lifts his head and turns to face me. I suppose I should have recognized the tattered green notebook open on the table in front of him. If I had, I wouldn't have bothered asking. I'm definitely not getting an answer out of *him*.

Robby Martinez's intense brown eyes settle on mine, and for a moment, I actually wonder if he's going to speak to me. If I'm going to hear his voice for the first time ever. But then he breaks away, shakes his head, and returns his attention to his notebook.

Robby only moved to our town two months ago, but in those two months, I've never seen him without that old green notebook. He's almost always scribbling in it. And I've never heard him say a single word to anyone.

For the first week of school, Harper was kind of intrigued by him. She might even have had a little crush on him. But that ended the moment she found out that Elliot Phillips liked her.

Or so I thought.

The memory of Elliot's pursed pink lips moving toward me pushes its way into my mind, and I shudder. At least I've successfully managed to avoid him all day. And I don't think he's going out of his way to talk to me either. I think it's best if we both just go about our lives, pretending last night never happened. Thank goodness we don't have any classes together.

Robby continues to scribble in his notebook, and I casually lean in to try to steal a peek at the page. I'm not sure what I expected to see—poetry, fan fiction, the same three words written over and over again—but I definitely didn't expect *that*. To my surprise, they're not scribbles at all.

Coming to life on a clean white page is a drawing of an old man, done entirely in black pen. But if I didn't actually see the pen in Robby's hand, I would have thought it was a black-and-white photograph. It's *that* good.

Robby is working on the man's eyes, and I can't help but notice they look haunted and full of sorrow, which makes me wonder if Robby is drawing someone specific or someone from his imagination.

I'm so mesmerized watching his hand move skill-fully across the paper, I don't even realize that lunch has come to an end until the bell rings, startling me out of a trance. I glance down at my half-finished tray of pizza and the still-empty seat beside me and the Tummy Tornado instantly starts to pick up speed.

Where is Harper?

Did she go home sick?

Did she even come to school at all?

Deciding to investigate the situation, I drop my tray at the dishwashing station and make my way toward the front office.

"Hello," I say when I reach the receptionist's desk. "Do you know if Harper Song left school early today?"

Ms. Watts glances up at me and then down at the clipboard in front of her. Her huge glasses nearly take up her entire face, making her look like a distorted bug. "I don't have her on the signout sheet."

"But she wasn't in the cafeteria at lunch, and—"

My words are cut off when, behind the receptionist desk, a door swings open and Ms. Jenkins, the guidance counselor, steps out. "I'm glad you came to me with this," she's saying to someone still inside her office. "I'll get it taken care of."

A moment later, to my great shock and disbelief, Harper walks out of the office, looking like she's been crying. Her eyes are all red and puffy, and she has a balled-up tissue in her hand.

The guidance counselor reaches out and gives Harper's shoulder a quick squeeze. "Don't worry, sweetie. It'll be okay. We'll get everything sorted out."

I stare at the exchange in complete bafflement. What is Ms. Jenkins talking about? What will be okay? What will get sorted out?

"Thank you," Harper says with another sniffle.

"You're welcome," replies Ms. Jenkins before returning to her office.

Harper turns toward the receptionist's desk and I can clock the very second she notices me standing there because she freezes, looking like an animal caught in the headlights of a fast-approaching car.

"Hi," I say, trying to sound bright and not at all like I just overheard her talking to the school guidance counselor. "I was coming to look for you. You weren't at lunch."

She squeezes the tissue in her hand. "Oh, yeah, sorry. I had to come talk to Ms. Jenkins about . . ."

I hold my breath, waiting for her to finish. But she never does. She just mutters, "Never mind," and continues out of the office.

"Harper, wait." I jog to catch up with her. "It's okay. You can tell me. Is something going on? Are you having trouble in one of your classes?"

She shakes her head. "No. It's nothing. It's not important. We should get to sixth block."

I can tell she's about to run away from me again, so I grab her arm to stop her. "Wait."

To my surprise, this time, she does. She turns toward me but for some reason won't meet my eye.

"Um." I fumble for something to say. But this is so new and unfamiliar. Since when do we keep things from each other? "I'm sorry I didn't meet you at my locker this morning. The Gargoyle stopped me and lectured me about the P-PUP but, oh my gosh." I glance over both shoulders for eavesdroppers before lowering my voice to an excited whisper. "I have to show you this new app I found on my phone this morning. It's the weirdest thing. I know it sounds completely bonkers, but I'm pretty sure the app—"

"I should get to class," Harper says, sounding rushed and slightly impatient. "I don't want to be late."

My entire body feels like a balloon that someone let the helium out of and now all it can do is sink and spiral helplessly to the ground. "Oh. Okay. But how about you come over after school today? I can show you then. Seriously, Harp, you're *not* going to believe this app. It's called iSpeak—"

"I can't," Harper says, cutting me off again. This time her voice isn't just a little impatient. It's downright dismissive.

I try to ignore the violent winds churning in my stomach. "Why not?"

She fiddles with the used tissue in her hand before suddenly seeming to remember that it's there and tossing it in a nearby trash can. "I have a lot of homework."

I don't have to be the school guidance counselor to know that's a lie. Something is going on with Harper. Something is not right with her. With *us*. I know it has to do with last night, but how can I fix it if she won't even talk to me?

My shoulders fall. "Okay."

The warning bell rings and Harper flashes me a hurried smile. "Maybe we can hang out later in the week?"

"Okay," I echo flatly, because for some reason, I can't bring myself to believe her.

BUBSYLAND AND THE REPUBLIC OF NICEASAURUS REX

I **WALK HOME** from school the way I came, with my head bent over my phone. Except this time, the screen is dark. My phone is still off from when I powered it down in the bathroom this morning. The whole way home, I stare at it, fingertip poised on the power button, trying to build up the nerve to turn it back on.

I try to convince myself that what I witnessed earlier was just my imagination. The stress of what happened at the carnival last night clearly went to my head. That's all. As soon as I turn it on, I'll see that it's just a normal phone that does *normal* things.

Then why can't I turn it back on?

BAM!

I'm so absorbed in my thoughts and what might be lurking behind my darkened screen, I don't even notice Grant standing on the sidewalk in front of me until I crash right into him and nearly fall onto my butt.

"Sorry," I mutter, trying to regain my balance.

"We should put some blinking hazard lights on you or something. You're clearly a danger to the road with that thing." He nods to the phone still clutched in my hand and flashes me that annoying, know-it-all smirk of his. It's like he thinks he's ten steps ahead of everyone else and is just waiting for us all to catch up.

My face flushes with irritation. "Look, I said I'm sorry."

Grant throws his hands up in the air like he's surrendering to me. "I was joking! You know, because you crashed into me."

"Yeah, I get it. Very funny." I don't have the energy to deal with Grant's sarcasm today. "And now comes the part where you give me a lecture about how dangerous it is for me to be looking at my phone while I walk. Or tell me some statistic you learned from a documentary about the number of phone-related accidents there are each year."

Grant's brow furrows. "I wasn't going to say that."

I cross my arms over my chest. "Yeah, but I'm sure you were thinking it."

"Hey, this is neutral territory, remember? I would never break the laws of international waters."

I squint at him like he's gone out of focus. "What?"

He points at the ground and I glance down to see we're standing on the grass that divides our two houses. Because Grant and I both live at the end of Hartfield Circle, our driveways fan out from the cul-de-sac like spokes of a wheel, creating little triangular patches of grass between them.

"International waters," I repeat as a memory starts to bubble up in my mind. "Oh yeah. This was the safe zone, right?"

"No one could be tagged here." Grant reminds me of

the rules we established when we were kids. "Because it was neutral territory between Bubsyland and the Republic of Niceasaurus Rex."

"That's right!" I chuckle as the rest of the memory comes rushing back. When Grant and I were seven, we decided to create our own countries and name them after our favorite stuffed animals. I named mine after my rabbit, Bubsy, and he named his after his stuffed dinosaur.

"Wait," I say. "Why did you name him 'Niceasauraus Rex' again? Something about T. rexes being given a bad rep?"

"They can't *all* be evil!" He starts to get all passionate, just like I remember him doing when we were kids. "I was convinced there had to be at least *some* nice T. rexes out there."

"Yeah, sure," I say with a teasing smile, and for a moment, it's nice to escape back to the past. Back to those days when Grant and I were friends. Before his parents pulled him out of school and started homeschooling him. Before Harper moved to town and became my new best friend.

The smile instantly fades from my face as soon as I think about Harper. Grant must notice because he asks, "Is everything okay?"

And just like that, I'm back from the past. Back in the present, where things are all wonky and nothing makes sense. I sigh. "Not really, no." And then, when it's obvious Grant wants me to continue, I add, "It's been a really weird day. I don't want to talk about it."

He nods like he understands, and I glance back down

at the ground, where I notice Grant's shoes are speckled with paint.

"If you want my advice . . . ," he says after a moment, and I swear if he tells me to watch a documentary about surviving middle school, I will throw something at his head. But to my surprise, he says, "Trace the problem back to the beginning."

"Huh?"

"Every problem has a cause, right? Every crack has to start somewhere. If you can trace it back to the beginning, maybe you can fix it."

Just then, a car pulls into Grant's driveway and Dev Thakkur jumps out of the passenger seat. Dev and Grant have been friends for almost three years now. They met at Ping-Pong Club in the next town over where Dev goes to school. I've watched Dev get dropped off at Grant's house countless times, which is why I immediately notice the difference in his appearance the moment he gets out of the car. He's still the same tall, lanky, dark-haired, dark-skinned boy with braces, but he looks really tired today. Almost drained. Like he didn't get enough sleep last night. His shoulders are sort of slouched, his hair is tousled, and he has faint shadows under his eyes.

I'm about to ask Grant if everything is okay, but before I can say anything, he blurts out, "Sorry. I gotta go." Then, without another word, he steps out of the "safe zone" and runs toward Dev like he's eager to get away from me.

I watch as Grant throws an arm around his friend's shoulders and guides him up the front steps of his house.

Something is definitely going on with Dev, but I have my own problems to deal with right now.

Spinning on my heels, I clutch my phone in my hand and head up my driveway. But a second later, Grant's voice calls out behind me, "Be sure to watch where you're going! The National Safety Council reports that over two hundred thousand people fall into trash cans every year from walking and looking at their phones!"

With a snort, I turn and yell back, "Thanks for the warning!" before we both disappear behind our separate front doors.

The house is quiet when I enter. I remember Mom telling me last night that she had a big meeting with the Nagmans today, so she's probably still there and the twins are probably in After School until she can pick them up.

It's not unusual for me to be on my own since Mom is a single parent. I used to go to After School with the twins, but when I started middle school last year, I convinced my mom I could stay home alone for a few hours. I'm just not allowed to cook, have friends over, leave the house, use sharp knives or matches, or open the door to anyone.

There's a grocery delivery on the front porch. I carry it in and put everything away so Mom doesn't have to deal with it when she gets home. I'm sure her meeting with the Nagmans is going to be super stressful because . . . well, they're the Nagmans.

After setting my phone down on the kitchen table, I scour the pantry for a snack and find one serving left of Isaac's favorite cereal. I pour it into a bowl, drown it in milk, and eat it standing up at the counter.

Five minutes later, I'm putting my empty bowl in the dishwasher when the garage door slams open and the house is instantly filled with noise and activity. The twins charge into the kitchen like two wild stallions let loose in a museum, dropping bags and lunch boxes on the ground, banging open cabinets and the refrigerator door in search of food.

There's a clacking of heels on the hardwood floors and I hear my mom call out from the next room, "Don't eat too much! We're having dinner in a few hours!"

"I-mack hack-u-nack-grack-yack!" shouts Isaac.

"I-mack stack-a-rack-vack-i-nack-gack!" Ben shouts back.

Mom appears in the kitchen, carrying about a thousand shopping bags filled with throw pillows, knick-knacks, and carpet samples. She drops everything onto the floor with a clatter and a humongous sigh. I can already tell the meeting with the Nagmans did not go well. When does it ever?

"Dack-o-nack-tack tack-o-u-chack mack-yack crack-a-cack-kack-e-rack-sack!" Ben says to Isaac with a glare in his eyes.

Mom collapses into a chair at the table and pushes her fingertips into her temples. "Boys! English! *Please.*"

"I dack-o-nack-tack e-vack-e-nack lack-i-kack-e thack-o-sack-e crack-a-cack-kack-e-rack-sack!" screams Isaac, blatantly ignoring her. He climbs onto one of the counters to reach the cabinet and pulls down a cereal bowl.

Mom looks like she's about to cry.

I glance over at my phone still sitting on the kitchen table and suddenly that same weird feeling is back. That pulling sensation. Like a magnet tugging at me. I take a step closer to my phone. I can feel that strange app taunting me from behind the darkened screen, daring me to turn it back on.

It was probably nothing.

Just my imagination.

Right?

I guess there's only one way to find out.

I press the power button and watch the screen illuminate. As the phone boots up, I wonder if it will even still be there. If the app will have magically transformed back into iSpeak Everything. Just a harmless translation app.

The home screen appears. With shaky fingers, I swipe to the third page.

And there it is.

The little blue icon with the white stick man stares back at me. And the text underneath blazes like a white-hot sun.

iSpeak Boy

I click on it. The app opens just as Isaac stomps his foot in front of the pantry and shouts, "Whack-o fack-i-nack-i-shack-e-dack mack-yack cack-e-rack-e-a-lack?"

And I watch in utter disbelief as a little green bubble appears on the screen.

Translation

Who finished my cereal?

My mouth falls open. I stand paralyzed and speech-less, staring at those words. This can't be happening. This can't be real!

Then, slowly, dazedly, I look up from my phone and in a loud, clear voice say, "I did. I finished your cereal."

It's a good thing the empty bowl Isaac is holding is plastic because it slips from his hand and clatters to the ground. In that moment, as I watch him share a look of disbelief and betrayal with his brother, the last shreds of doubt finally slip from my mind. And I know.

Something *did* happen to my phone when I fell into that Enchanted Lagoon. Something magical.

Where all your wishes come true . . .

I made a wish last night. When I was waiting for the rice to dry out my phone, I said, "I wish that boys weren't such a mystery."

My mind is spinning. I can't begin to understand what's happening right now and I'm not sure I even want to try. All I know is that this thing is real. It works.

It's impossible. It breaks all the laws of nature. But it's real. iSpeak Boy is still a translation app. But now it's a translation app for *boys*!

LOVE COORDINATOR, BACK IN ACTION!

THE NEXT MORNING, I get to school early and walk into the building with a new attitude. A new outlook on life. And a whole new plan. It feels good to have a plan again. It feels good knowing that, in my pocket right now, is the key to saving my friendship.

Last night, after convincing my panicked brothers that I didn't actually crack their secret language, but simply made a lucky guess about what Isaac was saying, I excused myself from the kitchen and ran straight to my bedroom. I sat on my bed for what felt like hours, staring at Harper's distorted, waterlogged drawing of me as the Love Coordinator, thinking about what Grant said earlier. How every crack has to start somewhere. And if you can trace it back to the beginning, maybe you can fix it.

This weirdness between me and Harper started because of Elliot Phillips. I thought he liked Harper. But I was wrong. And it broke her heart. That's what caused the crack in our friendship. Because I misread Elliot. Mis*understood* him.

But now I have a phone that magically reveals what

boys are thinking, making it impossible to misunderstand a boy ever again. If I can find a new boy for Harper— a new (and *better*) match—maybe I can mend her broken heart.

Rounding the corner of the main hallway, I position myself strategically across from Harper's locker. My phone is hidden inside my copy of *A Midsummer Night's Dream*. The screen is on. And the iSpeak Boy app is open and listening.

I've determined, after secretly using it a few more times on my brothers at dinner, that the app only works if a boy is speaking aloud. It listens to what the boy is saying and then translates that into what he's actually thinking. In other words, it's a dream come true! It's the secret to the universe. To world peace. To everything! No more guessing about what's going on in a boy's head. No more studying and analyzing and reading countless articles about decoding their thoughts. This app does it all!

Now all I have to do is listen to what the boys in my school are saying and the app will reveal if any of them have a crush on Harper. It's the perfect plan!

The hallway gradually starts to fill with people, and I hold back a giddy yelp as little blue and green bubbles start to pop up on my screen. I feel like a private detective in an old movie. I should have a cool trench coat and a matching hat!

A group of seventh-grade boys walks toward me and I slink back behind a bank of lockers so they won't notice me eavesdropping.

Jason Sanders

Have you seen Brianna Brown's face this morning? She has a zit so big, it looks like NASA landed a Mars rover on her forehead.

Translation

Am I getting a pimple? Please don't let that new freckle I found in the mirror today be a pimple.

Liam Cruz

I know! It's like, wash your face already!

Translation

I don't think that expensive acne wash my mom bought is working. And it smells like my dog's butt. I hope no one else can smell it.

Josh Gleeson

Or put some makeup on it or something! Why do we all have to suffer?

Translation

Can anyone tell I'm wearing my sister's concealer to cover this zit on my nose?

I stifle a giggle as they continue down the hallway. And I thought *girls* were paranoid about pimples!

Another group of boys approaches, and I raise up my

copy of *A Midsummer Night's Dream* to make it look like I'm highly engrossed in the play.

Ian Burke

Did anyone do the assigned reading for science?

Translation

Did I remember to change my underwear today?

Jeremy Mason

No, I totally forgot. Ms. Marshall is going to ream us.

Translation

What's my locker combination again? Is it 23-22-19 or 22-23-19?

Cole Campbell

I tried, but I practically fell asleep. I mean, who cares about cell membranes anyway?

Translation

There's that smell again. It's so heavenly, I have to find out whose perfume that is.

Archie Evans

Yeah, like we're ever going to use that in real life.

> If I get to the boys' locker room early enough, can I change into my gym clothes without anyone else seeing?

This is, hands down, the most useful, informative app I've ever had. It's even better than that app that does your math homework for you (not that I've ever used that).

I mean, this information has got to be worth millions of dollars! I'm pretty sure every girl at school would *die* for an app like this.

Which is exactly why I have to be extremely careful not to let anyone see it. I can't tell a single soul about it. Not even Harper. The ability to read boys' minds? Imagine if that power fell into the wrong hands. It could bring about the end of the world.

No. This has to be a secret. *My* secret.

I hear a locker door slam closed, and I look up from my phone to see a familiar head of shiny, dark hair bobbing down the hallway. It's Harper! I run to catch up with her but freeze when I realize she's walking the wrong way.

Today is an Odd Day, which means we have first block together. But the Computer Science classroom is the other way. Did she get the days confused?

I slip my phone into my pocket and my copy of *A Midsummer Night's Dream* into my backpack and start to follow Harper down the blue hallway. It's not really blue. Everyone just calls it the blue hallway because that's the color the hallway is on the map they give to all the sixth graders on orientation day. The longer I trail behind

Harper, dodging people and ducking around corners, the less I feel like a cool private detective and more like a creepy stalker. But I have to figure out where she's going.

She heads up the stairs and turns left down the purple hallway. I stay close behind, trying to blend into the crowd in case she turns around. All the while, with each group of chattering boys that I pass, notifications from the app are going off like little fireworks in my pocket. I'm so tempted to stop and look, but I force myself to focus on Harper.

I wonder if she's just coming up here to use the bathroom. The first-floor bathrooms are always crowded in the morning. But then I see her turn left into a hallway I've never been down before. I don't even remember what color it was on the orientation map. I stand at the corner and watch her, worry growing in my stomach. The first-block warning bell is going to ring any minute. She's going to be late to Computer Science. Mr. Weston might be the coolest teacher in school, but he's still not above giving out late slips.

With a huff of frustration, I start off down the hallway, weaving through clusters of mingling students and teachers monitoring the hallways.

Finally, Harper darts into a classroom and I pull to a stop and stare at the little black label affixed above the door.

ROOM 220—ART

Art?

What is she doing here? I mean, yeah, she's a great artist, but why isn't she in Computer Science?

Concealing myself behind the open door to the class-room, I peer inside and watch as Harper hands a yellow slip of paper to the teacher. My chest fills with a heaviness that feels a lot like dread.

Those yellow slips are transfer slips.

Suddenly, I remember what I overheard yesterday outside the guidance counselor's office.

"I'm glad you came to me with this. . . . I'll get it taken care of."

That's what Harper was meeting with Ms. Jenkins about? Transferring into Art class?

I can't help but think that this is not just about Harper wanting to take Art. This is about her wanting to get away from me. Computer Science was the one class that we had together and now Harper is no longer in it. The heaviness inside me spreads. It feels like someone is standing on my chest and I can't breathe. Tears prick the corner of my eyes and I turn around, preparing to run so no one can see me cry. The number one rule of middle school is no one sees you cry!

But I stop when I realize someone has been watching me. I jump at the sight of the boy in dark jeans and red T-shirt standing across the hallway with a tattered green notebook tucked under his arm. It's Robby Martinez. He's just staring at me. At least I *think* he's staring at me. It's hard to tell because his dark, shaggy hair is so long it covers his eyes.

Looks like I'm not the only creeper stalker in the building today.

Why is he just standing there, watching me like that?

The answer, I know, is sitting in my pocket. The iSpeak Boy app is still running on my phone, and if I can just get Robby to talk, I can use it on him. The problem is, I've never heard Robby talk to anyone, but I suppose it's worth a try.

I paint a smile on my face and, in a friendly voice, say, "Hi, Robby. Did you want something?"

He seems to startle at the sound of his own name, looking like a frightened rabbit who's been cornered.

I widen my smile and try again. "How are you today? Are you in this class? Are you an artist? I saw one of the drawings in your notebook. It's really—"

I was going to tell him it was good, but before I can finish the compliment, he scuttles into the Art classroom, casting me an angry look as he passes.

What did I say?

I watch as he sits down next to Harper and opens his notebook. Harper already has her sketch pad out and she's doodling on a fresh page. I feel a stab of something I can't identify as I notice how content she looks. The way she always looks when she's drawing. Like she's found her happy place.

But why can't her happy place be with me? In Computer Science?

The warning bell rings, reminding me that I have to get to class, and I reluctantly step away from the door, taking one last glance at my best friend before heading to first block alone.

RAINBOW UNICORN STAR FARTS

FOR THE FIRST ten minutes of the block, I stare gloomily at Harper's empty computer station next to mine. I feel so icky about what happened, I can't even get excited when Mr. Weston announces that for our assignment today, we're making our very own GIFs. And I *love* GIFs. But I just can't stop thinking about that look on Harper's face when she opened up her sketch pad in the Art classroom and started to draw.

"So first we're going to add a background into our code," Mr. Weston is saying as he types into his laptop at the front of the room. He's wearing his usual dark-vest-and-bright-colored-tie combination, and his wavy brown hair is tousled as usual. It always looks like he brushed it with a strip of Velcro.

"I'm going to choose this adorable, fuzzy unicorn," he goes on. "Because who doesn't like unicorns, right?" A few of the students laugh as a cartoon unicorn appears on the projector screen. I sit up in my seat and try extra hard to pay attention. Normally, it's easy to listen to Mr. Weston. He's the smartest, funniest, most interesting teacher in school. And I love how excited he gets when his code scripts work.

"See how we have four different frames to use?" Mr. Weston continues, hovering his mouse over four boxes on the screen. "In each frame, we can program something to happen. So let's say I want rainbow-colored stars to come out of the unicorn's butt." He pauses and strokes his short brown beard. "Because what's a unicorn without rainbow-colored stars coming out of its butt, right?"

More laughter. That one even gets me.

"In this first frame, I'm going to add red stars. Then, in the next frame, I'll add yellow stars, then green stars, then purple stars." I watch, mesmerized, as he maneuvers the mouse around, dragging and dropping components into his visual code editor. "Now, when we push preview, we'll see that each of the frames will play for one second, making it look like . . ." He pushes the little PLAY button and we all lean forward in our seats. "Presto!" The stars change from red to yellow to green to purple and then repeat. Mr. Weston throws his arms up in the air and does a waddling victory lap around his laptop. "Rainbow unicorn star farts!"

The whole class cracks up. I turn toward Harper's station to share a laugh with her, only to remember, once again, that she's not there.

Mr. Weston finishes his victory dance and returns to his computer. "So you see, it's that easy. Now it's your turn. Open up your code editor and show me what you got. Let's get GIF-ing!"

Everyone turns to their monitor and gets to work. I choose to animate a tube of lipstick, making the color change from red to pink to purple to blue. I try not to wonder about what Harper would have chosen to do if she'd been here. But I can't help but think she would have really enjoyed today's assignment. She loves GIFs as much as I do.

Whatever, I think, giving myself a quick doglike shake. I need to get over it. If Harper wants to take Art instead of Computer Science, fine. It doesn't have to mean the end of our friendship. It just means she would rather draw than code. So what? I'm not going to let this distract me from my mission to find her a new boy . . . or from my lipstick GIF.

"Wonderful job, everyone," Mr. Weston says as he walks around the room, checking people's work. "Jacks-in-the-box," he says, stopping at Jackson Harris's computer and giving him a thumbs-up. "A flying saucer with flashing lights! Excellent! Micah-langelo!" He moves on to Micah Lowenstein's station and adjusts his black-rimmed glasses. "Love the fireworks! *Bellissimo!*" He finally gets to my station and pauses, leaning over my shoulder to get a look at my screen. "Emm-meyster! Emm-o-matic! Emm-inem! You are a GIF-ing machine."

I giggle. Mr. Weston loves to turn all of our names into funny catchphrases. It always makes me laugh.

He continues to watch my cartoon lipstick change colors on the screen and gives me an approving nod. "Seriously, great job. You have a knack for programming. Does your mom have a background in coding?"

I laugh at the thought of Mom trying to code anything. I had to teach her how to use her phone to check the weather. "Not at all. She decorates houses."

"Huh," Mr. Weston says as something unreadable flashes over his face. But it's gone just as soon as it appeared. "You must get it from your dad, then."

I keep my eyes trained on the screen as a familiar anxious feeling tugs at my chest. It's the same sensation I always get whenever someone mentions something about my dad or makes some guess at what he might have liked or might have been good at. It's not the first time I've wondered if my dad is as into computers and devices as I am. If he were still around, would he be the one ordering food from an app whenever Mom works late? Would he have been the one setting up the smart thermostat so Mom can control the temperature of our house from her phone? Or fixing her calendar when it stops syncing?

I barely remember what life was like when my dad was around. He walked out on us when I was four and the twins were only a month old. All I have left of him is a box on the top shelf of my closet, filled with random things he left behind.

Having a dad that you barely remember is kind of like having a half-finished puzzle lying around your house forever. Every once in a while, you find a piece that fits, and that feels good, but you know the picture will never be whole.

"Yeah, I must get it from him," I whisper back, but

by then, Mr. Weston has already moved on to the next student.

"'Or, if there were a sympathy in choice, / War, death, or sickness did lay siege to it, / Making it momentary as a sound, / Swift as a shadow, short as any dream; / Brief as the lightning in the collied night / That, in a spleen, unfolds both heaven and earth, / And ere a man hath power to say "Behold!" / The jaws of darkness do devour it up: / So quick bright things come to confusion.'"

Ms. Hendrickson lowers her dog-eared copy of *A Midsummer Night's Dream* and gazes wistfully around the Language Arts classroom. She presses the book to her heart. "Is that the most beautiful thing you've ever heard?"

No one answers. I glance around to see if anyone else is as lost as I am, and I'm relieved to find a sea of blank, dazed faces staring at our teacher.

"Who can tell us what Shakespeare is saying here about love?"

Love? Is that what the passage is about?

Ms. Hendrickson peers out at the class and I try to make myself invisible, slouching down in my seat to hide behind the head of Garrett Cole. It should be easy, given that he's a football player with a huge head, but Ms. Hendrickson finds me anyway. "Emmy?"

I shift nervously in my seat and stare down at the

open page of my play. "Um," I say, stalling. But no matter how many times I read the passage, it just looks like gibberish to me. "I think he's saying that love is like . . ." The letters start to blur together, and my head starts to throb. I focus in on one of the words I can actually understand. "A disease of the spleen?"

The class is silent, apart from a few muffled giggles. Ms. Hendrickson stares at me like I'm a three-headed frog that's just hopped into her classroom. She sighs. "Emmy, look at the words. *Feel* the words. Go deeper into them. Do you really think Shakespeare is talking about a spleen disease?"

I can hear more tittering from a few of the students around me. I fight the urge to snap back at them, "Let's see you come up with something better!"

"I . . . ," I start to say, but I have no idea what comes next. Thankfully, I'm saved by Alexis Dawson, who's sitting next to me.

"I think Shakespeare is saying that love is fragile. No matter how strong or right it feels, it can always be destroyed in an instant. Basically, all lovers are star-crossed in the end."

Ms. Hendrickson's sour expression instantly turns to glee. "Excellent! Absolutely stellar. I can tell you're really absorbing the material, Alexis." She shoots a look at me as if to say, "See how easy it is?"

I'm just grateful to have the attention off me and my three frog heads.

"And what about the next passage?" Ms. Hendrickson

raises her copy of the play again and resumes reading. "'If then true lovers have been ever crossed . . .'"

"Hey," someone whispers, and I look up to see that Garrett Cole has turned around in his seat to face Alexis. "What's Shakespearean for 'kiss-up'?"

Garrett's football buddies all snicker behind their hands as Ms. Hendrickson shoots a scathing glare in his direction. I glance over at Alexis, who looks mortified and I feel a flare of anger. Alexis is one of the sweetest girls in our class. And she's smart. *And* super pretty. But it seems like every day, Garrett goes out of his way to make fun of her. Why is he so mean to her?

As soon as the question pops into my mind, a flicker of giddiness ignites inside me. I don't *have* to wonder about these things anymore, I remind myself. The days of boy-related questions are over.

While Ms. Hendrickson continues to read passionately from her copy of the play, I slink down in my seat and ever so delicately slip my phone out of the pocket of my backpack and onto my lap.

"'Therefore, hear me, Hermia. / I have a widow aunt, a dowager / Of great revenue, and she hath no child,'" bellows Ms. Hendrickson dramatically.

Double-checking that no one is looking, I click on the iSpeak Boy app and hold my breath as it loads, praying that it was able to hear Garrett through the fabric of my backpack.

Then, a second later, I stifle a sequel as the screen fills with blue and green bubbles. An entire morning's worth of unread translations are waiting for me. I don't have time to scroll through them all now, so I quickly swipe up until I find Garrett's last comment.

Garrett Cole

What's Shakespearean for "kiss-up"?

Translation

I could listen to Alexis interpret Shakespeare all day.

My eyes open wide and I reread the message again.

Oh my gosh. He's totally crushing on her!

Why on earth, then, would he make fun of her on a daily basis? Wouldn't that just push her away? Why not compliment her or ask her to help you with your Shakespeare homework or something?

I shake my head in utter bafflement. Even though I can literally read their thoughts, boys still don't make any sense to me.

"And remember, everyone," Ms. Hendrickson says right before the end of class. "The local Highbury Shakespeare company is putting on a performance of this very play, *A Midsummer Night's Dream*, this weekend. Anyone who goes and brings me their ticket stub gets extra credit."

The bell rings and everyone leaps out of their seat, eager for lunch.

"Well, we all know who's going to be in the front row," Garrett mutters to one of his friends. They both turn and watch Alexis shuffle out of the classroom. My gaze snaps right back down to my phone just as the translation appears on the screen.

Translation

> If there was any chance she wouldn't laugh in my face, I'd ask her to go with me.

I can't believe it. I just can't believe it. I never, in a million years, would have predicted that Garrett Cole was in love with Alexis Dawson. They're as different as two people can be. He's a football player who I've only *ever* heard talk about football. And she's a dancer who loves Shakespeare. Talk about star-crossed lovers!

But it doesn't matter whether I believe it or not. I am now in possession of very important information. Information that I wholly intend to put to good use.

Darting out of the classroom, I make a beeline for Alexis's locker. She's putting away her books from Language Arts and grabbing her sack lunch.

"Alexis." I skip the small talk and get straight to the point. "I have something important to tell you."

She looks surprised to see me and I don't blame her. We're not enemies or anything, we just don't normally talk much. "What?"

I glance over my shoulder to check for eavesdroppers before beckoning her to come closer. She shoots me a wary look but eventually leans in.

"Garrett Cole has a crush on you," I say in my best conspiratorial whisper.

Alexis's expression darkens. "That's not very funny, Emmy."

"It's not a joke," I assure her. "I'm totally serious. He wants to ask you to go see *A Midsummer Night's Dream* with him this weekend but he's too afraid you'll laugh at him."

She narrows her eyes, clearly not believing me. "I *would* laugh at him, because Garrett Cole hates me."

I shake my head. "No! He only *acts* like he hates you. Because he has a huge crush on you."

"He told you that?"

I hesitate. "Um, well, not exactly. He more like *implied* it."

Now she just looks confused. "How did he imply it?"

"It's complicated," I rush to say. "You just need to trust me."

"And then what? What am I supposed to do about it?"

"Well, what do you think of him?"

She shrugs. "He's cute, I guess. And he can be funny. When he's not making fun of *me*. And he has this really cute freckle right behind his left ear. Sometimes I stare at it during class." As I watch her eyes go all dreamy and her cheeks turn the faintest hint of pink, I can tell that despite her hesitation, there might be a chance she likes him back. Or *could*, anyway, if he stopped being such a jerk.

"You should talk to him!" I say eagerly.

The color instantly drains from her cheeks. "What?"

"Just start up a conversation with him. *Away* from his friends. Casually mention the play this weekend and how much you're dying to see it. I bet you *anything* he'll ask you to go with him."

Alexis crosses her arms over her chest. "Why are you telling me this? Why do you even care?"

I shrug. "If two people like each other, they should be together."

Ooh! I like the sound of that. That should definitely be my new motto.

"But hey," I add. "It's totally up to you. You can do whatever you want. I'm just the messenger."

Then, with a mischievous smile worthy of Cupid himself, I turn and stride off down the hallway, feeling pretty good about what I just did. I know I said I would use the app to help Harper find someone new. But it doesn't hurt to improve a few other lives along the way, does it?

THE (NOW NOT-SO) SECRET LANGUAGE OF BOYS

"WELCOME BACK, BERRINITES! This is Liza Wu and you're watching 'Crushin' on the Crush.'"

The voice of my favorite YouTube host streams through my earbuds as I walk the seven blocks home from school with my head bent over my phone.

"So, you might have heard," Liza continues in a conspiratorial whisper. "Berrin James? New song? Dropped last week and sent the Berrinite fandom into an internet frenzy?"

"Crushin' on the Crush" is my favorite Berrin James fan channel on YouTube. It used to be a fan channel for Summer Crush, but since they broke up last year and Berrin launched a solo career, the channel mostly focuses on him.

"You guys!" Liza leans in super close to the camera. "What is the deal with this 'Magnolia Street' song? The whole world is scratching their heads trying to figure out who it's about. And yeah, count me as one of those head scratchers."

I let out a gasp and nearly trip over my own feet. That's the song Harper and I were talking about on the way home from the carnival. Apparently, we're not the only two people who disagree about the meaning of the lyrics.

"I have been reading fan theories nonstop," Liza goes on. "One of the more popular theories is that the song is about Berrin's on-again, off-again relationship with Kelsey Kapur."

I nod vigorously, as if Liza can actually *see* me agreeing with her. This is exactly what I told Harper on Sunday night.

"And the lyric 'Pink-scribbled hearts on the sidewalk' does seem to corroborate that theory, given that Berrin and Kelsey *are* seen drawing pink hearts on the sidewalk in his 'Every Heartbeat' video."

"That's right!" I say aloud to the screen as Liza shows a clip from the video. I can't believe I missed that connection.

"While another popular theory," Liza goes on, "is that the song is about Berrin's difficult breakup with Julianna Allen, which we all know completely *crushed* him. And lyrics like 'Rose-tinted glass on the windows all cracked and faded to black' do seem to point to Julianna."

"So who is it about?" I shout at my phone.

"I think," Liza says with a nod, as though she's answering me personally, "the key to solving this puzzle is in the name of the song itself. Where is this mysterious Magnolia Street? So I started doing a little digging on Google maps and it turns out there are actually a *lot* of Magnolia Streets out there. But I did find that the very first song Summer Crush ever released was actually recorded in a studio located on . . ." She does a dramatic pause, making it look like the video has frozen. "Magnolia Street!"

"No!" I gasp, gripping the phone tighter.

"So, I don't know," Liza goes on. "Maybe the song is actually about Berrin's regret over the breakup of Summer Crush? Or maybe it's a hint at a possible reunion?" Liza holds up crossed fingers and I do the same. A Summer Crush reunion would be amazing!

I wonder if Harper has seen this video yet. I press PAUSE and immediately text her the link. Harper and I have been listening to Summer Crush since the third grade. It's pretty much the reason we became friends in the first place. Maybe the hint of a reunion will give us something to talk about.

We barely spoke at all today. At lunch, I tried to get her talking by casually mentioning that I missed her in first block, hoping she'd open up about her choice to change electives. But she just said, "Oh yeah, sorry. I meant to tell you. I wasn't really liking Computer Science, so I transferred to Art instead." And that was the end of it.

"Anyway, that's my favorite theory so far," Liza says after I've resumed the video. "But I'll keep searching. And if you have a favorite theory, be sure to leave it in the comments below. And don't forget to thumbs-up and subscribe!"

I arrive home just as the video is coming to an end. I click the thumbs-up button, tap out a quick comment casting my vote for Kelsey Kapur, and let myself into the front door. Mom and the boys are already there, and as soon as I walk inside, Mom asks, "Wanna go to Lickety Split?"

At the mention of our family's favorite frozen yogurt shop, the boys start shouting and zooming around the living room as though they're on a premature sugar high.

"What's the occasion?" I ask, only slightly suspicious.

Lickety Split is sort of like a Woods family tradition. We've been going there for celebrations and special occasions ever since the boys were little.

"No occasion. Just for fun." Mom smiles at me, but I can see in her eyes that she's hiding something.

We pile into the car and Mom waits until we're all buckled in and the car is already moving before she says, "I just need to make a *super*-quick stop at Home Mart first."

The boys and I let out a chorus of groans and boos. So *that's* the occasion: bribery. We're only going for fro-yo because Mom knows how much we hate going with her when she's shopping for her job.

"Wack-e hack-a-tack-e thack-a-tack stack-o-rack-e!" Isaac complains from the backseat, and although I still haven't cracked the code of their secret language— despite studying last night's translation multiple times—I can take a wild guess about what he's saying.

"You tricked us," I tell Mom as she drives out of our subdivision and onto the main road.

"I swear it'll only be a few minutes."

"You said that last time," I remind her, "and we practically spent the night in that store."

"Stop exaggerating, Emmy. I just have to pick up a

few things for the Nagman house. I finally found a couch they like, and they need some accessories to go with it. I'll be in and out and we'll be eating fro-yo in no time."

As predicted, Mom takes longer than a few minutes. The boys went into Home Mart with her, but I decided to wait in the car, where I could be alone with my phone. I have almost an entire day's worth of boy translations to read through, and I need to get back to my quest: finding a new match for Harper. With the app running all day long, picking up everything every boy around me said throughout the day, I'm guaranteed to find a lead. There's got to be at least one boy in our school who thinks Harper is cute or funny or smart . . . or all of the above! And like a needle in a haystack, I'm determined to find him.

I recline my seat a little, get comfy, and start scrolling through the hundreds of green and blue bubbles, giggling and gasping and sometimes feeling just flat-out disgusted.

With every translation I read and every new discovery I make, I feel like a tiny explosion is going off in my brain. Like, did you know how many seventh-grade boys can't stop thinking about their hair? Practically all of them. Almost half of these green bubbles are about hair. Does it look okay? Did I use too much gel? Did I not use enough gel? It's too short, it's too long, it's too straight, it's too curly. I wish it looked more like his hair.

And bras. Boys are *obsessed* with bras! They want to know which girls are wearing bras. How bras work. How do girls know what size bra to buy? Are bras comfortable? Uncomfortable? Too itchy? Too tight? It's fascinating! Even *I* haven't given that much thought to bras!

I've learned more about the boys in my class in the past twelve minutes than I have in the past twelve years of my life!

For instance, I learned that Tyler Watkins is super insecure about his height, Eric Garcia hates when his friends make fun of him but doesn't have the guts to say anything, Jackson Harris loves Berrin James almost as much as I do, Mitchell Valentine farts almost twenty times a day and always blames it on someone else, Archie Evans doesn't like changing in the locker room because he's worried people will make fun of his scrawny body, Cole Campbell is obsessed with some girl who wears delicious-smelling perfume, and Logan Lansing hasn't told any of his friends that his parents are having money problems.

Wow.

Mind. Blown.

I never would have imagined that boys think about this stuff. I thought they only cared about video games and sports. And while yes, there are a lot of those thoughts too, it's not nearly as much as I imagined.

Unfortunately, though, as fascinating as all of this is, I haven't yet found a single mention of Harper. Maybe it was too much to hope for that a boy would simply think about her, all on his own. Maybe tomorrow I need to be a little bit more proactive about it. You know, ask around, drop her name into the conversation.

A text pops onto my screen, and I click on it.

Mom: Sorry! Just a few more minutes!

I roll my eyes. That means another half hour. I don't know how she puts up with these people. Mom has been working for Nathan Wagman and his wife, Stephanie, for the past month and I swear, they haven't been happy with a single thing she's done. She's picked out three different couches for them and had their bathroom retiled *twice* already and the house is still nowhere near done. It's like they can't make up their minds about anything!

I flip back to the iSpeak Boy app. And that's when one of the little blue bubbles catches my eye. I'm not sure how I missed it during my endless scrolling, but now I'm not sure I even want to read it.

Because the name at the top says Mr. Weston.

I consider just deleting it. I'm still scarred from the mental picture of Assistant Principal Langley in his bubble bath. I don't think I can handle any more of my teacher's thoughts. But my curiosity gets the better of me.

Mr. Weston

> Seriously, great job. You have a knack for programming. Does your mom have a background in coding?

Translation

> Just act natural. Casual. Don't seem too interested.

Confused, I reread the translation, but it still doesn't make any sense to me. Why would he have to act natural? He's my teacher. Doesn't he always act natural around me?

I try to remember the conversation we had in Computer Science class this morning so I can play it back in my mind. He asked if Mom had a background in coding, I told him she decorated houses, and then he got an odd look on his face and said . . .

I quickly scroll down to the next message.

Mr. Weston
Huh. You must get it from your dad, then.

Translation
So she's beautiful *and* artistic. How could a woman like that possibly be single?

The inside of the car starts to spin.
Beautiful?

Why is Mr. Weston calling my mom beautiful? How does he even know what she looks like?

The hatchback door opens, and I twist around to see Mom loading shopping bags into the trunk. "Mom?" I say, and there's a desperate ring to my voice. "Have you ever met any of my teachers?"

"Come on, boys!" she calls to the twins. "Get in the car, please!" Then she turns to me. "Yes, of course I have."

"When?" I ask.

I don't even realize how accusing I sound until Mom laughs and says, "Am I under arrest? I had parent-teacher conferences last week." She finishes loading the shopping bags and closes the hatchback door.

"So you met *all* my teachers," I confirm the moment she sits in the driver's seat.

"That's what parent-teacher conferences are for." She turns to address the boys, who have just climbed into the backseat. "Seat belts, please."

Meanwhile, I'm glaring at her like she's the prime suspect in a murder case. "And were there any teachers you liked better than others? Or had a more interesting conversation with?"

She laughs again. "Why do I feel like I'm on trial here? What's going on? Did you get in trouble at school?"

I flash momentarily to the Gargoyle's face yesterday when he lectured me about having my phone out on school property. "No," I lie. "I just want to know if you . . . you know, hit it off with any of them."

As Mom reaches back to grab her seat belt, I just manage to catch sight of a fleeting smile that crosses her face. It's not a normal, everyday kind of smile. It's a different kind. The kind that holds a secret behind it.

"*Mom,*" I say, and I can't help the warning that slips into my voice.

"What?" she asks innocently. "They were all very nice. I enjoyed meeting with all of them." And then, like a guilty suspect with no alibi, she starts the car and changes the subject.

FRO-YO BEAU

THE LINE AT Lickety Split almost reaches halfway to the door. I don't mind, though. Because it means I get extra time to watch Frankie. He's the boy who works behind the counter. He's sixteen, with a face straight out of a clothing catalog.

"How was school today?" Mom asks the boys as we take our place at the back of the line.

My brothers start to ramble about their day while I steal secret glances at Frankie. He's dispensing strawberry-vanilla swirl yogurt into a cup, which he then hands to a waiting customer before flashing that adorable half smile of his. His cap sits slightly askew on his dark hair, and he hasn't even bothered to tie his apron. Now, if that's not a commercial for frozen yogurt, I don't know what is.

"And I won the spelling bee!" Isaac says, pulling my attention back to the conversation.

"You did?" Mom questions, and I can tell from the look on her face that she thinks this is a lie. Ben and Isaac have never excelled at anything academic. In fact, they've never excelled at anything except getting in trouble.

113

"You did not win!" Ben says. "*I* won."

"We both won! It was a tie!" Isaac shouts, his face turning red.

"Okay, okay," Mom soothes. "Calm down. No need to get excited. So you *both* won?" I can tell she's still suspicious. "The class spelling bee?"

Ben nods. "Yep. And Ms. Oliver says that next we're going to compete against winners from other schools."

Mom looks like she's going to faint from shock. "Really?"

But the boys don't reply because we've reached the front of the line and they both rush the counter, fighting to place their order first, which is a bit of a joke since they always end up ordering the same thing anyway.

"Chocolate-caramel swirl in a cup!" they shout in unison.

Frankie looks a tad overwhelmed by the outburst but nods and grabs two cups before turning back to the machines. I wait anxiously for my turn, my phone gripped in my hand, the iSpeak Boy app open on the screen.

Frankie hands the cups to Isaac and Ben, who both race to an empty table and start fighting over one of the four chairs.

Then, suddenly, those intense dark eyes are on me, and it's like I forget how to breathe. Forget how to think. My brain empties of everything and everyone. I forget all about the crack in my friendship with Harper, my mom's suspicious teacher-parent conference with Mr. Weston, even the phone clutched in my own hand. It's all fuzzy background noise against the symphony that's playing in those eyes.

"Emmy?" Mom says, and I blink and realize that both she *and* Frankie are staring at me with expectant looks. Oh gosh, how long did I zone out for this time? "He asked you a question."

"He did?" I whip my head back to Frankie and try not to trip over my own tongue as I rush to say, "Sorry, what was the question?"

Frankie looks at me like I might have left my brain back in the car. "Cup or cone?" he says, enunciating each word.

I stutter out a nervous laugh. "Oh, sorry. Cup, please. And I'll have the chocolate–peanut butter swirl."

"And a small blueberry in a cup for me, please," Mom adds.

Frankie turns to make our orders and I slouch against the counter in defeat. Well, that was embarrassing.

"Thack-a-tack-sack mack-yack chack-a-i-rack!" Ben shouts from the far end of the shop.

"I wack-a-sack hack-e-rack-e fack-i-rack-sack-tack!" Isaac yells back.

"Boys!" Mom hurries over to restore the peace and I use the moment to glance down at my screen. Even though I already know what that little green bubble is going to say. Frankie probably thinks I'm the biggest loser on the planet.

Frankie

Cup or cone?

> I can't believe she came. She's really here. I've been waiting forever for this.

Wait, WHAT?

My gaze snaps up just as Frankie is turning around with our cups of yogurt. He gives me a smile, but all I can do is gape. My stomach is spinning. It's not the Tummy Tornado, though. It's more like the Tummy Ferris Wheel.

He's been waiting? For *me*?

Say something else, I urge him with my mind, and to my delight he does. He flashes me another delicious smile as he hands over the cups. "That'll be fourteen twenty-five."

"Oh . . ." I glance awkwardly over at my mom, who's still trying to wrangle the boys into their chairs. "Mom! We have to pay."

She hurries over with her wallet, and while she's distracted fishing out her credit card, I suck in a breath and brave another peek at my phone.

Frankie

> That'll be $14.25.

> Now I just have to figure out how to talk to her.

My heart is galloping like a pack of wild stallions in my chest. This can't be happening. This can't be real!

He's been waiting to see me and now he wants to talk to me? What do I say? How do I start?

"S-so," I stammer, feeling ridiculous. I've never tried to talk to an older boy before. And definitely never one this cute. "How long have you been working here?"

Frankie runs Mom's credit card through the machine "Only a few months," he says before turning to give me another one of those killer smiles that makes my knees feel like they're made of pudding.

My phone vibrates in my hand.

Translation

Just ask her out. Don't mess it up. Just be cool and casual and say, "Hey, do you wanna hang out with me this weekend?"

"Yes!" I blurt out so loudly, even the twins quiet down and look over from their table.

"Yes, what?" Frankie asks as he hands Mom back her credit card. Mom is looking strangely at me.

But I don't care. It's like the rest of the world has disappeared. And all that's left is me and Frankie and those gorgeous brown eyes. "Yes, I would love to—"

"Excuse me, are you done?"

I turn around to see a girl is standing in line behind us, waiting to order. She looks to be about sixteen and she's drop-dead gorgeous, with long hair and long legs and perfectly applied eyeshadow.

"Yes, sorry." Mom grabs my shoulders and scoots me to the side like I'm an unruly little kid who needs to be ordered around. I open my mouth to argue. To tell both her *and* this random girl behind me that, no, we are most certainly not done. But then I see the expression on Frankie's face as the girl steps up to the counter. It probably looks a lot like the expression on my own face a few moments ago. His dark eyes are all sparkly, his lips are quirked into that adorable half smile again. And when he lifts his cap long enough to run his fingers through his thick hair, that's when I know.

This is not just a random girl.

"Hi, Janey," Frankie says, and I don't miss the slight tremble in his voice. "You came."

Janey gives a shy little shrug and pretends to be totally absorbed in the frozen yogurt flavors. "You know, I had a craving for fro-yo. And you said you worked here, so . . ."

"Yeah, I hear ya," Frankie says with a nervous laugh. "Fro-yo cravings are no joke. Why do you think I got the job here?"

Janey giggles like this is the funniest thing she's ever heard. I can feel my cheeks burn with heat. Of course, he wasn't thinking about *me*. Of course, he didn't want to ask *me* out. She was probably standing behind me the whole time.

Frankie leans forward on the counter and swings a towel over his shoulder like he's a bartender in an old-time saloon. "So, what'll it be, little lady? We got chocolate, we got peanut butter, we got chocolate–peanut butter *swirl*."

Janey giggles again as she continues to study the flavors. I stare down at my own sad, little chocolate and peanut butter swirl, certain that I've lost my appetite. Meanwhile, my phone is vibrating like crazy, but I don't dare look at the screen.

This is why I'm so much better off just playing Love Coordinator for everyone *else*.

"Emmy? Are you coming to sit down?"

I glance over to see Mom is already seated with the boys and I'm still standing off to the side, looking like a rejected puppy, while Frankie and Janey continue to fall in love over the frozen yogurt counter. Bowing my head, I scurry over to the table, plop into the chair, and scoot as far down as I can, trying to make myself invisible.

It's official. We can never come back to Lickety Split ever again.

LEVELING UP

TWO NIGHTS LATER, I sit at my desk, trying and *failing* to reread act 2 of *A Midsummer Night's Dream* for Language Arts. Ms. Hendrickson is giving us an oral test on it tomorrow, and I'm so not prepared. I keep rereading the same line over and over and I still don't have a clue what it means. Something about fairies and a queen and a king and I'm pretty sure someone is jealous of someone else.

Ugh.

I lean back in my chair and pick up my phone, checking if Harper has texted me. But I frown when I see the last message in our thread is a funny GIF I sent earlier this morning, trying to get at least an "LOL" out of her. I check my notifications to see if she tagged me in a photo or contacted me through another app, but the only thing there is, is an alert that Aurélie has started a new online Monopoly game. Harper barely even responded to the "Crushin' on the Crush" video I sent two days ago. She just said, "Thanks. I'll check it out." But then I heard nothing.

I sigh and make another attempt to text Harper, slowing typing out I M-I-S-S Y-O- before erasing the whole thing and starting over.

> **Me:** I've been listening to Magnolia Street and I think you might be right! I think it *is* about Julianna Allen!

I push SEND and hold my breath, waiting for the three little dots to appear. But they never do. Harper has never taken this long to text me back. Ever since we both got phones, we've been in constant communication. This silence has been torture.

I open my desk drawer and pull out Harper's drawing. It's completely dry now but the image is still all distorted and blurry from the Enchanted Lagoon. It was supposed to represent me as Cupid—as the Love Coordinator—but the water warped my wings and smeared my heart-tipped arrows.

I can't help but think that this picture is like our friendship now. All smudged and damaged, barely even recognizable. But if you squint hard enough, if you look close enough, you can still see what it used to be.

"I'm going to fix this," I whisper to the drawing. "I'm going to make this right."

Plink!

A pencil hits my window, startling me, and I turn to see Grant waving from his bedroom.

"Sorry about the other day," he says the moment I

open the window, and when my brow furrows, he clarifies, "For leaving so abruptly. Dev is going through some stuff, and I kind of need to be there for him."

I think back to the tired look on Dev's face and the way his shoulders were sort of hunched like his head was too heavy for his body. "What kind of stuff?"

Grant shrugs. "Just some personal stuff." He nudges his chin toward the drawing in my hand. "Nice. Did you do that? It's very . . ." He twists his mouth to the side, searching for the right word. "Frankenthaler."

I glance down at the drawing again. "Huh."

"Helen Frankenthaler was an abstract expressionist painter."

I still have no idea what he's talking about. "Harper drew it. And it's not supposed to look like this. It got wet."

Grant barks out a laugh like I've just made the most hilarious joke.

"What's so funny?"

He walks out of view of the window and comes back a second later holding a small canvas. I recognize it as the painting he's been working on for the past few days. I know I'm not an art expert, but it still doesn't look like much to me. It's just large patches of green and gray paint. "I've been trying to get *this* to look more like *that*." He points at Harper's drawing. "But so far, I haven't succeeded. Maybe I'll try pouring a bucket of water on it."

I chuckle. "Hey, whatever works, right?"

Grant sits down on his window seat. "Where is Harper anyway? I haven't seen her all week."

"We're . . . ," I start to say but I don't know how to

finish that sentence. I don't know what Harper and I are right now. The whole thing seems so uncertain. But Grant is leaning on the window frame, waiting for me to finish. I glance down at the distorted drawing of me and say the first thing that comes to my mind. "Things are a bit weird with us."

Admitting it aloud feels like a paper cut on my heart.

"Oh," Grant says, and something that looks like genuine sympathy crosses his face. "Do you want to talk about it?"

I shrug and try to swallow down the sting in my throat. "Not really. I just feel like there's a constant tornado in my stomach."

Grant's mouth twists again. "What rating?"

"Huh?" I say again.

"What rating of a tornado?"

I snort. "There are different ratings?"

"Of course. Tornados are rated on the Enhanced Fujita Scale."

And there he goes. Off on one of his know-it-all lectures.

"So, you've got your EF-0 tornados. These are relatively calm. Sixty-five- to eighty-five-mile-per-hour winds. Just some minor roof damage or broken tree branches. Then the next level is an EF-1. That's where we start seeing some more moderate damage. Broken windows, overturned mobile homes."

"How do you know so much about tornados?"

Grant opens his mouth to answer but I beat him to it. "Let me guess. You watched a documentary?"

He grins. "Don't knock documentaries. They're like school that you don't have to get dressed for. In fact, I was just about to watch a new one if you want to join."

I can't think of anything I'd want to do *less*. But I don't want to be rude, so I ask, "And what is this *epic* new documentary about?"

Grant's face instantly lights up. He shifts his weight on the windowsill like he's settling in for a long chat. "Okay, so it's about handwriting analysis and—"

"Handwriting analysis?" I echo tonelessly. "Seriously?"

"Yes! It sounds so cool. The police have been using handwriting analysis for years in criminal investigations, because a person's handwriting is almost as unique as their fingerprints. But this documentary goes into the future of handwriting analysis and all the cool things computers are going to be able to do with it. Like did you know that right now, you can upload a picture of something someone wrote, and a computer can instantly tell you over five thousand different traits about the person?"

Grant continues to talk passionately about handwriting analysis, but meanwhile, my mind is spinning. Something he said lit a spark in the back of my brain.

"*. . . you can upload a picture of something someone wrote, and a computer can instantly tell you . . .*"

I cast a glance back at my desk, where my phone is still sitting.

A picture.

iSpeak Boy is a translation app. But it used to be the

iSpeak Everything app. And with that app, I had the ability to upload a photo of something in a foreign language and the app would . . .

"Grant!" I cut him off midsentence. "You're a genius!"

He looks slightly confused. "*I* didn't come up with the algorithm. That was all the scientists at the university who—"

"No, I mean, you . . ." I glance back once again at my phone. "You . . . uh . . . gave me an idea. An exciting one."

Grant looks pleased. "Really? Well, glad I could help."

I reach for my phone, eager to try out my new theory. "Um, sorry. I need to go. But I really want to hear how the documentary is after you're done watching it."

Grant laughs. "Did anyone ever tell you you're a horrible liar?"

"Yeah, you. Almost every day when we were eight."

"Well, you haven't gotten better with age." He waves. "Have a good night."

"You too." I smile and shut the window, then the curtains, making sure they're completely closed before I open the app.

My heart is racing. If I'm right about this, it could be big. Like next-level big. It could open up all sorts of new possibilities.

I click on the little blue boy icon and the screen immediately floods with unread bubbles, all of them with Grant's name on it. Apparently, the app was listening to our entire conversation and translating everything Grant said.

I'm eager to try out my idea, but once again, my curiosity gets the better of me. The opportunity to peer into the thoughts of the all-mighty, know-it-all Grant Knight? It's too much to pass up. I quickly skim through the messages.

Grant Knight

Sorry about yesterday. For leaving so abruptly. Dev is going through some stuff, and I kind of need to be there for him.

Translation

Sorry about yesterday. For leaving so abruptly. Dev is going through some stuff, and I kind of need to be there for him.

Grant Knight

Where is Harper anyway? I haven't seen her all week.

Translation

Where is Harper, anyway? I haven't seen her all week.

Grant Knight

Oh. Do you want to talk about it?

Translation

Oh. Do you want to talk about it?

Grant Knight

> Tornados are rated on the Enhanced Fujita Scale.

Translation

> Tornados are rated on the Enhanced Fujita Scale.

That's weird. Is something wrong with the app? Did it stop working? Why isn't it translating anything Grant says? Maybe it just doesn't work on homeschooled boys. Maybe it just doesn't work on *Grant*.

But I can't worry about that right now. I still need to test my theory.

I sweep my gaze over the screen, locating the little OPTIONS button on the top left corner of the app. I click on it and let out a squeal when a little camera icon appears on the list. Just like in the iSpeak Everything app!

Hastily, I click it and the app changes to camera mode. I pan around my desk, searching for something to take a picture of. It needs to be something a boy wrote. A moment later, the camera focuses on a white page with crisp black text and I freeze.

Yes!

I line up the shot. Making sure the words are perfectly aligned in the frame.

OBERON:
    Fetch me that flower; the herb I showed thee once.
    The juice of it on sleeping eyelids laid

Will make or man or woman madly dote
Upon the next creature that it sees.

Then, with shaky, excited fingers, I click the shutter.
I hold my breath.
A little spinning wheel appears on the screen along with a pop-up that says "Translating."
I squeeze the phone tighter in my hand.
Then it happens. The picture of the text gets shifted to the top of the screen, and right below it, a new set of text appears. And suddenly, I'm reading William Shakespeare's own *thoughts*.

> I see myself in this Oberon character. I am the writer who unleashes comedy and anarchy onto my characters, like a powerful fairy playing tricks on mortals.

I throw my hands up in the air and cry out, "Achievement unlocked!"

IN SEARCH OF FAMILY RESEMBLANCES

I'M RUNNING, SPRINTING across my room to my closet. My whole body is thrumming with excitement as I pull down the small shoebox from the top shelf and flip off the lid. My hands move quickly through the contents: a movie ticket stub, a silver watch, a half-empty pack of cinnamon gum, a tube of ChapStick. Finally, I reach the photo. It's stuck to the bottom of the box and I have to peel it off with the delicacy of a crime-scene investigator.

Even though I've stared at this picture countless times over the past eight years, for countless hours, the three people in it still feel like strangers to me. Faces I can't remember.

My mom's huge belly hangs over her baggy pants, making it look like she's going to topple forward. But she's still somehow able to hold her four-year-old daughter in her arms.

Me.

Both of our faces are tilted upward, smiling at the tall, curly-haired man next to us. We're standing in front of a tree so huge, the top of it doesn't even fit in the picture. The look on my mom's face in this photograph fills me with so much joy and so much sadness at the same time. It's the same way I look at Bubsy, my stuffed rabbit, and the poster of Berrin James on my wall. The way the twins look at chocolate-caramel swirl frozen yogurt. The way Harper looks at art supplies and, up until a few days ago, the way she looked at Elliot Phillips.

Except a thousand times stronger.

One month after this picture was taken, my mom gave birth to rambunctious twin boys. A month after that, my dad was gone.

And I've never seen my mom look that way again.

She says he left without an explanation. Without a reason. But I know that can't be true. There's always a reason. There's always logic behind any decision. Any good computer programmer will tell you that. You just have to look hard enough until you find it.

Heart hammering in my chest, I turn the picture over in my hands and run my fingertips over the loopy, slanted handwriting. Hastily formed letters that spell out the date and the name of the state park that is visible in the background.

I don't know how many times I've studied those letters, searching for long-lost clues, trying to make sense of the spaces in between. Explanations that I've always been convinced are hiding in plain sight.

With trembling hands, I raise up my phone and point it at the back of the photograph. Centering the handwriting in the frame, I click the shutter and wait.

The milliseconds drag by. The air in my closet seems

to drop a hundred degrees in an instant. I shiver as my eyes stay locked on the screen.

Until finally, a message appears.

Error: Unable to translate.

Panic bubbles up in my chest. *What?* What does that mean? I take the picture again, making sure to keep my hand rock steady. But I get the same error message.

Which can mean only one thing.

My dad didn't write it.

But there has to be something in this house that he *did*.

It takes me less than thirty seconds to stuff everything back into the box and return it to the top shelf. Then I'm on the move again, traveling through the house at rocket-launch speeds, searching room after room and calling out to my mom.

"Emmy!" Mom finally finds me in her office with file cabinet doors flung open and papers strewn everywhere. "What's going on? What are you doing?"

"I need to find . . . ," I say, trying to catch my breath. But the words come out choppy and gasping. ". . . something with . . . Dad's . . . handwriting . . . on it."

Mom flinches at the mention of his name. It's not a name that comes up often in our house. "Why?" she asks uneasily.

I continue to riffle through the open cabinet, pulling out folders and boxes of old stuff. "I just really need it.

You must have kept something that he wrote. A letter, a postcard, a legal document, anything?"

"Emmy," Mom says, and I see the concern flash in her eyes. "What's this about?"

"I . . . ," I begin, but I don't know how to finish. I can't very well tell her the truth. I can't just blurt out that I have a magic app that can translate boys' thoughts, and if I can just take a picture of something my dad wrote, then I might finally be able to answer the question that's been weighing on my heart for the past eight years.

"I . . . ," I say again while Mom stares at me, waiting for me to finish. I glance around at the mess I've made of her office and through the window, I can just make out the light of a TV screen, shining through the curtains of the Knights' living room next door. "Handwriting analysis!" I blurt out.

Mom's forehead crumples. "Huh?"

I blink and focus back on her. "I . . . um, watched a documentary on handwriting analysis. And I need samples to analyze. Did you know that a person's handwriting can reveal over five thousand different traits about them? I thought maybe analyzing samples from Dad would be interesting to compare to my own and see if there's any, you know . . ." I swallow. "Family resemblances."

"Handwriting analysis," Mom echoes, clearly still stuck on the first part of my rambling explanation. "You watched a *documentary*? On handwriting analysis?"

"Uh-huh," I say, praying I've somehow become a better liar in the past thirty minutes. "I watched it with Grant."

Now she looks shocked. "Next-door-neighbor Grant?"

"Yep."

"Your ex–best friend who you now can't stand?"

I flush with irritation. She really needs to stop paying such close attention to everything I tell her. I stand up straighter. "Actually, he's not as bad as I thought."

Mom studies me, and I can tell she's trying to digest this new information. "Okay. Well, I'm sorry. I don't think I have any handwriting of your father's. I threw away most of his things when he left. You know that."

"But couldn't you just . . . *check?*"

Mom gives me an apologetic look. "I'm a bit swamped with work right now, Em. How about I write something down for you and you can analyze that for"—she pauses like she's trying to remember the exact wording—"family resemblances."

The hope slithers right out of me and I feel myself deflate. But I also don't want to make Mom feel bad, so I force myself to smile and say, "Okay, sure. That would be great."

HUNCHED

WHEN I SEE the dark-haired girl standing next to my locker on Friday morning, I feel a swoop of hope in my chest.

Harper! She's back! She's finally forgiven me!

But when the girl turns around, to my surprise, it's not Harper. It's Darcy Cohen, one of Alexis Dawson's friends from the dance team. She has a huge grin on her face like she just won the lottery. "Hi!" she says, and I wonder if she's always this chipper in the morning. Maybe that's one of the requirements for being on the dance team.

I peer over my shoulder, searching for Alexis or Isla, certain that Darcy must be talking to one of her friends and not to me. But there's no one else there.

When I turn back around, Darcy is squinting at me like I'm one of those abstract expressionist paintings Grant was talking about. "Soooo, what's your deal?"

I blink, wondering if I misunderstood her. "I'm sorry. My deal?"

"You know, your secret. How did you do that?"

I'm still not following. "Do what?"

"How did you know Garrett liked Alexis?"

Comprehension suddenly streams through me. "Did she tell you about that? Did something happen between them?"

"Uh, yeah," Darcy says as though it's the talk of the school and where have I been? "She talked to him yesterday. She said *you* told her to do it because Garrett had a crush on her. She mentioned how much she wants to go see *A Midsummer Night's Dream* and now they're going together this weekend."

"They are?" Colorful fireworks are exploding inside me. I feel so warm and fuzzy and giddy. I'm basically the heart-eyes emoji come to life.

Darcy squints at me again. "Yes, but you *knew* that would happen, didn't you?"

I shrug and take my reaction down a notch. "Well, I didn't *know*. I had a . . ." I search for the right word. "A hunch."

The expression on Darcy's face is making me just the slightest bit uneasy. I can't tell if she believes me or not. "A hunch?" she repeats, continuing to scrutinize me like I'm an especially complicated line of Shakespeare.

"Yeah."

I'm just searching around for an escape route so I can get out from under that inquisitive stare of hers when she says, "Do you think you can do it again?"

My gaze snaps back to Darcy. "Do what?"

Once again, she speaks like the answer is obvious and why am I so bad at keeping up? "Have a hunch. About a boy."

And then it hits me. She wants my *help*. She wants

me to play Love Coordinator for her like I did for Alexis and Garrett!

I still can't believe they're going out on a date because of me. Well, technically because of an app on my phone, but still, *I'm* the one who made it happen. The app only gave me the information. I successfully coordinated the match!

The sensation I'm experiencing right now is unlike anything I've ever felt. In fact, it's the exact *opposite* sensation I had when Elliot leaned in to kiss me. That feeling was icky, and sour, and uncomfortable. This one is bubbly and sugary and sparkly. I suddenly have an urge to run down the hallway with my hands raised triumphantly in the air, the way Mr. Weston does when he writes a code that works.

And the feeling only fuels my determination to find a new boy for Harper. Which I will. Trust me, I totally will. I'm not going to lose sight of that. But . . .

There's no harm in helping a few others along the way, is there?

I flash Darcy a mischievous smile and with a raise of my eyebrow say, "Sooooo, tell me about this boy."

I can't believe it. The boy Darcy has a crush on is Dev Thakkur! Yes, as in Grant's best friend. He goes to school at Weymouth Academy—a private school in the next town—but he and Darcy apparently go to the same dentist and that's where they met. According to Darcy, they hit it off in the waiting room, and by the time the hygienist was done polishing her teeth, she already had a text message from him! They've been texting for two weeks.

"But the problem is," Darcy explains as we walk to first block, "I don't know if he likes me as just a friend, or more than a friend. He's kind of hot and cold."

Friday is another Odd Day, so we have blocks 1, 3, 5, and 7, and Darcy's math classroom happens to be on the way to my Computer Science classroom, so I offered to walk her there while she told me all about the boy.

"What do you mean by 'hot and cold'?" I ask in my most professional-sounding tone. I've decided this is my new Love Coordinator voice. Calm. Thoughtful. Authoritative. If people are going to come to me with their boy problems, I need to act the part.

"Like he'll be really into texting and we'll text back and forth nonstop for hours and then I won't hear from him for over a day. It's super weird."

"Hmmm." I stroke my chin pensively. "That *is* weird."

My mind flashes back to what Grant said last night about Dev having some kind of personal problems. That could be contributing to this behavior.

"I just want to know if he likes me!" Darcy cries as she pulls her phone out of her pocket and glares at it like it's her biggest enemy. Then, with what appears to be a sudden bolt of determination, she says, "I'm going to tell him to stop texting me altogether. Right now. This is too stressful. I can't handle it."

"No!" I say, reaching for the phone just as Darcy's

fingers start to tap furiously against the screen. "Don't do that. We can figure this out."

The warning bell rings and I carefully hand Darcy back her phone, making sure she returns it to her pocket. I give her shoulder a reassuring squeeze, the same way I watched Ms. Jenkins, the guidance counselor, do to Harper earlier this week. "Don't worry. It'll be okay. We'll chat more about it at lunch, okay?"

Darcy draws in a huge breath and nods. "Okay. Thanks, Emmy." She waves goodbye before veering off toward the green hallway.

I walk the rest of the way to first block with a new pep in my step. It's nice to feel useful and needed. Darcy definitely needs me. From what she told me about Dev and these texts, the whole thing sounds *very* confusing. But I'm sure it's nothing me and my trusty app can't handle.

THE TRICKSTER FAIRY

"THIS ORAL EXAM will make up ten percent of your final semester grade," Ms. Hendrickson tells us later that morning in Language Arts. She's sitting on the edge of her desk, twirling her reading glasses between her fingers. "So be sure to take it seriously. I don't want to hear any jokes. I've read all the Shakespeare cheat sheets out there, so I will recognize anything taken straight from a Google search."

For the first time *ever,* I've actually been looking forward to Language Arts today. I spent all of Computer Science (normally my favorite class) glancing anxiously at the clock, waiting for the bell to ring. And, of course, glancing anxiously at Mr. Weston too, just in case he made any more worrying comments about my mom. But he appeared to be all business today. By the end of class, I almost managed to forget that he thought my mom was beautiful. Maybe I read too much into it. It was probably just a one-time thought. I mean, she *is* beautiful.

"Now, I will call you up one by one and read you a random passage from act two of *A Midsummer Night's*

Dream and you will give me your *own* winning interpretation of that passage. Are we understood?"

Alexis Dawson leans over from the next chair and I think she's going to make some comment about the oral test, but instead she whispers, "Thanks for your help the other day." Her eyes dart to Garrett in the row in front of us. "With you know what."

The permanent grin that has been glued to my face all morning widens even further. "No problem," I whisper back.

"Hey!" Garrett turns around and his eyes dance when they land on Alexis. "Are you two girls whispering about me?"

Alexis flashes him a smile. "You wish." She makes a show of angling her body toward me, playfully shutting Garrett out of the conversation.

I lean in a bit closer. "So, I hear you guys are going to—"

"Emerie Woods," Ms. Hendrickson calls out, startling me back upright. "I hope your excess chatter means that *you* are volunteering to go first."

Normally, that scornful look on Ms. Hendrickson's face would be enough to make me break out into a cold sweat. But not today.

"Absolutely!" I say, launching from my seat and strutting confidently to the front of the room. I stand next to Ms. Hendrickson's desk and face my fellow students, like I'm an actor in the very play I'm being asked to analyze, ready to give the performance of my life.

Ms. Hendrickson looks slightly put off by my eagerness, but she slides her reading glasses onto her nose, grabs her copy of the play from her desk, and flips to one of the hundreds of colored flags sticking out from the top. "Okay, how about this passage, spoken by Robin Goodfellow, better known as Puck." She clears her throat and begins to read. "'Thou speak'st aright; / I am that merry wanderer of the night. / I jest to Oberon and make him smile.'"

I instantly feel giddy. I remember this part. I stayed up late last night, running every page of act 2 through the iSpeak boy app and revealing Shakespeare's *true* meaning behind what he wrote. In other words, I got this in the bag.

"'And sometime lurk I in a gossip's bowl, / In very likeness of a roasted crab, / And when she drinks, against her lips I bob / And on her withered dewlap pour the ale.'" Ms. Hendrickson looks up from the play and stares expectantly at me over the top of her glasses. "Can you tell us what you think Shakespeare is saying here?"

I beam back at her. "Of course! And an excellent choice, Ms. Hendrickson." I turn to address the class and speak in my most scholarly voice. "I especially love this passage because on the surface, it seems that Mr. Shakespeare is simply showing us how much of a trickster Puck, the fairy, is. He calls him the 'merry wanderer of the night,' and talks about how he likes to turn himself into an apple at the bottom of an old woman's drink and then makes her spill it on herself when she takes a sip. But I think it goes much deeper than that. I don't think Shakespeare is just creating a funny character who likes to cause trouble and interfere with people's lives. I think

Shakespeare actually feels sorry for Puck. Puck is anxious and lonely and desperate for validation from King Oberon. The 'merry wanderer' could also be translated as a '*restless* wanderer who can't sit still and can't be happy.' And that's why Puck does what he does. To hide his own loneliness behind the chaos he creates."

When I finish talking, there's a long silence in the classroom as everyone's eyes ping-pong between me and Ms. Hendrickson. She looks like a robot who ran out of power. She sits statue-still on the edge of her desk, her mouth slightly open, her eyes unmoving. Like the shock has overloaded her circuits. Then she blinks and refocuses on me, but her mouth still seems unable to form words. "That . . . well . . . that . . . yes . . . I . . . very good." She blinks again and quickly adds, "Emerie," before turning to find someone else to call on.

I practically skip back to my seat, feeling as light and giddy as a trickster fairy. When I slide into my chair, Alexis leans in again and whispers, "I think you broke her."

And I have to hold my hand over my mouth to keep the laugh from escaping.

ODE TO A BUTT

"I THINK HE just wants to be friends," Darcy says miserably as she scowls down at her phone.

It's lunchtime, and I'm walking to the cafeteria with Alexis, Darcy, and Isla. I was going to try to meet Harper at her locker and walk with her, but Alexis intercepted me in the hallway after Language Arts and we got to talking about her upcoming date with Garrett and, well, long story short, now I'm walking with her and her friends while Darcy shows us every text Dev has ever sent her.

But that's okay. I'll just find Harper once I get to the cafeteria.

"I don't think so," Isla says encouragingly. "I think he really likes you."

"Let me see the one he sent you after the dentist again," Alexis says, and Darcy hands the phone over. "'I can't feel the left side of my face,'" she reads aloud from the screen. "'Good thing we're texting and not talking. My mouth is totally numb from that cavity filling. No more candy for me ever again!'"

"See?" Isla says. "He's talking about his *mouth*. Boys

don't talk about their mouths unless they're thinking about kissing you."

Alexis lowers the phone and purses her lips thoughtfully. "Yeah, but he's saying his mouth is numb. That's not exactly romantic. It seems like more something you'd joke about with one of your friends."

"Ugh!" Darcy throws her hands up toward the ceiling like she's trying to summon a thunderstorm. "Why are boys so confusing? Maybe I should just go over to his house after school, knock on his door, and say, 'Do you like me or not?'"

"Don't do that," Isla and Alexis both say at once, and I can tell from the looks on their faces that they half think Darcy is serious.

"Can I see the text?" I ask, and Alexis passes me the phone.

"Yes!" Darcy squeezes my arm. "Please, Emmy. Tell us what you think. What does your hunch say?"

"Her hunch?" Isla wrinkles her forehead.

Darcy nods. "Emmy is awesome. She has these hunches about what boys are thinking. She's the reason Alexis is going to the play with Garrett this weekend."

Isla's eyes go wide. "That was *you*?"

I hope they can't see the warm glow of pride on my cheeks. "Kinda."

"OMG!" Isla says. "That was amazing. How did you know Garrett had a crush on her? We all thought he hated her."

"I—" I start, but Darcy answers for me.

"It was a *hunch*!"

"So what does your hunch say now?" Isla asks. All

144

three of them have stopped walking and are staring at me like I'm a trapeze artist about to attempt a daring, life-defying catch-and-release move.

I squint at the screen, pretending to study the text message. To be honest, I have no idea what it means. The text *is* super cryptic. Fortunately, I don't have to interpret it myself.

"Can I take a picture of this?" I ask Darcy, who dazedly nods in response, probably assuming this is all part of my mysterious "hunch" process.

I pull out my own phone and, making sure to angle the screen away from the girls, open iSpeak Boy and snap a picture of Darcy's screen. I hand the phone back to her and continue to study the message, pretending to be pensive as the little wheel spins and the app analyzes Dev's words.

Darcy, Isla, and Alexis are all still watching me, completely rapt and silent, waiting to hear what my verdict will be. I have to admit it feels good to talk to someone about boys again. Ever since Sunday's disastrous carnival and Harper's semi-disappearing act, I haven't really had any girls to talk to about this kind of stuff.

The app finishes its magic and the translation appears on the screen.

> I can't believe I'm texting with a girl! And she's cute! This is terrifying. What if she doesn't think *I'm* cute? What if she thinks I'm too scrawny? Or doesn't like my butt? Girls at Weymouth are always talking about cute butts. What makes a butt cute? I better talk about my numb mouth to keep her mind off my butt.

I give an incredulous snort as I read the words on the screen. Really? *This* is what Dev was thinking when he wrote that text? He's worried about what she thinks of his butt? I never would have guessed that in a million, zillion years. I thought only girls were insecure about their bodies. But with Archie Evans's fear of changing clothes in the locker room, Tyler Watkins's obsession with his height, and now this, it would seem boys are just as insecure as girls.

Was this the personal problem Grant mentioned yesterday? Is Dev losing sleep over Darcy and whether or not she likes his butt? I snort again at the thought.

"What?" Darcy asks, looking extremely worried. "What's wrong? Is it bad?"

I peer up from the phone to see all three girls still staring at me with wide, wondrous eyes. "No," I say quickly to reassure Darcy. "It's not bad. Not at all."

"So, do you think he likes her?" Isla asks.

I nod vigorously. "He *definitely* likes you."

She collapses dramatically against Isla's shoulder in relief.

"Then why do you think he's being so weird?" Alexis asks. She looks a bit skeptical of my answer.

"I think . . . ," I say, pausing to make it look like I really have to dig deep for this one. "I think he might just be insecure. And he's not sure if *you* like *him*. That's why he's been a little shy and reserved. In case you don't like him back."

"But I do!" Darcy practically shouts.

"Compliment him," I say, nodding to her phone. "Tell

him you like his hair. Or his eyes. Or his . . . um . . ."
I give a little cough. "His butt."

"His butt?" Darcy looks horrified. "Why would I tell
him I like his butt?"

I shrug. "Boys are super insecure about their butts."

"They are?" Isla and Alexis ask at once, their jaws
dropping like they're cartoons.

"Oh yeah," I say with authority. "And they're obsessed
with their hair."

Isla groans. "I could have told you that. My brother
is in tenth grade and he spends longer primping in the
morning than I do. And when he's done, his hair always
looks like he just got out of bed! I don't get it."

"Boys are weird," Alexis says.

I roll my eyes. "You have no idea."

"Should I text him now?" Darcy asks, looking eagerly
at each of us.

We all nod. "Yes!" I say.

Darcy bites her lip nervously as she stares down at
her phone. She starts to type something but then stops
and jabs at the DELETE key. "I don't think I can compliment his butt. Like, how do you even write that?"

Isla theatrically clears her throat. "'Dear Dev's Butt,
I think you're very cute and nice to look at. And you
make me sparkle. Sincerely, Darcy's Eyes.'"

We all bust up laughing, and it feels so good I wonder
when the last time was that I laughed this hard. Probably Sunday night before the carnival. With Harper.

"You *have* to write that!" Alexis says to Darcy.

"No! I can't write that!" Darcy wipes at her eyes,

which are now watering from laughing. "How about I just stick to his hair. That feels safer."

"Good idea," Isla says.

Darcy bites her lip again and returns her attention to her screen. She's just starting to type something when a deep gargoyle voice booms behind us, "I know you girls don't have your phones out during school hours."

We all race to shove our phones in our pockets before turning to face the wrathful gaze of Assistant Principal Langley, who has snuck up on us in the hallway.

"Of course not," Darcy chirps innocently.

Mr. Langley peers down at us, his dark, beady eyes flicking to each of our faces one by one. "Aren't seventh graders supposed to be at lunch right now?"

"We were just on our way, Mr. Langley," Alexis says before grabbing me by the elbow and pulling me down the hall to the cafeteria. Darcy and Isla scurry behind us, and as soon as we turn the corner, we all start laughing again.

We're still giggling when we tumble into the cafeteria and plop down at one of the empty tables. I packed a lunch today because the cafeteria menu said tuna casserole, and if the first rule of middle school is not to let anyone see you cry, then the second rule is don't go anywhere near the tuna casserole.

I pull my lunch from my backpack and begin to unwrap my cheese and pickle sandwich as Darcy brainstorms her text message to Dev aloud.

"How about something not so obvious, like 'Hey, I was just wondering what shampoo you use because your hair looks really soft.'"

"I like that," Alexis says, crunching into one of her carrot sticks.

"Or maybe," Isla says after a sip from her juice box, "you could compare him to a hot celebrity and tell Dev his hair reminds you of him."

Alexis points her half-eaten carrot stick at Isla. "That's even better."

I'm just taking the first bite of my sandwich when I feel someone's eyes on me. It's like a prickle on the back of my neck. I whip my head around and nearly choke on my food when I see Harper staring at me. She's sitting at a nearby table surrounded by a few girls from her new art class. One of the girls is talking animatedly, and Harper is nodding like she's listening, but her eyes are focused on me.

I've known Harper since the third grade. I know all of her looks. Which is why, as I watch her gaze swivel from me to Darcy to Isla to Alexis and then back to me again, I immediately recognize the jealousy in her eyes.

I leap out of my seat, fully prepared to run to her. The words are already forming in my mind: *You have no reason to be jealous! You're still my best friend. You will always be my best friend. I swear I was going to come find you and—*

But the imaginary words are cut short as Harper's gaze breaks away from mine. The movement is so sharp, so sudden, it feels like a string being cut. A string that was somehow holding me up and now I'm falling.

Harper goes back to her conversation without another glance in my direction, and I slowly lower back down in my seat just as Darcy is saying "What do you think, Emmy?"

"Hmm?" I swallow the lump of sandwich lodged in my throat.

"About comparing Dev to a celebrity. You're the boy expert."

Boy expert.

The phrase bounces around the inside of my brain, echoing deep in my eardrums, reminding me that I still haven't fulfilled my promise to help the one person who matters.

I steal one last glance at Harper before turning back to Darcy, forcing my lips into a smile. "Yeah, I would go with that."

KNIGHT IN NOT-SO-SHINING ARMOR

Leo Burns

Yeah, I know Harper Song.
She's in my social studies class. Why?

Translation

I have to beat level 13 before Victor does. But how am I ever going to defeat that stupid forest gnome without a shrinking spell?

Tyler Watkins

Harper is nice. We used to carpool together in elementary school.

Translation

Can anyone tell I stuffed my shoes with socks? I definitely think it makes me look taller.

Jackson Harris

Harper Song? Didn't she draw a picture for me in the third grade?

Translation

"Now I've walked every block
And I've roamed every road
I've wandered in circles, to find my way home.
To Magnolia Street."

Matt Clemens

Why does Harper want to borrow my science notes? She has a better grade than me.

Translation

Harper wants to borrow my science notes!? I think I'm going to throw up.

Kyle Bates

Sorry, I don't know which one is Harper Song's locker.

Translation

I wonder what they'll blow up today on Dude-Possible.

The next Thursday, I walk home from school with a heavy and hopeless heart. With every step I take and every green translation bubble I read, I can feel Harper's happiness (and my joyful reunion with my best friend) slipping further and further away.

It's been nearly a week since Harper started sitting with her new Art friends at lunch. I've spent the past few days desperately trying (and failing) to find her a new match. I must have dropped Harper's name into conversations with at least a dozen boys this week, in hopes of revealing some secret crush somewhere, but I got nothing. All the boys I talked to were so preoccupied with other pointless things, they never gave Harper a second thought.

The closest I came was yesterday, when I mentioned to Matt Clemens that Harper wanted to borrow his science notes, and he thought he might throw up. But I kind of think, given what I've read of that boy's mind, he would have had that same reaction if *any* girl asked to borrow his notes.

Ugh. Why is this so difficult?! I don't get it. Harper is charming and sweet and beautiful and funny! Any boy in our school would be lucky to have her as a girlfriend. Obviously, the boys in our class are just blind and stupid and immature. I wonder if I should widen my search to include eighth graders.

I turn left on Hartfield Circle and scroll back through my recent translations, just to make sure I didn't miss anything.

Kyle Bates

That new alien movie with Carey Divine is coming out this weekend. Who wants to go?

I have to get out of the house. If I have to listen to my parents congratulate my brother one more time on his debate team championship, I will lose it.

Logan Lansing

Dang it! I can't go. I promised my parents I'd clean out the garage. Lame.

Translation

Not that I could afford it anyway. When is my dad going to get off his butt and get a new job already?

Archie Evans

I'll go! Carey Divine is hot!

Translation

If I survive gym next period. I wonder if anyone would notice if I changed in the bathroom instead of the locker room.

Elliot Phillips

Count me in. But we should go Sunday night instead of Saturday night. It'll be less crowded.

And because I heard Aggie Hawkins is going to see the movie with her friends on Sunday night and maybe we'll bump into them.

I scowl at my phone. I'd almost forgotten about that one. I don't even know how the app managed to overhear *anything* Elliot Phillips said, since we've been doing such a stellar job avoiding each other for the past two weeks. But at least it appears he's moved on to someone else. I just hope Harper never finds out. It would break her heart all over again.

The low-battery alert pops up on my phone, telling me I have less than ten percent power remaining. The one downside of this app is that it eats up a lot of battery, especially since I basically keep it running all day long. I'm about to switch off the screen when I hear someone shout, "Don't fall into any trash cans!"

When I look up, Grant is standing in front of his open garage, holding a Ping-Pong paddle in his hand. He uses it to mime someone walking and texting . . . and then tripping and tumbling theatrically onto the grass.

I stifle a laugh at the charade and call back, "I'll do my best!"

As Grant stands and brushes the grass from his knees, I notice that his Ping-Pong table is set up inside the garage. Grant *loves* Ping-Pong. I don't know how many times I've sat in my room, trying to do homework to the sound of *pop! ping! pop! ping!* outside my window.

Grant saunters down the driveway, twirling the

paddle in his hand like a pro. "So, how's everything?" he asks me. "Are you feeling better? Were you able to fix your"—he leans forward conspiratorially—*"problem?"*

I frown. "What problem?"

"From last week. Were you able to find the 'crack' you were looking for?"

I think about Harper and the way she looked at me last Friday in the cafeteria, and I drop my gaze back down to my phone. "I'm working on it."

"Good. Well, let me know if you ever need to talk. I live right here, you know." He jabs his thumb over his shoulder.

I bark out a laugh and feel a strange flush of warmth in my cheeks. Grant can be kind of sweet when he wants to be. You know, when he's not criticizing me or lecturing me about how I'm living my life all wrong. And, okay, so maybe he's a *little* cute. But only when his hair is all messed up from playing Ping-Pong, like it is now.

I glance over his shoulder at the Ping-Pong table and suddenly realize there's no one else in the garage. Was he playing by himself? How?

Just then, the door to the house swings opens and Dev steps out carrying two cans of flavored sparkling water. "Your mom sent me back out with drinks," he says, then notices me standing there. "Oh, hey, Emmy."

"Oh my gosh! Dev!" I shout, and sprint toward him like he's some kind of celebrity. The poor boy nearly trips over his own feet in surprise. I admit, my reaction is a bit much, but after having read messages between him and Darcy for the past week, I sort of do feel like he's a celebrity. Ever since she sent him that text about his hair on Friday, they've been texting almost nonstop.

"Hi," he says nervously, his eyes darting every which way, like he's unsure where to look.

"Sorry." I calm myself down. "I'm just excited to see you."

"Why?" Grant asks, his gaze bouncing between us.

"He's been texting with a girl from my school," I explain. "Darcy Cohen."

At the mention of her name, a huge grin spreads over Dev's face. "I didn't know you know Darcy."

"We've recently bonded," I reply vaguely. He doesn't need to know that we bonded over *him*.

"Who's Darcy?" Grant asks, and I feel a flicker of pride that for *once*, I know something Grant doesn't.

Dev shrugs, looking caught out. "Oh, she's this girl I met at the dentist. We're going to her school dance together next week."

"You are?" Grant and I both say at once. The difference is, he sounds like a school principal interrogating a disobedient student, while I sound like a squealing fan at a Berrin James concert.

Dev's smile widens. "Yeah. We've been texting a lot, and she just asked me. Right before I came over."

"That's amazing!" I say, trying to keep my voice at a regular volume. I knew she was going to ask him today (it was sort of my idea, actually), but I didn't know he'd already said yes! I can't believe they're going to the dance together! That's exactly what I'd hoped would happen with Harper and Elliot, until . . .

I push the memory from my mind before it can drain all my excitement. I need to stay focused on Dev and Darcy right now. This is a huge win for them. (And yes, it's also a win for my credibility as a Love Coordinator, but mostly for them.)

"What's this about a dance?" Grant asks, and I feel just the slightest bit sorry for him. He still looks totally lost, and honestly, a little left out.

"It's just school stuff," I tell him. "Highbury Middle School is having a seventh-grade dance. I'm sure you wouldn't be interested."

He scoffs. "You're right. I wouldn't. That sounds horrifying." He pretends to shudder, which makes Dev laugh.

I laugh too, but a part of me feels slightly stung. I get that he's homeschooled and doesn't want to take part in any regular school stuff, but he doesn't have to be *so* forceful about it. I mean, he didn't have to *shudder*.

Dev passes one of the cans of sparkling water to Grant and holds up the other to me. "Do you want one? I can run back in and get another."

"Sure. Thanks." I take the can from Dev, who hurries back up the driveway to the house.

The moment he turns around, my gaze automatically falls to the back of his jeans and I tilt my head a little to get a better angle.

Hmm, I think. His butt is a *little* on the scrawny side, but it's definitely still cute.

"Were you just checking out his butt?" Grant asks after Dev disappears into the house.

My face warms to approximately the temperature of the sun. "Wha— N-no!" I sputter. But I can tell from the gleam in Grant's eyes that he doesn't believe me. I *very* quickly change the subject. "How cool is it that my friend and your friend are going to a dance together?"

Grant looks uncertain as he pops the top of his water and takes a sip. "I don't know." He glances back toward the garage door. "Dev is going through some things right now, and I'm just not sure it's a good idea."

"Of course it's a good idea! Didn't you see the smile on his face when I mentioned her name? He's happy! And totally smitten! You're *welcome*."

Grant's eyes slide suspiciously to me. "What do you mean?"

"I got them together," I say casually as I open my water and then take a long gulp.

"What?"

"It's true. Darcy wasn't sure if Dev liked her, so I helped her figure it out."

"And how exactly did you do that?" His voice is dripping with sarcasm, and it immediately raises my hackles. I know I should probably just let it go and enjoy this little victory all by myself, but there's something about the way Grant is looking at me as he takes another sip. It's as if he's challenging me. And I do not like backing down from a challenge.

I flash him a smirk. "Let's just say I have a knack for understanding boys."

Sparkling water shoots out of Grant's mouth like a fountain, spraying all over my shirt.

"Ew!" I cry, jumping back. "Drink much?"

Grant wipes his mouth. "Sorry. I thought I heard you say you have a knack for understanding boys."

I stick out my chin defiantly. "That *is* what I said."

"You?" he asks dubiously, and now my hackles are *way* up. Why does he have to do that? Why does he have to be all nice one second and then turn back into his snobby, arrogant self the next?

"Yes!" I say. "*Me.* Some people even say I'm a boy expert."

He crosses his arms over his chest, resting the can of soda against his opposite elbow. "And *how* exactly are you a boy expert?"

"Well," I begin importantly, slipping back into my professional mode. "You see, boys don't always say what they mean. And they don't always mean what they say. Sometimes they say one thing but are thinking something completely different."

"Uh-huh," Grant says flatly.

I take another sip of water, drawing out the moment before I continue. "But *I* can bridge the gap."

He raises an eyebrow. "The gap?"

"Yes. I have a talent for deciphering exactly what a boy is thinking, no matter what he says."

"Really?"

Grant's tone is starting to annoy me. "You don't believe me?"

He barks out a laugh. "Not even a little bit."

"Fine, I'll prove it to you." Keeping my phone by my side, I angle the screen away from Grant as I stealthily open the iSpeak Boy app. "Say something. Anything."

Grant looks at me like I've lost my mind. "You're serious, aren't you?"

I steal a quick peek at my screen as Grant's little blue speech bubble pops up, followed shortly after by the green translation bubble.

Grant Knight

You're serious, aren't you?

Translation

You're serious, aren't you?

I let out a small harrumph. Why does it keep doing that?

"Say something else," I urge him.

"Like what?"

Grant Knight

Like what?

Translation

Like what?

"I don't know! Anything. Tell me what you think of me."

Grant stops to contemplate for a second and I know that the app *has* to work this time. I can *see* him thinking right now.

"Well," he begins pensively, "you act a little strange sometimes, like right now, and sometimes I miss hanging out with you like when we were kids. But . . ." He shrugs. "I still like having you as my neighbor."

I bite my lip, waiting for the app to process. The anticipation is killing me. *Come on, come on, work!*

Grant Knight

> Well, you act a little strange sometimes, like right now, and sometimes I miss hanging out with you like when we were kids. But . . . I still like having you as my neighbor.

Translation

> Well, you act a little strange sometimes, like right now, and sometimes I miss hanging out with you like when we were kids. But . . . I still like having you as my neighbor.

What. The. Heck?

Why doesn't this stupid thing work on Grant?

"Problems?" Grant asks, and I realize I've completely abandoned the façade of hiding my phone. I'm now holding it right in front of my face, glaring at the screen with a murderous expression.

"Never mind," I mutter. "It doesn't . . . I don't . . ."

I blow out a breath. "My abilities don't seem to work on you."

Grant chuckles. "That's because I have no gap."

I scowl at him. "What?"

"I always say what I mean."

I roll my eyes. I know that can't possibly be true, but it does explain why this keeps happening. One of these days, though, he's going to think something and not say it and I'm going to be there, ready and waiting to prove him wrong.

"Well, whatever." I shove my useless phone into my pocket. "My abilities may not work on you, but I'll have you know that I have successfully coordinated *two* matches in the past two weeks. Two! Because I *am* a boy expert and I *can* tell what boys are thinking." I wave my half-empty can dismissively toward Grant. "Most of the time, anyway."

"What do you mean, you've 'coordinated two matches'?"

"I mean two couples are now together because of me. That's four lives that I've improved."

Grant lets out an infuriating little snort. "Improved?"

"Yes, *improved*. You said so yourself, Dev has been going through some personal stuff, and today, he actually looked happy. I did that."

For a long time, Grant doesn't speak. He looks contemplative and a little frustrated, like he's racking his brain for a good comeback but failing. And just when I'm convinced he's about to give up, he says, "Be careful, Emmy."

I take a step back, confused. "What does that mean?"

"It just means be careful. Getting involved in other people's lives can be tricky. Someone can get hurt."

I scoff and take another sip of my drink. "You know what I think?"

Grant chuckles. "I haven't the *slightest* clue."

"I think you're jealous."

"Jealous? Of what?"

"Of Dev and Darcy. Your best friend has a girl in his life now, and you're afraid of losing him. *Or* maybe you're just jealous that he gets to go to a school dance and you don't."

At that, Grant actually throws his head back and laughs. I would be insulted if his reaction weren't just the slightest bit over-the-top. Which immediately makes me wonder if I've hit the nail right on the head.

"Okay, *boy expert*," he says once he's stopped cackling like an old woman. "That's the most ridiculous thing I've ever heard. I couldn't care less about going to a middle school dance. They sound awkward and awful, and there are *so* many things I'd rather be doing with my time."

His voice is sharp and bitter, but for some reason he won't look at me. Instead, he takes a sip of his water, like he's trying to cover his face.

The door to the house slams, and Dev is back, carrying another can of sparkling water. He flashes me a smile, completely oblivious to the animosity bouncing between me and Grant like a Ping-Pong ball.

"Are you going to stick around and play?" Dev asks me, nodding to the table.

I down the last of my water and toss the empty can into the recycle bin in Grant's garage. "No thanks," I reply with an artificially sweet smile before cutting my eyes to Grant. "There are *so* many things I'd rather be doing with my time."

Then I turn on my heels and walk briskly toward my house. The moment I'm behind my front door, I yank my phone out of my pocket and jab at the screen. There's no way Grant was being entirely truthful just then. There's no way he was saying *everything* he thought. I know he was hiding something.

But when I glance down at my phone, the battery is dead.

INSTANT CELEBRITY

WHEN I GET to school the next day, there are colorful, glitter-covered banners hanging in all the hallways. Streamers dangle from classroom doors, and some of the lockers are decorated with signs that say things like "They can't stop what they can't catch!" and "Have no Fear, #21 is here!"

I forgot today is Spirit Day. Which means we're expected to get all excited about the eighth-grade football game this weekend.

I roll my eyes as I pass by a giant poster with a football player's picture on it. I don't get it. I really don't. These people chase a ball around a field and slam into each other . . . *on purpose*. How is that more important than, say, building a website, or painting a mural, or starring in a play? Because I don't see the entire school celebrating any of *those* things. I don't see the lockers of the Robotics Club decorated each week. In fact, I doubt most of these people know that we even have a Robotics Club (which we do).

Apparently, though, I'm in the minority, because everyone in the hallways seems super pumped about the game tomorrow afternoon. The eighth-grade foot-ball players are dressed in their uniforms and are high-fiving everyone they pass. There's even a huge crowd of girls gathered around one of the players up ahead, prob-ably wanting to take selfies with him in his uniform, like he's a real celebrity or something. And it happens to be right near my locker. Which means I'll have to shove them all aside just to dial in my combination.

I blow out a breath and plow on, ready to elbow and shoulder my way through the crowd. But as I approach, I notice that there is no football player standing in the middle of that crowd. The group of chattering girls is gathered around a locker.

My locker.

Why are they—

"Emmy!" someone shouts, and then a hand reaches out and yanks me forward. The girls spread out, like they're making room for the queen of England, and sud-denly I'm thrust into the center of a circle of at least eight pairs of eyes staring eagerly at me.

"Um . . . ," I begin awkwardly. I have no idea what's going on right now, but it sort of feels like an ambush. "Good morning."

Brianna Brown giggles. But it's not an evil, teasing giggle. It's more like the kind of giggle you hear when a cute boy tells a lame joke.

"Can I . . . help you?" I spin in a slow circle, taking in the faces of my captors.

Then, suddenly, they converge, moving toward me and talking all at the same time. It's so loud and jarring,

I only catch bits and pieces of what is being practically shouted at me.

". . . and then he said that he liked my socks . . ."

". . . but I can't figure out why he only picks on me . . ."

". . . except I don't know what to think because he never even looks at me . . ."

". . . brother is driving me crazy . . ."

". . . totally cute and likes all the same things as me . . ."

". . . he's best friends with my brother so it's complicated . . ."

". . . partner on this school project but he won't do any of the work . . ."

". . . what do you think that means . . ."

". . . but I just want to be friends . . ."

". . . I don't even know if he likes me!"

"Wait a second!" I call out, raising my hand to try to silence the noise. Surprisingly, all the voices fall quiet. I glance around again, into their matching eager faces, and suddenly I understand. I can't believe it, but I understand.

"Are you . . . ," I begin, unsure of how insane it will sound aloud. "Are you all here to talk to me about *boys*?"

Some of the girls nod and a few others mumble "yes," and something that sounds like "of course." Then Brianna Brown steps forward, like she's the official spokesperson of the horde, and says, "I heard you were some kind of a boy expert."

My mouth falls open in shock. "Really?"

"I heard that too," says another girl.

"And me," says a third.

"Darcy Cohen told me you helped her get together with a cute boy she met at the dentist!" a sixth-grade girl named Chelsey Costas exclaims.

"And Alexis Dawson said you were the one who figured out that Garrett Cole had a crush on her," a small blond girl calls out.

"Well, I mean, yeah, that's *technically* true." I try to keep my voice calm and humble, but inside my own head I'm screaming, *All these girls think I'm a boy expert! They've all come to me for help with their boy problems. ME!*

Take that, Grant Knight.

Chelsey steps forward. "Can you tell me if Tyler Watkins likes me? Or if he thinks I'm just his best friend's annoying little sister?"

"And Matt Clemens!" says the small blond girl, stepping forward. "What do you think it means when he says he likes my socks?"

"Kyle Bates is totally blowing off our school project and I'm doing all the work myself!" complains Brianna.

"Jackson Harris and I have been friends for two years," says another voice, and I turn to see Hilary Pasquale peering at me with desperate eyes. "How do I know if he wants more than that?"

"Do you know Micah Lowenstein?" someone else shouts over the quickly growing chatter. "Do you know if he likes anyone in our school?"

"You have to tell me what is up with my brother,"

says a girl named Lesley Schwimmer. "He locks himself in his room for hours and won't come out. It's driving the entire family crazy! We have no idea what he's doing in there!"

"But first you *have* to tell me what this SnipPic comment from Archie Evans means!"

And suddenly, the crowd converges again, all shouting to be heard over each other. I now understand how Berrin James feels when he's mobbed on the street by fangirls. I want to curl into a little ball until it all disappears.

"Hey! Hey! Hey!" someone shouts over the noise, quieting everyone in an instant. I assume it must be a teacher, given how commanding and effective the voice is, but when I glance up, I'm relieved to see Darcy waving her arms wildly to part the crowd. "Give the girl some space. Jeez!"

Darcy shoos everyone away and extends her arm out in front of me, creating a blockade. "Okay," she begins, once again sounding a lot like a teacher. "We will do this in a calm, orderly fashion. One at a time. The line starts here."

Everyone scrambles to line up in front of her. "Wow," I whisper to Darcy, impressed. "You should be a professional bodyguard."

She flashes me a grin. "I helped my dad run the pie-throwing booth at the carnival. You should see the crowds when you tell people they can throw a pie at their teacher's face. This is nothing."

I giggle and stand up straighter, trying to collect myself.

Darcy pulls out her phone and, with an air of authority, calls the first person in line. "Name?" she prompts.

"Vivi Lee," the girl replies.

"Boy problem?" Darcy asks, and I stifle another giggle.

"I'm not sure if Micah Lowenstein likes me or not. I catch him looking at me sometimes and I want to talk to him, but I don't know what to say."

Darcy types furiously into her phone. "Got it. Emmy will investigate and get back to you with any insights. Next!"

"Delia Nazari," announces the next girl.

"Boy problem?"

"Archie Evans left this weird comment on one of my SnipPic posts about dragons and I want to know what it means."

"Dragons, got it," Darcy says before beckoning the next girl forward.

By the time the warning bell rings, Darcy has impressively worked through the entire line, taking down names and notes on each boy-related mystery.

"Thank you!" I say, breathing out a deep sigh of relief. "You're a lifesaver."

She waves this away. "It's nothing. Just helping out a friend in need. Like you did for me."

I smile at her casual use of the word "friend." Darcy definitely feels like someone I could become good friends with. I like her. She's funny and quirky and kind of spontaneous. Like you never know what she's going to do or say next. Actually, I wonder why we never became friends before. Maybe because I was so busy with Harper and she was so busy with Alexis and Isla that we never really had the chance to get to know each other. But now, because of my magic app, I'm not only helping tons of girls solve their tricky boy problems, (not to mention saving my grade in Language Arts!), but I'm also starting to make some new friends.

"Wanna walk to first block together?" she asks.

I grin. "Sure! But I still have to get my stuff out of my locker. I don't want you to be late."

She shrugs. "I can be late. I don't mind."

I quickly dial in the combination, pull open the door, and empty my backpack. I'm just grabbing my stuff for Computer Science when my phone chimes in my pocket and I check the screen to see a new email from Darcy.

"I just sent you all the notes I took," she explains at my puzzled look. "So you have it all in one place."

"Thanks!" I say, closing my locker door. "Now I just have to figure out how I'm going to talk to all of those boys."

"Actually," Darcy says as we head down the hallway, "I happen to know a place where they will all be at exactly the same time."

"Where?"

She nudges her chin toward the nearest hand-painted banner on the wall.

IN it to WIN it!
Come support your Highbury Bobcats
Saturday at 3:00!

I let out a groan. "Ugh. I hate football."

"Oh my gosh!" Darcy squeals. "Me too!"

"It's so lame!"

Darcy lowers her voice to a low grumble to imitate a football player. "Oh, look at me. I'm a big strong man who can steal the ball from other big strong men."

I laugh and break out my own practiced imitation. "Yeah, and I can fall in a big dog pile on top of other dudes."

Darcy rolls her eyes. "So stupid. Alexis and Isla both want to try out for cheerleading when we get to high school because you get to use your dance skills, but I'm sorry, why should girls be on the sidelines cheering on *boys* playing sports? Why can't everyone cheer on everyone?"

"Yeah!" I say. "I've never thought about it that way before, but you're so right."

The hallways are starting to clear out as people disappear into their classrooms and Darcy and I pick up the pace. We're definitely going to be late.

"So, do you want to come to the game with me tomorrow?" I ask as we round the corner into the blue hallway. As much as I hate to admit it, Darcy is right. The football game would be the best place to talk to all the boys on this list. And the P-PUP doesn't apply there, so I wouldn't have to hide my phone from teachers. "We can suffer through it together."

Darcy beams in delight. "Yes! Oh, wait, no. I can't. We're hanging out with my grandma all day. She gets kind of lonely since my grandpa died, so we try to spend as much time with her as possible."

"Oh, okay," I say, slightly disappointed. "No worries."

"But how about we meet at your locker first thing Monday morning. And you can rehash all the lame details of the game . . . and the boys."

I giggle. "Perfect."

"It's a date," she says with a smile before she hurries to her math class and I continue on to Computer Science.

The final bell rings, and I'm about to turn down the yellow hallway, when out of the corner of my eye, I see a flash of movement. I turn just in time to see someone slip a piece of paper through the slats of a locker door. I can tell from the back of his head and his light-brown fauxhawk that it's Cole Campbell, but what on earth is he doing? He stands on his tiptoes to try to peer through the slats of the locker door, presumably to make sure whatever he stuffed in there is all the way in. Then he turns and scurries down the hallway. It's not until he leaves, and his body is no longer blocking the locker, that I see the number on the door, and my heart immediately starts to flutter.

That's Harper's locker!

Why is Cole Campbell secretly slipping something into Harper's—

I let out a quiet gasp as a memory floods back to me. It was something the app translated last week, when I first discovered it on my phone.

There's a girl with a locker near mine who wears the most amazing perfume. It smells like heaven.

Starry Skies!

It's Harper's favorite body spray. We both wore it on the night of the carnival. The girl Cole has been obsessed with this whole time is Harper!

Okay, so technically, he's obsessed with the way she *smells*, but that's a solid start, right? No relationship can succeed if you don't like the way the other person smells. And isn't there an old saying about the way to a boy's heart is through his nose? Or maybe that's his stomach.

Anyway, I'm practically overflowing with excitement and relief. I knew there had to be some boy at this school who liked Harper. And I've finally found him. It's Cole Campbell!

He's pretty cute, now that I think about it.

In my mind, a new plan is already brewing. I have to figure out the perfect time and place to get them together. Maybe at the football game!

I start toward Mr. Weston's Computer Science classroom with a new lightness to my step. By this time tomorrow, Harper won't even remember who Elliot Philips is!

Wait a minute.

My feet drag to a halt as that name ricochets around my brain, bringing all the painful memories from the carnival with it. Before I set *any* plan into motion, I have to be one hundred percent certain this time. There can be no more mistakes. No misunderstandings. What if Cole is actually obsessed with another girl's heavenly smelling body spray and he was just returning some borrowed notes to Harper or something? Or what if that secret love note was meant for someone else and he confused the locker numbers?

There's only one way to be sure.

I peer down the hallway after Cole and watch him disappear into the boys' bathroom. Then I turn back and look toward Mr. Weston's door.

One room I'm supposed to be in right now; the other I'm not supposed to be in *ever*.

But I have to fix my friendship with Harper. And right now, Cole is my best lead. My *only* lead.

What choice do I have?

INVISIBLE HAIRBALLS

I'VE NEVER BEEN inside a boys' bathroom before. It's even worse than the girls' bathroom. It feels dirtier somehow, and there are balled-up paper towels all over the floor around the trash can, as though boys have terrible aim. And that might also account for the smell. It bombards my nostrils the moment I ease open the door. I make an effort to breathe only through my mouth.

"What are you doing?" Cole asks, and I'm relieved to find him standing at the sink, washing his hands and not doing something else. He's staring at me like I'm an alien who has just crash-landed on earth. I suppose there's some truth to that. I do feel like I'm in enemy territory right now.

And completely out of my comfort zone. My hands shake as I grip my phone. I tuck them behind my back so he can't see the iSpeak Boy app open on the screen, or the trembling of my fingers.

"I need to talk to you," I say as steadily as I can, pushing back my shoulders to try to look more confident.

"In the boys' bathroom?" He grabs a paper towel

from the dispenser, dries his hands, and then tosses it toward the trash can. It misses by a foot.

"Sorry about the, um"—I clear my throat—"location, but it couldn't wait."

Cole darts his eyes toward the door, like he's thinking about bolting. I casually sidestep to block his path.

"Okay, so talk," he says, and I don't like the tone of his voice. If he's going to be Harper's boyfriend, he has to be a bit nicer.

"It's about Harper Song."

He shrugs. "What about her?"

My phone vibrates in my hand and I steal a peek at the screen.

Cole Campbell
What about her?

Translation
Crap! What did she see? I thought the hallway was empty!

That little green bubble renews my confidence. I'm on the right track. "Why were you putting something in her locker?"

Cole's face loses about three shades of its natural coloring. He drops his gaze to the floor. "I wasn't putting anything in her locker."

Cole Campbell
I wasn't putting anything in her locker.

She did see! So much for being stealthy.

I grit my teeth. "I saw you. I saw you put something in her locker. Do you like her or something?"

"Like her?" Cole makes a choking sound like there's a giant hairball in his throat. "I mean, she's nice and everything, but I don't *like* her."

Cole Campbell

Like her? I mean she's nice and everything, but I don't *like* her.

Translation

I have no idea what's going on, but I have to get out of here. This girl has lost her mind!

With a surge of frustration, I take another step to block the door and press on. "So you don't think Harper Song is pretty?"

The invisible hairball chokes him again. "Pretty? No! What are you even talking about?"

Cole Campbell

Pretty? No! What are you even talking about?

Translation

Of course she's pretty! She's the prettiest girl in school. But what does she expect me to do about it?

Bingo!

There it is. The proof. The certainty. The win!

The Love Coordinator has struck again.

I try to keep the triumphant smile from overtaking my face, but I'm not doing a very good job. My joy is impossible to contain. I can't *wait* to tell Harper.

"Um, hello?" Cole says, waving a hand in front of my face. It's only now I realize I still haven't looked up from my phone. "Are we done here? Can I go now?" He nudges his chin toward the door that I'm still blocking.

"Oh, right. Sorry. Yes." I quickly jump aside and let him pass. But as soon as he's gone, I remember something else. I shove the door open with my shoulder and barge into the hallway. "Wait! Cole! Are you going to be at the football game tomo—"

The words die on my lips when my shoulder smashes painfully into a rib cage and I glance up to see someone looming over me. I watch with dread as the Gargoyle's beady little eyes slide from me to the door (which is very clearly marked with the word "Boys") before finally coming to rest menacingly on my lit-up phone.

MONKEY WITH A NEW COMPUTER

"HOW MANY TIMES have I told you to put this thing away?" Mr. Langley bellows. We're sitting in his dusty office that smells like old lemons. My phone is lying on his desk, the screen on, unlocked, and open to the iSpeak Boy app, which is still running.

Unfortunately, I wasn't able to close the app before Mr. Langley swiped the phone right out of my hand. Fortunately, he's too focused on scolding me to notice what's on the screen.

For now, anyway.

"I'm sorry. It'll never happen again." I lean forward to grab the phone, but he slides it out of my reach with his fingertip.

"All of you are obsessed with these . . . *things.*" He gives the phone a disgusted flick. "These are the real addictions in our society. These are the real threats to our future! These *distractions.*" He raps on his desk. "Ms. Woods!"

My gaze whips up from my phone, and I try to focus on Assistant Principal Langley. But it's pretty hard when my phone is buzzing incessantly with every word he says. Sweat is pooling at the back of my neck. I can see the screen filling with little green bubbles right before my very eyes. Right before *his* very eyes. But it's like he can't even see it. He's too distracted by his own rambling.

"Where is the dialogue?" Mr. Langley asks. "The conversation? The witty repartee? Gone. It's all gone. Now it's all about likes and comments and retweeps." He makes a noise between a grunt and a snort. "Likes and comments are not going to help you live a more fulfilled life, Ms. Woods."

My phone vibrates again, rattling against the wooden desk. With a groan, Mr. Langley scoops it into his hands and shakes it. "How do you even concentrate with all this buzzing?" He jabs frantically at the screen, looking not unlike a monkey that's just gotten its hands on a computer. "How do you turn this thing off?"

I'm pretty sure my heart is going to explode out of my chest. He's staring *at* the screen. *At* the app. All he has to do is read *one* of the messages on the screen, see his own name, and this will all be over. My secret will be out. I might be expelled. I don't know. I doubt it says anything in the P-PUP about punishment for students who bring mind-reading apps to school.

I hold my breath as Mr. Langley continues to fumble with my phone, his mustache twitching, his cheeks turning beet red. "Why does it keep buzzing at me?"

"Um," I say, slowly reaching toward the phone, terrified of making any sudden movements. "I can shut it off." He flicks his dark, beady eyes to me. I swallow a gulp and hastily add, "If you want. I mean, if it's bothering you."

He stares at me for a long time, then back at the phone in his hand. I honestly can't tell which one he hates more right now.

"Fine," he says, sliding it across the desk to me. I catch it with two hands and shudder in relief. "I don't want to hear it again."

"Yes, Mr. Langley. I'm sorry." I jab at the power button until the thing is completely off and then collapse against the back of my chair.

"And we haven't even gotten to the *other* infraction yet." Mr. Langley points a thick finger at me. "What, may I ask, were you doing in the *boys'* bathroom?"

"Um," I say again, gripping the wooden arms of the chair like I'm on a terrifying roller coaster. "I . . . I went in by mistake."

"By *mistake?*" He clearly doesn't believe me.

I glance down at the phone in my lap, as though it might be able to offer me some kind of help, even without the power.

And, actually, it does.

"I was distracted!" I say with sudden inspiration.

"Distracted?"

I hold up the phone and shrug sheepishly. "You're so right. They *are* distracting. I was texting my friend and not looking where I was going, and I walked right into the wrong bathroom." I flash him a pitiful look. "Better than falling into a trash can, I guess."

I snort out a laugh, but he clearly doesn't get the joke.

"I don't know what I'm going to do with you, Ms. Woods." Mr. Langley shakes his head and makes a *tsk* sound. "A lot of kids at this school have a problem following the Proper Phone Use Policy, but you seem to have the biggest problem of all. I can't count the number of times I've seen you—this week alone!—sneak your phone out of your pocket when you think no one is looking."

"It won't happen again."

"You're right it won't. And to make sure you understand the consequences of your actions, I'm giving you detention after school today."

"What!" I screech, which I immediately realize is the wrong thing to do. Mr. Langley's brow furrows.

"You're lucky it's just one day."

The Tummy Tornado starts to swirl relentlessly. I wonder what level on the Fuji-whatever scale this one would be classified as. I've never been sent to detention before. "Are you . . . are you going to tell my mom?" I ask shakily.

"You bet your hot dog buns I'm going to tell your mom," Mr. Langley says, sounding way too pleased with himself. "And then you can explain to her why you'll be coming home late from school today." He nods to the phone in my lap. "I'm sure you, of all people, can figure out how to reach her."

CONTAGIOUS EXCITEMENT

THE MOMENT I see Harper walk out of her Art classroom at the end of the block, all memories of Mr. Langley's office and my upcoming detention fade into the background. I sprint up to her, practically squealing, and loop my arm through hers. The action is supposed to be friendly and reassuring, to remind her of how close we used to be (and could be again!), but it's also, admittedly, to make sure she doesn't try to run away.

"Harper!" I exclaim as she glances curiously at our interlocked arms. "You won't believe what I just found out."

"What?" she asks, and I'm relieved to hear she does sound mildly interested.

"Bye, Harper!" someone shouts from behind us. It's one of Harper's new Art class friends. "See you at lunch!"

"Bye, Jojo!" Harper calls back to the girl. "Bye, Robby!" Robby Martinez has just appeared in the doorway of the classroom as well. He, of course, doesn't respond.

As I watch Harper waving to her new friends, I try to flick away my jealousy, reminding myself that after she hears what I have to say, there's no way we won't be BFFs again and back to sitting together at lunch.

I give Harper's arm a little tug, coaxing her down the hallway. "Are you ready for this?" I ask, doing my best to build up the suspense. "Are you sure? Because it's big! Like, seriously big. Bigger than when Berrin James announced his solo career after Summer Crush broke up! Bigger than when we found out—"

"Emmy, just tell me already!" She laughs when she says this, but there's a tinge of impatience in her voice.

I should probably just get to the point. "Okay, here it goes." I take a deep breath. "Cole Campbell likes you."

Harper stops walking so suddenly, I'm jerked back by our intertwined arms. I can tell from the look on her face that she's as surprised as I was to learn this. Her eyes are wide and kind of glazed over, like she's thinking back to every encounter she's ever had with Cole and trying to find all the signs she missed.

"Isn't that exciting?" I ask after Harper hasn't spoken for a solid ten seconds. "He's pretty cute, right? And smart. Even though he acts like kind of an idiot when he's around his friends, but most boys do that."

We're stopped in the middle of the hallway and Harper is still standing motionless with her mouth slightly open. She's clearly too shocked to speak. So I keep going. "Anyway, I was thinking tomorrow, we should go to the football game together, because he's most likely going to be there, and I'm working on a plan to—"

"No." The word is so fast and so forceful, it feels less like a word and more like a slap.

"What do you mean no?"

"I mean *no*. I don't want to be involved in any more of your plans."

I sigh. Okay, so she's still upset about the last one going wrong. That's fair. But she needs to know that this is nothing like the last time. This will not be another Elliot Phillips disaster. This time I have proof. Maybe she just needs to see it for herself. I know I said I would keep the iSpeak Boy app a secret, but Harper is my best friend. I can trust her. And she needs to believe me.

"I should really get to class," Harper says, but I grip her arm tighter.

"No, wait!" Wading through the hallway traffic, I drag Harper behind me until we're tucked into a quieter corner, away from all the commotion. "Okay," I say in a hushed voice. "I understand why you're hesitant. I know I've been wrong about this kind of thing in the past. But this time I'm absolutely one hundred percent certain. Cole likes you." I glance over both shoulders to check for eavesdroppers and then draw my phone out of my pocket and power it back on. "You see, I found this app last week, and—"

"Emmy!" Harper shouts, causing me to flinch. "Stop! Just stop! No more apps! No more plans. No more schemes. No. More."

Now I'm certain she must have slapped me, because the sting is so bad, my eyes are starting to water.

She must notice it, because when she speaks again, her voice is much softer. Remorseful, even. "Em, I'm sorry. I just . . ." She lets out a weary breath and tugs at the ends of her hair. "Did you ever think to ask who *I* like?"

I blink rapidly, trying to squeeze the water from my eyes. "What?"

"You're all excited about Cole Campbell *supposedly* liking me—"

"Not supposedly!" I interject, holding up my phone. "He *does*. I swear. If you would just look at this—"

"It doesn't matter!" Harper says in exasperation. "Because I don't like him! But you never seem to care about how I feel. Or who *I* like."

"Th-that's not true!" I'm so baffled by what she's saying, I can barely get the words out. "You *liked* Elliot."

Harper shifts uncomfortably. "That's the thing. I've been thinking about it a lot since the carnival, and I don't think I really did."

Okay, now she's just lying to make a point. "Of course you did. You told me."

"No, *you* told *me*."

"Huh?"

Harper blows out another breath. "Do you remember when you first used that horoscope app? And you found out Elliot's birthday was compatible with mine? You were so excited about it. You kept talking him up, telling me what a good match we would make, why we were perfect for each other. Then, when you thought he was looking at me at the assembly, you got even more excited. And I think I just . . ." She shrugs. "I just got caught up in *your* excitement. I'm not sure I ever had any of my own."

I'm trying hard to grasp what she's saying, but it's

like trying to catch water in a net. "So, wait, if you don't like Elliot, who *do* you like?"

"Why do I have to like *anyone*?" she fires back. "Why is it so important to you to match me with a boy?"

"I already told you," I say, rapidly losing my patience. "Because you're my best friend."

Harper shakes her head. "No. I don't think this has anything to do with me."

I squint because she's suddenly gone all fuzzy and out of focus. "What are you talking about? Of course it has to do with you. Why else would I go through so much trouble to set *you* up?"

For a moment, Harper looks almost disappointed in my answer. Like I've just failed a test I didn't even know I was taking. She drops her gaze to the ground again. "Well, I don't need you to set me up with anyone, okay? I don't need you to be my Love Coordinator anymore." Then, just before she takes off down the hall, she adds in a sad, almost regretful voice, "I just need you to leave me alone."

A PICTURE IS WORTH A THOUSAND WORDS

NO ONE TELLS you the worst thing about detention. It's not the boredom. It's not that you're not allowed to do any homework. It's not even the teacher glaring at you from her desk in the corner.

No, the worst part of detention is your own brain.

When you have nothing else to do, nothing to distract yourself with, all you're left with are your thoughts. And trust me when I tell you that right now, mine are pretty messy.

All I can think about is Harper and what she said to me in the hallway this morning. She was barely making sense! She's claiming never to have liked Elliot at all? That's baloney! I saw the look on her face when I told her I thought he was looking at her. I saw the pink in her cheeks every time he liked one of her SnipPic posts. She was totally into him.

Maybe she's just protecting herself after what happened at the carnival. Maybe her heart hurts less if she pretends she never liked him at all.

But then, you would think she would be super excited about a new boy. It's something to chase away the pain of the old one! But she acted like she wanted nothing to do with Cole Campbell.

Or me.

The tears instantly well up in my eyes again, and I blink hard to chase them away. Okay, so she doesn't want to be set up. Fine. But there's got to be another way to fix this. The problem is, I haven't the slightest clue what that is.

I feel a gentle tap on my shoulder, and when I turn around in my chair, I'm surprised to see Robby Martinez sitting behind me. He must have come in after I sat down, because otherwise, I definitely would have noticed him.

He glances down at his green notebook, which is open on his desk, and spins it around so I can see the drawing he's working on. I nearly gasp. Once again, the artwork is amazing. The black lines are so crisp and precise, and the face of the subject is so real, it looks like a photograph. But that's not why I react the way I do.

I lean in closer, studying the girl on the page. She's standing in front of a locker, her arms crossed over her chest, her mouth pulled into a tight line, like she's trying to keep a tidal wave of emotion locked inside. She looks sad. She looks rejected. She looks like her best friend just walked away from her, leaving her alone in the middle of the hallway.

I know all this because the girl is me.

I peer up at Robby with questioning eyes. He saw me after my fight with Harper in the hallway? He *drew* me?

He turns the notebook back around and hunches

over the page, his pen gripped tightly in his hand as he carefully adds something to the drawing. It must be really tiny, because the tip of his pen barely moves.

I peek at the teacher's desk in the corner. Ms. Gladstone is leaned back in her chair, her chin resting on her chest, her eyes closed, clearly as bored as we are.

I feel another tap on my shoulder, and when I turn back around, the notebook is facing me again. I immediately notice the change.

In the drawing, Robby has added tears to my face. Delicate, raindrop-shaped tears rolling down my cheeks. The kind of tears you're not supposed to cry in a middle school hallway, in view of everyone. But clearly, the girl in this picture doesn't care about that.

When I look up from the notebook, Robby is watching me. His long, dark hair is tickling the tops of his eyelashes, and his round, inquisitive eyes seem to be asking me a silent question. He tilts his head, and I understand what he's trying to say. He's asking me what happened.

I give him a small, one-shouldered shrug. I'm not sure I want to talk about it. Especially not with a *boy*. And I'd probably get assigned an extra week of detention for talking.

Robby pushes his pen into my hand and nods toward his notebook.

I stare down at my fingers, wrapped loosely around the slender black pen. It feels safe somehow. Safer than words, anyway.

Robby flips to the next page in his notebook and nudges it toward me. I've never been much of an artist. That's always been Harper's department. But I do my best. I draw two stick figures, holding hands, a little heart floating above their heads like a sun that never sets. Then, holding back another flood of tears, gently and mournfully, I draw a big jagged line—a crack— through the center of the heart, breaking it in half.

I turn the notebook back to Robby, and he stares at it for a long time. At first, I wonder if my drawing is so bad, he can't even figure out what it is. But then he flips back through his notebook, page after page, until he finds what he's looking for and shows me the drawing.

I recognize it instantly. It's me and Harper, sitting at our usual table at lunch. It must have been drawn before the carnival disaster, because Harper has her head thrown back and she's laughing that beautiful laugh that I've always loved. Laughing at something *I'm* saying.

It's the perfect snapshot of our friendship.

A perfect moment captured in time by someone I never knew was watching.

I start to turn to the next drawing but stop and look up at Robby for permission. He nods and I push back the page to reveal another snapshot. Another captured moment. This time, it's Tyler Watkins. He's standing in the middle of his group of friends, looking up at them. But Robby has drawn the other boys to be as tall as giants and Tyler barely comes up to the height of their knees.

The next drawing is of Matt Clemens. He's peeking his head out of the boys' bathroom, looking terrified as a group of girls walks by.

I nod knowingly and flip to the next page.

This sketch shows Kyle Bates leaning against a wall, his body kind of hunched over, his shoulders slumped. Hanging directly above him is a framed picture of a boy who looks a lot like him—his brother, I would assume—positioned right under the words "Wall of Fame."

Page after page, I find more drawings. More truths. While I've been listening, Robby Martinez has been watching.

I glance up at him and give him a look that I hope conveys just how impressed I am. He smiles weakly in return, and I think it might be the first time I've ever seen his teeth.

Checking to make sure Ms. Gladstone is still asleep, I point around the classroom and then at Robby, trying to ask him how he got put in detention.

He seems to understand, because he grips his pen in his hand, flips to a blank page, and starts sketching. He works astoundingly fast. He would be, hands down, the best partner to have in Pictionary. Well, until it came to his turn to guess.

When he rotates the notebook back toward me, I have to cover my mouth to stifle a gasp. This time, he's drawn himself. And I recognize the setting immediately. He's standing at the front of Ms. Hendrickson's Language Arts classroom, his hands stuffed in his pockets, his mouth sealed shut by an actual zipper, while Ms. Hendrickson—who has been depicted as a dragon clutching a copy of *A Midsummer Night's Dream*—breathes fire at his face.

The meaning is clear. He refused to take the oral test. And she sent him here.

I shake my head, commiserating on how unfair that is. He just shrugs. I guess he's used to getting in trouble for not talking. Funny how for most of the boys in our school it's the opposite.

I guess you really can't win.

When the clock finally ticks over to 3:30, Ms. Gladstone wakes up from her catnap and releases us. I wave goodbye to Robby and sprint for the door, anxious to get home before Mom does. Today is the boys' regional spelling bee and it's being hosted at the elementary school in our neighboring town. I'm hoping that means I'll have enough time to get home and prepare the house. My plan was to clean everything and organize all of Mom's client files (something she's always meaning to do but never has enough time). No doubt Mom has already been alerted by the school about my detention and the aftermath is not going to be pretty. I figure a little kissing up can't hurt.

But that plan goes completely out the window the moment I burst through the front doors of the school and stop dead in my tracks. Mom's car is parked at the curb.

CRIME AND (COMPLETELY UNFAIR) PUNISHMENT

TO MY SURPRISE, Mom doesn't start yelling as soon as I get in the car. In fact, she's very calm and quiet. Which is way worse. Because it means she's had time to process the news of my delinquency and come up with a strategy. And it's never a good thing when Mom strategizes.

"Yack-o-u-rack-e i-nack track-o-u-back-lack-e," Ben says from the backseat, and I don't even dare to look at my phone for a translation.

"Tack-o-tack-a-lack-lack-yack back-u-sack-tack-e-dack," says Isaac, and I swear he almost sounds sorry for me.

Mom pulls away from the curb and starts to drive. After three minutes of silence, the anticipation is killing me, and I decide to just get this over with. "Mom. I'm really sorry I got detention. I promise it will never happen again. Ever."

More silence. I glance over at Mom to make sure she's still awake and hasn't fallen asleep at the wheel. When she finally speaks, her voice is quiet and remorseful. "No, Emmy. It's me who needs to apologize."

I'm sorry, but WHAT?

"I've been so distracted with this Nagman project,

I haven't even noticed what's going in my own house. Under my own nose. With my own children."

If this is some kind of reverse psychology trick, it's working. My heart instantly cracks at the sound of her sad, broken voice. I can't let her take the blame for *my* detention. I just can't.

"No, Mom," I say. "This is *so* not your—"

But she raises her hand to alert me that she's not finished. "It is. I'm the parent, but lately I haven't been acting like the parent. I've been acting like a selfish teenager." She sighs. "It's hard sometimes, juggling it all. But my family comes first. And I need to be paying more attention to what's important. That's why on Monday morning, I'm going to call Nathan Wagman and tell him that I can't work with him anymore."

"WHAT?" Isaac, Ben, and I all shout at once.

Mom nods and I search her face for a hint of what she's feeling, but her gaze is trained on the road and I can't make it out.

"B-b-but," I stammer. "The Nagmans are your biggest client."

"Yes, but they're also the reason I've been so distracted lately. It's not fair to the three of you. Something has to give."

The Tummy Tornado starts to howl inside me. I knew I was going to feel guilty as soon as I got in the car, but I didn't think it would feel like this. I didn't think my actions would cause Mom to drop her biggest client. Yes, the Nagmans are a drag, but they also pay her a *lot*, and I know she worries about money. She never tells us that, but I've seen the anxious look on her face every time she logs in to her bank account online. Like she's bracing herself for bad news.

I feel more than guilty. I feel sick and slightly dizzy.

"Mom, please don't drop the Nagmans. I'm *really* sorry I got in trouble. I swear I'll start following the P-PUP. I'll never have my phone out at school again."

"And that's another thing," Mom says, ignoring my pleas. "I've been far too lenient with you and that phone. That is going to change too."

She pulls to a stop at a red light and extends her hand to me. She doesn't even have to say anything. Silently, I pull my phone out of my pocket and drop it into her hand. She immediately goes to work, moving at such a fast, practiced speed, I know she spent some time re-searching this.

The light turns green, and when she hands the phone back, my eyes nearly pop out of their sockets. My apps! They're . . . they're . . .

Grayed out.

Like a giant rain cloud has settled over my phone and my life.

"What did you do?"

"From now until further notice," Mom says with that same eerie calmness, "you will have access to your apps from four to six p.m. every day. And that's it. You can still use the phone feature to call me in case of emergencies."

"What about texts?" My voice sounds like some kind of exotic, screeching bird.

"Only between four and six p.m."

"Mom!"

"I'm sorry, Emmy. But I have to start setting some boundaries. We both could benefit from a little balance. You with your phone and me with my work. Four to six will be your phone time. The rest of the day, you can focus on school, homework, and spending time with your family."

The twins, who have been unusually quiet in the backseat, start to whisper in their secret language. Tears are now springing to my eyes for the third time today.

"Mom, you can't do this to me. I *need* this phone."

"You don't *need* the phone," Mom replies. "Believe it or not, people once survived without phones. And you'll have your phone. For two hours a day."

"What about weekends?" I ask, thinking about the football game tomorrow and the list of girls who have requested my boy expertise. Harper might not want my help anymore, but there are still tons of girls who do. And they're counting on me.

Mom teeters her head from side to side, the way she does when she's thinking. "I suppose I can widen the window slightly for the weekends."

This is not happening. This is *not* happening. I mean, I knew Mom's punishment would be bad. But I didn't know it would be *life ending*.

Mom puts the car into park and kills the engine and it's only now I realize we haven't driven home. We're in the parking lot of Lickety Split, the frozen yogurt shop where I made a complete fool of myself last week.

This day really can't get any worse, can it?

"What are we doing?" I ask as the twins eagerly unbuckle their seat belts and begin bouncing in their seats.

"We're celebrating!" says Isaac.

Baffled, I look to Mom for an explanation. "Celebrating what? You firing the Nagmans or ruining my life?"

Mom gives me that "Don't be dramatic" look that she's gotten so good at over the years. "No," she says, reaching for her seat belt. "The twins won first and second place at the regional spelling bee."

SPRINKLES AND FORTUNES

LICKETY SPLIT IS crowded again. Thankfully, though, Frankie isn't working today, so I don't have to face up to that humiliation. But it's a very small consolation compared to the way the rest of my day is going.

"What's everyone going to get?" Mom says as we approach the counter. Her voice is *way* too chipper, as though she hopes to distract me from her life-destroying punishment by talking about yogurt.

The twins stand on their tiptoes to read the flavors on the board. "They have chocolate banana!" exclaims Isaac.

"Yuck!" says Ben. "Bananas are gross."

"You're gross," Isaac fires back.

"Shack-u-tack u-pack!" Ben bellows.

"That's enough," warns Mom.

"Can we get toppings today?" Isaac asks. "Since we're spelling bee championships?"

"*Champions*," Mom corrects. "And I suppose so."

"Then I want strawberry with rainbow sprinkles!" Ben announces.

"Me too!" says Isaac.

"Did you know that adding rainbow sprinkles to your

yogurt means you're a fun person who likes life to be colorful and adventurous?" A deep male voice speaks from behind us in line and we all turn around.

My jaw instantly drops when I see who's standing there.

Mr. Weston obviously just came from school as well because he's dressed in his usual outfit of dark jeans, button-down shirt, colorful tie, and vest. His hair is as wild and untamed as always and his eyes twinkle at me from behind his black-rimmed glasses. "Hey, Emm-omatic." He holds up a hand for me to high-five.

"Who are you?" Ben asks, glaring suspiciously at the newcomer.

"And what do they say about chocolate sprinkles?" Isaac asks, pushing me aside to get closer to him.

"That you will live a long time and make lots of money," Mr. Weston says with a wink.

Ben looks up at Mom. "Can I have chocolate sprinkles too?"

"Me too?" asks Isaac.

Mom laughs and turns to Mr. Weston. "Well, thank you for that."

Mr. Weston seems to notice my mom for the first time and stands up a little taller, tugging at his vest to straighten it. "Hello again. And sorry about that."

"Can we, Mom?" Isaac asks.

Mom sighs. "I guess."

"We're celebrating," Ben tells Mr. Weston. "We won the regional spelling bee."

Mr. Weston looks genuinely impressed. "Wow! Can you spell 'congratulations'?"

Ben rolls his eyes like he's Einstein and has just been asked what two plus two is. "C-O-N-G-R-A-T-U-L-A-T-I-O-N-S."

"Pretty good," says Mr. Weston with a nod.

"Give me one!" Isaac demands.

Mr. Weston strokes his thin beard. "Hmm. Let me see."

"A hard one," Isaac warns him.

"Oh, a hard one? Okay. How about . . ." He glances around the shop, as though searching for inspiration. When his gaze lands on Mom, I catch a faint gleam in his eye as he says, "How about 'fortuitous'?"

I don't know what "fortuitous" means, but I definitely know what the look on Mom's face does. And I *don't* like it.

Is she *blushing*?

I quickly pull out my phone to check the translation of what Mr. Weston just said but frown when I see my apps are still grayed out. I forgot I won't have access to them for another fifteen minutes.

"That's not a real word," Isaac complains.

Mr. Weston blinks, as though coming out of some kind of trance, and looks down at my brother. "Sorry. How about 'coincidence'?"

Satisfied for having been given a second chance, Isaac straightens up, like he's back on the spelling bee stage and says, "Coincidence. C-O-I-N-C-I-D-E-N-C-E. Coincidence."

"It certainly is a nice one," says Mr. Weston, who has gone back to looking at Mom.

A bashful smile creeps over her face and she looks away.

Oh my gosh. Are they *flirting?*

No! No, no, no, no, NO.

Mr. Weston is my *teacher.* He cannot flirt with my *mom.* That has to be against some kind of rules. The rules of the universe, perhaps? Or maybe just the rules of common sense. Teachers and parents should not flirt. Or do anything else together besides talk about things like test grades and class participation.

I am the Love Coordinator here, and I say it's forbidden.

I clear my throat, trying to interrupt whatever is going on here. "So, um, Mr. Weston," I say in my most casual, *non*-interrogation voice. "Do you come to Lickety Split often?"

"All the time," he says jovially. "Best yogurt in town." His expression suddenly turns serious. "Although, it looks like I might have to find a new fro-yo shop."

"Why?" Isaac asks.

"Because Emmy's my student," Mr. Weston says. "And now she knows my secret identity. My cover is blown."

"What's your secret identity?" Ben asks. I can tell my brothers are completely enchanted by Mr. Weston. Like I used to be. Back when he was just my Computer Science teacher and not some tall, well-dressed man flirting with my mom in a fro-yo shop.

He bends down and beckons the twins closer, like

he's about to reveal government secrets. They lean in, their eyes glimmering. "I'm a fro-yo addict."

"Us too!" says Ben.

"Well, you know what they say about *that*, don't you?" Mr. Weston asks.

Ben and Isaac both shake their heads, entranced.

"That you get a *lot* of brain freezes."

I roll my eyes. I'm used to Mr. Weston making lame jokes, but this one is especially bad. Apparently, though, I'm the only one who thinks so because the boys are cracking up like they're sitting in the front row of a comedy club and Mom is giggling into her hand.

The line moves up and it's our turn. The boys immediately order strawberry yogurt in a cup with both rainbow *and* chocolate sprinkles. Ben turns back to show Mr. Weston his order and Mr. Weston nods approvingly.

I've pretty much lost my appetite, but I still get a small chocolate-vanilla swirl and Mom orders her typical blueberry before turning to Mr. Weston. "What would you like, Jim? It's our treat."

Jim?

My mother knows Mr. Weston's first name? And now she's buying him fro-yo? This is not good. Not. Good. At. All. The Tummy Tornado is ramping up fast.

"You don't have to do that," Mr. Weston says.

"I insist," replies Mom with a smile.

Mr. Weston thanks her and orders a chocolate banana in a cup.

"I told you bananas weren't gross," Isaac whispers to Ben, and I notice they're not speaking in their secret alien language. In fact, they haven't uttered a single "ack" since Mr. Weston appeared.

Mom invites him to sit with us and we carry our yogurts to a table in the back of the shop. As we play the musical-chairs game, I make sure to nab the seat next to Mom, forcing Mr. Weston to sit as far away from her as possible.

"How do you know so much about sprinkles?" Ben asks between spoonfuls of yogurt.

"Well," Mr. Weston says confidently. "I *am* a teacher."

Ben and Isaac both giggle.

"You teach Computer Science," I say, and it's probably a *tad* rude, because everyone looks at me with startled expressions. I shrug and drop my gaze to my cup. "Well, he does," I mutter under my breath.

"Emm-inem is right." Mr. Weston scrapes his spoon around the edge of his cup. "I do teach Computer Science. Fro-yo fortune-telling is more of a side hobby."

"Fro-yo fortune-telling?" Isaac repeats with wide eyes, like someone has just given him the directions to Bigfoot's house.

"Yup. It's an old Weston family tradition. We read each other's fortunes based on what yogurt flavor and toppings we choose."

"Do Emmy!" Ben says, pointing way too enthusiastically at my yogurt. "Read Emmy's fortune!"

Mr. Weston turns to me and pretends to study my cup with intense concentration. "Hmm. Chocolate-vanilla swirl. Yes, I'm definitely getting a vibe." He places a hand to his head and closes his eyes, like he's receiving a message from another dimension. The boys snicker. "I see a big test in your future. A *very* big test. Next week, actually." He flicks his eyes open and gives me a friendly wink.

I chuckle along with the rest of the table because, despite the fact that I'm still angry, that was kind of funny.

"Now do Mom!" Isaac says giddily.

"Okay," says Mr. Weston, and I watch in horror as his eyes slide across the table and land on Mom. She doesn't look away. Her gaze meets his somewhere in the middle, and for a long moment, they're just sitting there, staring at each other.

I can practically *see* the cartoon hearts flowing between them like a scene out of a bad movie. Mom is blushing again. Mr. Weston's eyes are sparkling again. And the Tummy Tornado is raging. This is all kinds of disastrous.

"I have a better idea!" I exclaim, breaking through their trance. "Ben, why don't *you* try to read Mom's fortune?"

Ben looks delighted and practically climbs on top of the table to peer into Mom's cup. "Hmm," he says, imitating Mr. Weston's intense focus. "Blueberry. I predict you will have a very blue tongue."

Mr. Weston throws his head back and laughs. Isaac giggles delightfully and turns toward Ben. "My turn! I predict all of those sprinkles will turn your poop rainbow colored!"

"Ewwww!" Ben says through his snorts of laughter.

Mom scowls. "Isaac. That's not funny."

"I thought it was funny," I say casually, taking a bite of my yogurt.

Ben gets a hold of his laughter long enough to turn to Mr. Weston and say, "And I predict that chocolate banana will give you diarrhea."

"Ben!" Mom looks humiliated. "I'm sorry," she says to Mr. Weston and I notice, with satisfaction, there is a *whole* different kind of blush on her face now.

But Mr. Weston just smiles politely. "It's okay. A fortune is a fortune. We can't control them." He flashes Ben an apologetic look and says, "I'm extremely sorry for both of us."

This makes Isaac crack up.

"And I predict," I announce loudly, pulling everyone's attention back to me, "that Mr. Weston will never want to play this game with us ever again."

Mr. Weston doubles over laughing. Mom joins in. I don't think either of them realizes I wasn't joking.

THE LONGEST PAUSE OF MY LIFE

"**ALL THE WORLD** continues to speculate on the meaning behind the mysterious lyrics of Berrin James's new song 'Magnolia Street.'"

The Xoom! channel is playing on the TV in the living room. It's one of those "Xoom! Scoop" segments, where a teen correspondent stands in a brightly lit studio, delivering the latest celebrity news. I'm barely listening as I scroll through pages and pages of grayed-out apps on my phone, all of them locked now that I'm in the hours of my "phone curfew," as I'm now calling it.

It's after nine p.m., the twins are in bed, and I can hear the quiet tapping of keys down the hall. Mom is in her office, probably sending off a few last-minute emails before she calls it quits on the Nagmans on Monday morning.

"There's also a theory floating around the internet that the song is actually about Berrin's decision to change his name a few years ago from Berrin Mack to Berrin James," the teen correspondent continues. "To this day, no one really knows why he did that."

I reach the last page of grayed-out apps on my phone.

The only features that actually work outside the curfew hours are the settings, the camera, and the phone. But honestly, who even makes phone calls anymore? And what good is the camera if you can't post the pictures anywhere?

"So now Berrin has got us all scouring maps of the country, searching for this elusive Magnolia Street in hopes it might give us some clues."

I open the settings and scroll through the options until I find the controls for the phone curfew. It's under the parental settings. But it's locked with a four-digit PIN. I try a few obvious options—my birthday, the twins' birthday, Mom's birthday—but none of them work.

"But we here at the Xoom! channel decided to go straight to the source. We caught up with Berrin James on tour this week and asked him for the inside Xoom! Scoop."

Curiously, I lower my phone and focus on the TV just as the scene cuts from the studio to what looks like some kind of backstage dressing room. Berrin is lounging on a comfy leather couch, one ankle crossed over the other knee. He looks amazing. He's dressed in tight black jeans, black sneakers, a white T-shirt, and a black leather jacket. His dark hair is styled in its signature "swoop," and he's tapping his fingers lightly against his propped-up knee, like he's practicing a drum solo.

"Berrin, Berrin, Berrin," the teen correspondent says from the chair opposite him, looking positively giddy to be in the same room as him. I would probably throw up. "I know you've been asked this a million times, but what is the deal with these lyrics? Why are you leaving us all guessing? Why not just set the record straight right here and now and tell us who 'Magnolia Street' is really about?"

Berrin laughs his deep, throaty laugh. "Well, Abby. First off, you're right. I have been asked about a million times. Maybe a million and a half."

Abby and I both laugh in perfect unison.

"And as you know," Berrin continues, "I write all of my own lyrics and I always try to make them personal. I think music *should* be personal, and my lyrics are how I process what's going on in my life. But sometimes the lyrics become a little too personal and you just . . ." He shrugs and shakes his head. "I guess you just want to keep some secrets for yourself."

I glance down at my phone and try another four-digit combination, this time our street address. Still nothing.

"Well, there you have it," says Abby, who is back in the Xoom! studio. "Berrin James is keeping his secrets locked up in the vault. Until next time, Xoomers! This is Abby Mitchell for 'Xoom! Scoop'!"

I try a handful of more passcodes, some as easy as 1-2-3-4, and others as top secret as Mom's ATM PIN, but my phone stays as locked as Berrin James's lips.

When I look up again, a new episode of *Ruby of the Lamp* is playing on TV. It's a show Harper and I used to watch obsessively when we were younger. We stopped when the lead actress, Ruby Rivera, quit and they cast some new girl to replace her who wasn't very good. And then Ryder Vance, the cute boy on the show, also quit to star in some cheesy movie called *Mean Tween Drama*

Machine and the show kind of fell apart. I'm not sure why they even keep making it.

"What are you doing up?" Mom asks, surprising me. Guiltily, I drop my phone in my lap, hoping she didn't see the passcode screen open when she walked in.

I point to the TV, where the *Ruby of the Lamp* opening credits are playing. "Just watching some old favorites."

Mom peers at the screen and smiles. "You and Harper used to love that show. Whatever happened to Ruby Rivera?"

I shrug. "She quit acting. Last I heard she's in high school."

"Good for her," says Mom. "I'm going to bed. Don't stay up too late, okay?"

I nod. "Okay."

I listen to her footsteps pad through the kitchen and up the stairs. The moment I hear her bedroom door close, I'm off the couch and on the move.

As I silently creep down the hallway, toward my mom's office, I feel like a character in one of those corny superspy versus supervillain movies. Except I'm not really sure which character I am right now. The superspy or the supervillain? I've definitely been behaving like a villain lately, busting into the boys' bathroom, getting detention, sneaking around the house, trying to hack my own phone.

But I have to unlock these apps. I can't live like this.

I reach Mom's office and, thankful for the soft, quiet carpet, scurry over to the desk and start to carefully open drawers. Mom keeps all her passwords written in a small black notebook. I've seen her referring to it when she gets locked out of accounts or websites. The PIN code she set on my phone has to be in there.

But after more than ten minutes of riffling through drawers and cabinets and stacks of papers on Mom's desk, I have yet to uncover it. Maybe it would be easier if her office wasn't so disorganized and chaotic. Her client files are even messier than I remember. How does she manage to find *anything* in here?

I'm just about to give up and close the last of the drawers when something catches my eye.

A name.

It's scrawled across the top of one of the client folders in red pen.

But it's *not* the name of a client. I would know. I've listened to Mom gripe about every client she's ever had. I could recite all of them backward and forward, *including* what color paint is on their walls.

It's another name. A name I've barely ever heard uttered aloud in this house. A name I'm not sure I've even seen written before. But a name I will never forget for as long as I live.

Henry Simmons.

My *father's* name.

As my eyes take in the hastily scrawled letters across the top of the folder, it feels like someone pulled a drain plug in my body and now all the blood is gushing down to my feet.

Carefully, I ease the folder out of the stack and open it, bracing myself for what I'll find inside.

But it's empty.

My heart sinks like a stone. Why would Mom keep an empty file folder in her drawer with Dad's name on it? Did something *used* to be in here?

Then my gaze falls on the left side of the folder and I notice a little yellow sticky note attached to the bottom. On it, someone has written a phone number. The area code is not anywhere near here. In fact, I don't even recognize it.

I peer up at the open door of Mom's office and listen for movement. Footsteps. Voices. The low rumble of a TV. But the house is asleep.

Quietly, I tiptoe to the door and ease it closed. Then, with trembling hands, I dial the unfamiliar number, press my phone to my ear, and sink to my knees on the carpet. The line rings and I make a promise not to take another breath until someone answers.

I realize it's late and it might even be later wherever this number is, but I don't care. I can't wait. I'm done waiting.

The voice that picks up on the other end sounds groggy and old. And definitely *not* my dad. It's a woman's voice. "Hello?"

I open my mouth, but no sound comes out. As my mind scrambles for a word—any word!—I glance down at the sticky note with the number scribbled on it. It has to be his number. Why else would Mom keep it in a file with his name on it?

"Hello?" the voice repeats. "Is anyone there?"

Still nothing. I can't speak. I finally let out the breath

I've been holding, and it makes a loud muffled sound into the phone. Like wind through a very tiny tunnel.

"I can hear you breathing!" says the woman, her voice thick with some kind of East Coast accent. "Is this another one of those prank calls? Because if it is, I'm hanging up and reporting this number to the pol—"

"Hello!" The word zooms out of me like a rocket.

There's a pause on the other end of the line before the woman says, "Who is this?" Her voice is less angry and more suspicious now. My mind reels with questions. Could it be his new wife? A girlfriend? His mother? Mom always said that she never got along with Dad's parents and that's why we never saw them after he left. Could I actually be talking to my grandmother right now?

"Um," I fumble for something to say. Something that doesn't sound ridiculous. But I realize that anything sounds ridiculous coming eight years out of the blue. "Hi. I'm hoping you could help me. I'm looking for . . . um . . ." It feels like a lifetime before I'm actually able to say his name aloud. "Henry."

Another long pause in which I feel the Tummy Tornado start to stir. "Henry who?"

At first, the answer confuses me. Is this woman so old she doesn't even remember her own son's name? But then realization hits me like an explosion, destroying all of my hopes in the blast.

"Uh . . . Henry Simmons?" The last name that used to be mine feels clunky and strange on my tongue.

"Simmons, Simmons," the woman repeats, like she's

trying to jog her memory. "Oh, yeah, there was a Simmons here once. He lived in this apartment before I did. Used to get all of his unpaid utility bills, the bum. Who moves and doesn't forward his address? I guess the kind of person who doesn't want to be found."

The walls of my mom's office start to cave in. Everything feels like it's collapsing around me. The ceiling, the sky, the stars. I try to take a deep breath, but no oxygen comes. It's just empty, useless air.

"But I tracked him down. I used to work in a police station, you know? I know the workarounds, the tricks. I called and I told him he better come back here and pick up all of his mail or I'd report him to the—"

"You have his number?" I'm on my feet, pacing, unable to sit still.

"You bet your butt I do. I wasn't about to pay for *his* cable TV. No way, no how."

Oxygen fills my lungs. It's beautiful and delicious and addicting. I can't get enough of it. "Can you give it to me?"

There's silence on the other end and I want to reach through the phone, shake this woman, and shout, *Stop with the long pauses! You're killing me! Don't you know you're my last hope? The only hope I've ever had?*

But I keep my lips glued shut.

The woman mutters incomprehensively for a while. There's a lot of grunts and grumbles and harrumphs. I press the phone tighter against my ear, trying to make sense of what she's saying. Finally, I lose my patience. "I'm sorry, *what?*"

"I said, that was a long time ago. I don't know if I still have it. I mean, it's probably around here somewhere but—"

"Please." I can feel my hope slipping away again. "Please, you have to find it. You have to look for it. It's . . . it's . . . very important."

The woman falls silent again. When she finally speaks, the suspicion is back. "What's it to you? Who are you, anyway? And what do you want with a bum like Henry Simmons? You don't sound older than ten."

I bristle at the insult and fight the urge to tell her that I'm twelve—and a *half*—thank you very much. "Please," I say again, trying to inject a lifetime's worth of desperation into that one word.

The next pause is the longest one of my life. I swear the woman already hung up and has gone back to sleep. I swear that night has turned to day outside the window and the world has moved on. But I don't dare hang up. I clutch the phone like I'm drowning and it's the only thing keeping me afloat.

"Okay," the woman finally says with a begrudging sigh. "I'll have a look and call you back if I find anything. But I wouldn't hold my breath if I were you."

I thank her over and over again before hanging up the phone. Of course, I don't tell her that her warning is too late. I've been holding my breath for eight years.

ALIEN AMBASSADOR

"YACK-O-U TACK-O-U-CHACK-E-DACK!"

"Dack-i-dack nack-o-tack!"

The sound of alien screaming fills the house the next morning and I drag my eyes open to find light streaming through the window.

What time is it?

I check the clock on my phone. It reads 8:00 a.m. Way too early for aliens.

"Lack-a-vack-a! Lack-a-vack-a!"

The yelling seems to be accompanied by some type of thudding coming from downstairs. They're probably bouncing on the furniture again. If Mom catches them, they'll be in so much trouble.

"Dack-o-nack-tack tack-o-u-chack!"

I bolt upright in bed, my pillow falling to the floor. That last voice was definitely *not* one of the twins. It was lower, a little deeper. And somewhat familiar.

One of the boys squeals with laughter, there's another thudding sound, and then the deeper voice bellows in an even deeper tone, "I-mack thack-e gack-o-dack o-fack lack-a-vack-a!"

More giggling, more thudding. And finally, I can't take it anymore. I have to find out what's going on and who is in our house. I throw open the bedroom door and hurry downstairs. The thudding sounds get louder.

I reach the first floor and come to a crashing halt when I see what's become of our living room. All the cushions have been removed from the couch and are spread out around the floor. Ben and Isaac are giddily hopping from one cushion to the next. And standing in the center of it all, his arms triumphantly raised over his head like he's just won some kind of cushion-hopping Olympics, is Grant.

"Vack-i-cack-tack-o-rack-yack i-sack mack-i-nack-e!" he shouts.

I'm so stunned and confused by the whole scene, it takes me a moment to find my voice. "What is . . . what is going on here?"

All three boys turn to me in surprise, like they forgot someone else lived in this house. But it's Grant I'm gaping at. "They taught you their secret language?"

"He already knew it!" Ben answers for him, taking an ambitious leap between two very distant cushions. "We're playing Lava! Only the islands are safe!"

"You're not supposed to jump on the furniture." I toss him a chiding look.

"We're not!" Isaac says defensively. "We took the cushions *off* the furniture. See?" He dives for the nearest "island" but misses and steps right into the sea of lava.

Grant points at him. "Yack-o-u lack-o-sack-e!"

I turn back to Grant. "Wait, you already *knew* the secret language?"

He shrugs. "Kind of." He looks me up and down and smirks. "Nice pajamas."

It's only now I realize I'm still wearing my night-gown. I've had this particular one since I was ten, so it's a bit too small. *And* it's covered in ponies.

I quickly cross my arms over my chest but it's too late. The damage is done. Grant has already seen my pony nightgown. My life is over.

"What are you doing here?" I demand, trying to change the subject.

"Your mom said she wanted to let you sleep. But she had to run to the store for a client, so she asked if I would chill with the twins until you got up."

"This is chilling?" I ask, gesturing to the disaster zone in front of me.

He shrugs again. "The game was their idea."

"Grant!" Isaac shouts. "Cack-o-mack-e o-nack!"

Grant nods to him. "Just hold on a second."

I squeeze the bridge of my nose, trying to clear away some of the sleep and confusion still lingering in my head. Grant is babysitting *and* he knows my brothers' alien language? What universe did I wake up in?

"I thought they made up that language," I say.

"Wack-e dack-i-dack!" Ben shouts midleap. He lands on the couch cushion with an *oomph* as it goes sliding across the floor and nearly collides with the TV.

Grant glances at the two boys before stepping off his cushion and beckoning for me to follow him into the kitchen.

"Yack-o-u gack-o-tack back-u-rack-nack-e-dack!" Isaac calls after him.

"O-u-chack!" Grant calls back, which makes both the boys giggle hysterically.

Once we're alone in the kitchen, he leans closer to me and whispers, "My mom and I used to do the same thing but with ogs."

Now I *know* I've woken up in a different universe. "Huh?"

"The language," Grant explains. "The words are spelled out. And for every consonant you add 'og' to the end of it. Or in their case 'ack.' And for every vowel you just say the letter." He grabs a pen and a sticky-note pad from the counter and scribbles the word "HELLO."

Then, with the tip of the pen, he taps on each letter as he quietly says, "Hack-e-lack-lack-o."

I stare in astonishment. One simple word that has just solved a six-month-long mystery.

"And for two consonants in a row that form a single sound, you combine them. Like this." Grant scribbles the word "CHAIR" and then taps on each letter again. "Chack-a-i-rack."

My wide eyes snap up to him. "Are you serious?"

"Yack-e-a-hack," Grant replies with another smirk.

"You mean they've been spelling out every single word they say?"

He nods. "You have to. That's how the language works."

"That explains the spelling bee!"

"Shh!" Grant puts a finger to his lips. "They warned me not to tell you. They said it was a boys-only language."

I lower my voice. "So that's how they keep winning? They've basically been practicing spelling for hours a day."

Grant shrugs. "I guess so."

"Thank you," I tell him. "You've just saved me and my mom a *lot* of agony."

"Wack-e-lack-cack-o-mack-e."

I giggle and turn to grab a piece of bread from the bag on the counter. I've just now realized how starving I am. "Want some toast?"

He shakes his head. "I should probably get home, now that you're awake."

"Did my mom say when she'd be back? I'm supposed to go to the football game this afternoon."

"She said by noon. And I didn't know you liked *football*." The way he says the word, you would think we were talking about a disease. Not a sport.

"Don't *you* like football?" I ask as I drop two pieces of bread into the toaster.

Grant makes a face. "No."

"But you're a boy."

He doesn't seem to be following my logic. "So?"

"So don't all boys like football?" I pull open the fridge door and start rooting around for the butter. "Isn't it, like, in your DNA or something?"

He snorts. "That's like saying all girls like ballet or unicorns. It's gendering."

"Gendering?" I repeat the unfamiliar word from behind the fridge door.

"It means you automatically associate something with one gender or another." His eyes light up. "There's a great documentary about it on—"

"That's okay," I say with a laugh. "I'll take your word for it."

"Anyway," he goes on, undeterred, and I can tell he's already slipped back into his know-it-all professor mode. Why does it always seem like just when I get a glimpse of *normal* Grant—hopping around make-believe islands—he disappears. "Boys are allowed to dislike football, just like girls are allowed to like it."

"Then why did you look so horrified when I mentioned it?" I grab the butter and jam from the fridge and set it down on the counter.

"I wasn't *horrified*," he corrects, shuffling his feet awkwardly. "I just didn't think you liked football."

"I don't." I flash him a playful smile

"Then why are you going to a football game?"

I think about the long list of names that are waiting on my phone. Clueless girls frustrated by the cryptic boys in their lives. "I have important work to do."

"Important work?" Grant repeats dubiously. "At a football game?"

My toast pops up from the toaster and I put it on a plate and start buttering. "I'll have you know that *many* people have now requested my services as a boy expert."

He rolls his eyes. "This again?"

"Yes! Some people actually appreciate my skills."

"Being a boy expert is not a thing."

"Yes, it is."

"It can't be!"

"Why not?"

Grant gestures helplessly with his hands. "Because of what I just said. Even to claim that you're a boy expert is gendering."

"How?" I challenge before taking a noisy bite of toast.

"Because it assumes all boys are the same."

I open my mouth to argue but I'm not sure how to respond to that. Of course I know not all boys are the same. If I've learned anything from the iSpeak Boy app it's that. But I can't very well explain that to him, so I just mutter, "Never mind," and take another bite of my toast. It's impossible to win an argument with Grant.

"Wouldn't you be offended if I said I was a *girl* expert?" he asks.

"No, because I'd know you were lying."

"Ha," Grant says scornfully. "Very funny."

For a long time, neither of us says anything and the only sound in the kitchen is the occasional thudding and yelling from the twins in the next room and my crunchy toast chomping.

Finally, with a surrendering sigh, Grant says, "Fine!" as though he's been having an internal debate with himself. "I suppose I'll just have to see it for myself."

"See what?"

"This 'boy expert' thing." He makes quotation marks with his fingers to let me know how skeptical he still is.

"You want to come with me?" I ask, scrunching up

my forehead. "To a middle school football game?" For some reason the thought makes my stomach flutter.

"No. But you don't give me much choice, do you? I have to see the almighty Boy Expert in action."

"Fine," I say, matching his tone. "The game is at my school and it starts at three. I'm leaving at two-forty-five."

"Fine," he says again, turning toward the front door. "I'll be here."

"Fine," I call just before the door closes, because there's no way I'm letting him have the last word.

THE NEW KNOW-IT-ALL

"**SO THIS IS** a middle school football game," Grant says as we gaze out at the field.

When I told Mom I was going to the game with Grant, she raised an eyebrow as if to say *Really? Grant Knight?* And that's the same question that was going through my mind the whole walk here.

"This is it," I tell him, heading for the stands in search of an empty seat. "What do you think?"

"It's . . ." He glances around, looking a lot like an explorer visiting an uncharted land. ". . . different than I thought it would be."

The game hasn't officially started, but there's already a buzz in the air. Apparently, this game is pretty important. Something about if our school wins, we go to some kind of world series of football. I don't know.

We find a fairly empty bleacher and slide in. "Let me guess," I tease Grant. "You watched a documentary about middle school football before you came?"

"No," Grant says with a defensive scoff, and then, a moment later, adds, "It was just a regular movie. I couldn't find a documentary about middle school football."

I laugh. "Maybe that's because it's not interesting enough to make a documentary about." I probably should have said this a little quieter, because the three boys sitting in front of us all turn at once to give me dirty looks.

A whistle blows and all the players run onto the field to a chorus of whoops and cheers. There's no booming announcer like there is on TV. The game just kind of starts. The ball is thrown to someone in a white jersey (I think that's our team but I'm not entirely sure. We could be the blue guys.) White jersey catches the ball and is immediately tackled by three players at once. The poor kid's head hits the ground with a painful-looking bounce.

Grant winces. "Ouch! People actually *choose* to do this?"

"I know, right?"

Miraculously, the player leaps back to his feet, looking unharmed, and jogs over to his team. "Are these guys really our age?" Grant stares incredulously at the helmeted, overly padded boys lining up in the center of the field.

"This is eighth grade," I explain. "One year older than us. Seventh grade plays flag football."

"What's the difference?"

I start to answer before realizing, "I don't know, actually."

"I suppose one involves the use of a flag?" Grant guesses.

I chuckle. "Maybe it's like capture the flag?"

One of the boys in front of us turns around again. He rolls his eyes like we are the most inconvenient thing in his life. "Flag football," he begins huffily, "is when the players wear belts with flags, and instead of tackling, the other team has to grab a flag from the player with the ball to end the down."

"Ah," Grant and I say in unison, even though I'm pretty sure neither of us has any idea what that guy just said.

"Obviously *he* found a documentary," Grant whispers to me, and I cover my mouth to stifle a laugh. "Should I ask him what streaming service he found it on?"

I get my giggles under control long enough to say, "I can tell you right now, it's the Never-Gonna-Watch-Flix streaming service."

Grant and I practically fall out of our seats. The boys in front of us turn to give us more dirty looks, and I decide it's probably time to get to work before we get kicked out of the stands.

I pull out my phone and click over to the list Darcy made for me. Thankfully, I was able to convince Mom to expand my phone time on weekends. I now have full use of all my apps between the hours of eleven a.m. and seven p.m. on Saturdays and Sundays.

The first name on my list is Vivi Lee. She says she noticed Micah Lowenstein looking at her a few times and wants to know if he likes her. I remember overhearing Micah talking to his friends at the carnival. He was gabbing about some girl in a video game who wears glittery pants. Will he even be here? Or is he at home looking for another fictional girl with boots made of gold?

I cast my gaze over the stands. Coming here was a good idea. I recognize tons of people from my class and, to my surprise, I actually spot Micah chatting with some friends near the snack stand.

"Well," I say, rising to my feet with a dramatic sigh. "Duty calls."

Grant squints up at me, shielding his eyes from the sun. "Is it time to boy expert?"

I nod and he leaps to his feet, looking relieved to not have to sit here and actually watch the game. As we make our way toward the snack stand, I open the iSpeak Boy app and keep my phone clutched in my hand where it's easily accessible and within hearing range of all my conversations.

"So what exactly does this entail?" Grant asks.

I put my finger to my lips. "Watch and learn."

He mimes zipping his mouth shut and dutifully follows me as I walk up to Micah and tap him on the shoulder.

Micah looks surprised to see me, and I can't blame him. I'm not sure I've said more than two words to Micah Lowenstein in all of middle school.

I decide this will all go a lot faster if I just cut to the chase. I have a long list to get through and I don't really have time to make small talk. "Hi, Micah. I was just wondering if you know who Vivi Lee is."

He blinks, confused. "Yeah, she's in my science class. Why?"

My phone vibrates and I casually glance down at the screen.

Translation:

Yeah, she's the cutest girl in my science class. Why?

"No reason. Thanks!" I chirp, before turning and walking away, leaving Micah to stare after me, wondering what just happened.

"That's it?" Grant whispers once we're out of earshot.

I nod. "That's it."

"But he barely said anything."

"I got what I needed."

He glances back at Micah, then at me. "What could you have possibly gotten from that?"

"He thinks she's cute," I say smugly. I won't lie and say I'm not totally enjoying the bewildered look on Grant's face right now.

"How did you get *that* from that?" He jabs his thumb at the stunned boy we just left behind.

"I told you." I tap my forehead. "Boy expert."

Grant studies me suspiciously. "This is a joke, right?"

"Nope. No joke. Watch." We've just arrived back at the bleachers. Tyler Watkins, another boy on my list, is sitting in the first row with his best friend, Logan. "Hey, Tyler!" I say in a cheery voice as we approach.

He leans around me to see the field. "You're blocking the game."

"I'll only be a second." I flash a smile. "So, Logan's little sister, Chelsey?"

"What about her?" Tyler groans and shares an eye roll with Logan like just the mention of her name is annoying. But the app is revealing something very different.

Translation:

What about her? Did she say something about me? Did she say I was too short for her? Does Logan know I like her? He'll hate me if he does!

"Never mind. Nothing. Enjoy the game!" Once again, I walk away, mentally checking another task off my list. Behind me, I can hear Logan asking Tyler what that was about and Tyler muttering something about me being a weirdo, but I don't care. I got what I wanted and so did Chelsey.

Grant jogs to catch up with me. "So?"

"So what?" I ask, acting as if I have no idea what he's talking about.

"So that guy Tyler thinks Chelsey is super annoying, right?"

I give him a tender look and pat his cheek. "Oh, you sweet, innocent boy."

"But I saw his face. He can't stand her."

"No," I correct him. "He's only *pretending* he can't stand her because she's his best friend's sister and he's worried how his friend will react."

Grant stops walking and gapes at me. "You got all

that from . . ." He does a funny, slack-jawed impression of Tyler.

I chuckle but can't help feeling a flicker of pride at the disbelief in Grant's voice. Who's the know-it-all *now*?

Grant narrows his eyes. "How do I know you're not just making this all up?"

"I'm not."

"But how do I *know* that?"

I snort. "Do you want me to prove it to you?"

Grant crosses his arms over his chest, looking pleased by the idea. "Yeah. I do, actually."

"How?"

Grant spins around, his gaze scanning the crowd until it lands on a sixth-grade boy standing in line at the snack stand. Grant runs up to him, says something in a voice I can't hear, and then beckons me over.

I have no idea what he's up to but I'm not worried. I clutch my phone tighter in my hand and saunter over to them.

Grant beams like he's about to win a very long and hard-fought game of checkers. "I've just been talking to my new friend here about what food he's planning to buy at the snack stand. Do *you* know what he's planning to buy, Emmy?" He raises his brows at me.

I raise mine back, accepting the challenge, and then turn and smile sweetly at the boy. "Hello. What's your name?"

Confused, the boy looks between me and Grant, probably wondering if this is some kind of trap. "Uh, Collin," he mumbles.

I steal a peek at my phone and beam back at Grant. "Nice try. He wants nachos."

"Wrong!" Grant shouts, pointing at me and startling poor Collin.

I hold up a hand, letting him know I'm not finished. "He *wants* nachos. But they don't have nachos, so he's settling for popcorn. Although he really can't understand why a football game doesn't have nachos. His older brother goes to high school football games and *they* have nachos."

Collin's mouth falls open as he gapes at me in wonder. "How did you know all that?"

I turn my triumphant expression on Grant, who's *also* gaping at me. "Believe me yet?"

Grant blinks, like he's trying to wake himself up from a strange dream. "I . . . I think I'm starting to." And from the tone of his voice, I can tell he's just as shocked by his admission as I am.

INTERNATIONAL WATERS

BY HALFTIME, I'M completely exhausted, and my phone battery is dead, but thankfully, I have answers to every single question on my list.

I now know that Archie Evans has had a crush on Delia Nazari since the fifth grade when they showed up on the first day of school with the same dragon backpack. I know that Matt Clemens only told Caitlin O'Hare that he liked her socks because he was too afraid to look her in the eye and that Jackson Harris only wants to be friends with Hilary Pasquale, which makes him feel guilty because he's fully aware that she wants to be more than that. I also know that Lesley Schwimmer's brother has been locking himself in his room for hours every night because he's taking dance lessons on YouTube to prepare for the middle school dance next week and that Kyle Bates has been blowing off his school project with Brianna Brown because he's worried that he's not smart enough to be paired with her and figures if she does all the work, he can't let her down.

It's all very enlightening and everything, and I'm glad that I'm able to help all these girls, but I kind of feel like my brain is going to explode. Is it possible to know *too* much information?

"Well, I don't know about you, but I need a nap," Grant says as we walk home. Neither of us wanted to stay for the second half of the game, so we bought a few snacks from the stand and left.

"I know," I mumble between bites of my enormous chocolate chip cookie. "I just want to binge-watch something for the rest of the day and not talk to anyone. Solving the world's boy problems is exhausting."

Grant laughs as he opens up his bag of chips and pops one into his mouth. "So, about that," he says after a thick swallow. "All the girls on this list of yours, they asked you to help them and you just said yes?"

I nod but don't meet his eye. "Yup."

Grant twists his mouth to the side. "Why?"

"What do you mean, *why*?" I fire back. "Don't you like to help people?"

"Of course. I just think . . . I don't know, isn't this whole thing kinda weird? I mean, why are you so interested in all of these people's lives?"

"I'm not *interested* in their lives," I say, feeling the same defensiveness I felt in the hallway yesterday, when Harper asked me why I wanted so badly to set her up. "I just want to help. Why is that so hard for everyone to believe?"

"Everyone?" Grant asks.

"Never mind." I take another bite of cookie, but this time it tastes bitter.

"I just wonder if . . . ," Grant begins, but his voice trails off, like he's changed his mind.

"What?" I ask, frustrated, even though I have no idea what he's going to say.

Grant licks his lips nervously. "Do you remember when we were little, and you wanted to make all of our stuffed animals get married?"

I'm trying to figure out where he's going with this. "Yeah."

Grant chuckles. "You were obsessed with pairing them all up with the perfect match."

I chuckle too, remembering how Grant wanted Simon the Seagull to marry Fiona the Fish and I argued that it would never work because where would they live? I guess I've always been a Love Coordinator.

Grant clears his throat. "It was right after your dad left."

"So?" I ask.

"So do you think maybe . . ." But once again his voice trails off like he's had second thoughts. In the distance behind us, I can hear the crowd cheering. The game must have started up again.

"Maybe what?" I prompt.

"Nothing," Grant mutters, and then, with the awkwardness of someone clearly trying to change the subject, he says, "Who knew that all this time I was living next door to a real-life superhero."

"A superhero?"

"I mean, the boy expert thing. It's sort of like a super-power."

"It's not a superpower," I reply with a snort, even though I kind of like the idea of having a superpower.

"It's totally a superpower!" Grant holds an invisible microphone to his mouth and deepens his voice, assuming the role of a news anchor interviewing a celebrity. "And here we are live with the Boy Expert herself, after she's just saved the world—or rather her middle school—from the dangers of cryptic boys. So, Boy Expert Emmy, can you tell us, have you ever used your superpower for your own benefit?"

I roll my eyes, trying not to laugh. "What?"

"I mean," Grant goes on, deepening his voice even more, "have you ever used your boy expertise to find out if someone likes *you*?"

And there's that funny flutter in my stomach again. It feels like I'm on a roller coaster even though I'm on solid ground. "Sort of, yeah."

Grant drops his invisible microphone, looking surprised. "Really?" he asks in his normal voice. "You figured out that a boy likes you?"

I nod and bite my lip, flashing back once again on that horrific moment when Elliot's lips drifted toward mine. "Well, not in the same way I did today. I sort of *stumbled* on the information. Accidentally. It's really awkward, though. And complicated. He's . . . well, he's not someone that *should* like me."

I watch Grant's shoulders rise and fall as he takes a deep breath. "Why not?"

"Because he was supposed to like Harper."

Grant's forehead crumples. "Your best friend, Harper?"

A crushing wave of sadness washes over me as I flash back to our fight in the hallway. Are we still best friends? Are we even *friends* anymore?

"Yeah," I mutter as we turn left into our subdivision. "I could have sworn he liked her. I even tried to set them up. But it turned out he liked me the whole time."

Grant is staring into his bag of chips with a serious expression, like something is bothering him. "Is that why you and Harper aren't friends anymore? Is that the thing you were telling me about? The crack?"

I shrug. "Pretty much."

"Oh," Grant says cryptically, his eyes shining with something I can't identify.

"And now Harper is saying she never really liked him at all, but I don't know if I believe her. I think she's still just totally heartbroken."

"Oh," Grant says again, and when I glance over at him, he's staring at the sidewalk. I wish my phone battery wasn't dead right now because Grant is acting totally strange. He actually looks like he might start to cry. I never knew he cared so much about me and Harper's friendship.

"So," he begins haltingly, "you never even *thought* about liking him back?"

"Never!" I say, drawing an X over my heart. "I never thought about him that way. I mean, he's a nice guy and all but he's just not my type. He's so much more Harper's type, you know?"

"Yeah," Grant says earnestly, but there's still something off about his voice. He sounds like a bad actor trying to read lines from a script.

We both go quiet and all I can hear is the sound of our side-by-side footsteps as we turn down Hartfield Circle, passing all the familiar landscapes of our childhood: the perfect piece of flat sidewalk where we used to play hopscotch, the mailbox we used to race to on our scooters, the giant tree I would hide behind when Grant was trying to tag me.

I'm about to ask what's wrong when he blurts out, "Why isn't he your type?"

I draw in a huge breath and think about all the reasons Elliot and I would never work. "I don't know. I mean, he's really cute. But we're just into totally different things and he makes these really lame jokes that I just don't get."

Grant laughs but it doesn't sound like his normal laugh. "That's . . . not good."

"And even if I *did* like him," I go on, "nothing could ever happen between us because I would *never* do that to Harper. She's my best friend. Or at least, she was."

"Yeah," Grant says again, but this time it's quieter, more distant, like he's wandered back into his own thoughts and gotten lost. "You and Harper are really close. I wouldn't want anything to come between that."

Why do I get the feeling that we're having two different conversations right now? The one we're having aloud and the one Grant seems to be having silently in his mind? Unfortunately, with my phone battery dead, I can only follow one of them.

"I hope Harper and I can be friends again someday," I say with a sigh.

"You will." Grant stops walking, and it's only now I notice we've reached the end of the cul-de-sac and are standing on the small triangular patch of grass between our two driveways, halfway between his house and mine. We both look down and seem to recognize the spot at once.

"International waters," I say with a smile.

"Safe zone," Grant says, but his smile, like his laugh, feels off somehow. Empty, almost. Then, after another long pause, he says, "Friendships are complicated. Things happen. People grow apart."

And, to be honest, I don't know if he's still talking about me and Harper, or if he's talking about me and him.

Is that what happened with us? Did we just "grow apart"?

Now that I think about it, I can't remember *why* we stopped being friends. Or when we started fighting so much. There's not a clear point in my memory when things went off track with me and Grant. His parents pulled him out of school after the second grade and started to homeschool him. Then Harper moved to town in the third grade and I guess she sort of filled the hole Grant left behind.

But it soon becomes clear that Grant was not talking about us when he says, "You and Harper will be friends again." There's a clear confidence in his voice, like he's some kind of authority on the subject of friendships.

"How do you know?" I ask. "You and Dev never grew apart?"

Grant makes a weird sound in the back of his throat. It sounds like a grunt.

"What?" I ask.

He shrugs. "Nothing." But I can tell from the look on his face that it's clearly not nothing.

"What's going on?" I ask. "Did you guys get in a fight or something? Is this about Darcy?"

Grant shakes his head. "No, it's nothing like that. We didn't get in a fight. Dev is just sort of . . ." He huffs. "Like I said before, he's going through some stuff."

I nod. I don't want to pry, because I know it's none of my business, but Grant looks pretty upset. I can tell there's something he wants to talk about but can't. I don't know how I know that. It's just a feeling. A *hunch*.

"Are you worried about him?" I ask.

"Yeah," he says, staring absentmindedly at his garage. "I just don't know how to—" He stops himself and squeezes his hands around his empty bag of chips. "If I tell you something, will you promise to keep it a secret? You can't tell anyone. Especially not Darcy."

"Of course," I say.

"Pinkie swear?" He offers me his pinkie, just like when we were kids.

I latch onto it with my own and we make the oath.

Grant exhales heavily, like a weight's been lifted from his shoulders. "Dev's parents are getting a divorce. He's taking it really hard."

I feel a small pang in my heart for the cheerful,

happy-go-lucky boy who always bounces out of the car at Grant's house. No wonder he's looked so burdened lately. "Poor Dev."

Grant nods. "His parents have started sending him to therapy three times a week to talk to someone. I want to be there for him. I want to help! But I don't know what to say or do. He doesn't seem to want to talk about it. I think he's embarrassed about it or something. Like it's his fault."

"But it's not!" I blurt out passionately.

"I know that," Grant says. "And I'm sure his parents have told him that too, but I guess when you're the one going through it, it's harder to believe."

I drop my gaze to the ground, feeling a familiar squeeze in my chest. "Yeah," I say softly, almost too soft to hear. "It is."

I can feel Grant's stare on me. I can feel the question marks bouncing off him. I don't know why, after eight years, I suddenly feel the urge to say this. To Grant of all people. But it's like I can't keep it in any longer. Like I'll burst if I don't say it.

"I sometimes wonder," I whisper, my throat thick, "if it was my fault that my dad left."

"What?" Grant's voice is full of disbelief. "Emmy, no. Of course it wasn't your fault. Your dad left because—"

"Because what?" I fire back. "I don't know. Mom says he left without an explanation. But I know that can't be true. People don't leave for no reason. There has to be a reason. What if the real reason is me and that's why Mom won't tell me?"

"I'm sure that's not true," Grant says, and I can hear the confidence in his voice.

I drag my foot against the grass, still unable to lift my head and look him in the eye. "You're probably right," I say. "But it's harder to believe when you're the one going through it."

Grant sighs. "Yeah."

I study him for a long moment. I can tell this Dev thing is really eating him up. "He'll be okay, you know?"

"Yeah," he says again, but I hear the doubt in his voice. "Thanks, Emmy."

My brow furrows. "I didn't do anything."

He glances down at the grass and then back up at me. There's something different in his eyes now. Peaceful waters where there was once a storm. Words where there were once only question marks. "You did."

And then, before I can say another word, he's gone.

S'MORES FOR TWO

I CAN'T SLEEP. My conversation with Grant is replaying in my head on a constant loop. I think about poor Dev, dealing with his parents' divorce. I think about Grant's theory that maybe Harper and I just grew apart. But mostly, I think about how weird Grant was acting when I told him about Harper and Elliot. It felt like I was watching a foreign language movie with no subtitles and couldn't follow the story. Why did he keep going all quiet and pensive every time I mentioned Harper? Maybe he was just really worried about our friendship? Or maybe he was preoccupied by his own friendship with Dev?

I saw Grant again earlier tonight through the window. He was in his room, standing at his easel. Unfortunately, I couldn't see what he was painting because the easel was angled away from me, but I could tell from the little creases between his eyebrows that he was concentrating really hard on it. I thought about throwing a pencil at his window, but he looked so focused, I didn't want to bother him.

Now, in my bed, I toss and turn and fluff my pillow

a thousand times before coming to the decision that it's hopeless. Sleep is definitely not happening tonight.

I sit up and turn on my bedside light. As soon as my eyes adjust, they immediately land on Harper's drawing. I hung it on the wall across from my bed as a reminder of my promise to fix our broken friendship. I've almost gotten used to the blurry water stains and smeared colors now. It almost feels like Harper drew it that way on purpose.

My eyes focus on the caption, the only thing still legible through the water stains.

Emerie Woods: Love Coordinator.

Well, at least that part is still true. I spent the rest of the afternoon texting every girl on my list and reporting back what I discovered at the football game. Another handful of successful matches to add to my growing collection, I suppose.

I throw off my covers and scurry down the stairs. My plan is to get a cup of water and maybe a snack from the kitchen, but the moment I reach the first floor, the sound of computer keys clacking stops me short.

I tiptoe down the hall and peer into my mom's office. My shoulders sag. She's working late again. When was the last time she got a full night's sleep?

Quiet as a mouse, I backtrack into the kitchen and start gathering supplies from the pantry.

The microwave dings a few minutes later and I pull out the plate. I've made our traditional late-night snack of "Everything but the Campfire S'mores." They're super easy. You simply place a piece of chocolate and a marshmallow on top of a graham cracker and pop it in the microwave for thirty seconds. They might not have that "campfire" smokiness, but they're still pretty tasty.

I remember when Mom and I used to have slumber parties back when I was little. After Dad left I went through a phase when I had nightmares almost every night. Mom would rush to my room, and when I refused to go back to sleep for fear of being plunged back into the dream, we would come downstairs and make s'mores. I don't remember the nightmares, I barely remember my dad, but I remember the s'mores like it was yesterday.

Sometimes I wish I had better memories of my dad. Less wispy and more complete. And sometimes I wish I was like the twins: too young to remember him at all. I can't decide which is better.

Balancing the plate in one hand and a glass of milk in the other, I creep down the hallway and rap gently on the open door with my foot. Mom turns around and her face clouds over with concern. "Emmy? Is everything all right?" Her gaze falls to the plate in my hand. "Did you have a nightmare?"

I shake my head. "I heard you down here and I thought you might be hungry."

She smiles that lazy, wistful smile she has when I've done something right. "I'm sorry. Did I wake you?"

I cross the room and place the plate down on the desk first, then the glass of milk. "Nah. I was up. Couldn't sleep."

"Annoying client?" Mom guesses.

I giggle. "Yeah. And let me guess." I point at her lap-top. "Problems with your best friend?"

She laughs too and grabs one of the s'mores. She takes a bite and closes her eyes, making her "this is the best thing I've ever tasted" face. It immediately eases the Tummy Tornado that's been storming all night.

When she opens her eyes, she seems to have regis-tered what I just said. "Wait, what's going on with you and Harper?"

I wave the question away. "No big deal. Just typical middle school stuff." I really don't want to weigh Mom down with my problems when she clearly has enough of her own. I gesture toward her laptop. "What's going on with work?"

Mom takes a long sip of the milk, finishing almost half the glass in one gulp. She wipes her mouth with the back of her hand. "All I can say is, I'll be very glad when Monday morning comes, and I won't have to talk to Nathan Wagman ever again." She peers back at her screen, where her inbox is open. Every single email is from Nathan. They seem to go on forever, disappearing even past the scroll zone. And they all have annoying, bossy subject lines like "Installer needs those new tile samples ASAP!" and "Where's the new look board for the guest bedroom?" and "Why hasn't the new end table for the living room been delivered yet?"

My hands clench at my sides. I swear, if I ever meet Nathan Wagman in person, I'll punch him in the face. What is his problem? Mom is doing the best she can.

"Maybe it's a good thing that you're dropping him," I

say, once again feeling the sting of guilt for getting sent to detention.

Mom sighs. "Yeah, I guess. I just wish I could figure out what he wants."

As soon as the words are out of her mouth, an idea pops into my head.

I'm not sure why I didn't think of it before. Maybe because I was so focused on my own problems, I didn't even *think* that I could possibly solve Mom's too.

"Hold on a second," I say, and before she can respond, I bolt from the room. I'm up the stairs and back down in a matter of seconds, gasping for breath.

"What are you—" Mom starts to say, but I thrust my phone into her hand.

"You have to unlock this. Just for a second."

Mom gives me a stern look. "Emmy. We've been over this. You need limits."

"I know, I know, but I just have to look at something really quick. It'll only take a second and then you can lock it up again. I swear."

Mom tips her head back and drains the last of the milk before lowering the glass to reveal a foamy white mustache on her upper lip. "Fine." She grabs the phone from me, and I watch her fingers rapidly move across the screen as she enters her PIN code. She passes me the phone, picks up the empty glass, and stands. "You have until I get back with more milk."

"Thank you!" I watch her shuffle out of the office and the moment she disappears into the hallway, I open the latest email in her inbox, click on the iSpeak Boy app on my phone, and hastily snap a picture.

The translation appears a moment later and I gasp aloud.

That's why Nathan Wagman keeps changing his mind?

It suddenly makes so much sense! If the whole thing hadn't caused Mom so much grief over the past few months, I would laugh. It's almost funny.

I hear footsteps coming down the hall, and I rush to close the email. Just as it vanishes from the screen and her inbox reappears, I spot a new message at the top of the list. It must have just come in because it definitely wasn't there before.

I would have noticed *that*.

The Tummy Tornado kicks up again as I glare at the name of the sender.

Jim Weston.

"Everything all right?" Mom asks, and I startle and look up from the screen.

"Yeah. Fine." As promised, I hand my phone back to Mom to lock up and she hands me the full glass of milk in exchange. Even though my stomach is still swirling violently, I take a sip and casually say, "You got an email from Mr. Weston."

"Oh?" Mom asks, and I detect a hint of interest in her voice. She sits back down at her desk and clicks on the email. I try to read it over her shoulder, but she closes it too quickly.

"What did he want?" I ask, trying to keep the suspicion

out of my tone, but it's like trying to yawn with your mouth closed. I snatch up the last of the s'mores from the plate and take a bite.

"Oh, nothing," Mom says dismissively, clicking over to a web browser where she's been looking at coffee tables. "He just wanted to thank me for the frozen yogurt yesterday. He's a sweet man."

"Are you going to go out with him?" The question explodes out of me like a volcano erupting, complete with a spray of graham cracker crumbs.

Mom flinches but quickly composes herself. "What? No. You think I have time to date with all that's going on right now?" She laughs, but it sounds a tad too forced. "Besides, he didn't ask me out. He just wanted to thank me for the yogurt."

"But what if he *did* ask you?" I press. "What would you say?"

I feel pressure building in my head, like my brain is trying to shove its way out of my skull. I need her to say no. I need her to say, "Never in a million years. I don't want anyone else in my life. Our family is complete with just the four of us."

But of course, she doesn't say that. She doesn't say anything at first. She seems to fall into some kind of trance, and for a minute, I wonder if she actually fell asleep with her eyes open. People can do that, you know. Grant told me he saw a documentary about it once.

Just when I'm about to wave a hand in front of her face to wake her up, Mom blinks and says, "I don't know.

But honestly, Emmy, I don't think it's something you need to worry about."

My heart sinks like a stone to the bottom of my chest. Because I know my mom. I know her looks. Her sounds. The way her eyes mist over when she's about to cry. I know what she does with her feet when she's nervous, how she wears her hair when she's stressed, what she smells like when she's happy. I know every single one of her twelve types of laughs. I know her better than she knows herself. Because even though she claims she doesn't know what she'd say if Mr. Weston asked her out, I do. I just saw it in her eyes. To anyone else, it would have been invisible. A flicker, a twinkle of a star in the middle of the night. But to me, it was as bright and glowing as a spotlight.

Yes.

She would say yes.

I swallow the rest of the milk even though it tastes like sludge. "Okay," I say, forcing myself to smile. Because that's what I do. I smile when she frowns. I order food when she's hungry. I clean up when she forgets to. I help the boys with their homework when she's too busy. It's what I've always done. Because I never wanted her to need anyone else.

Mom's laptop dings and she turns back to the screen as another email appears in her inbox. This one is from Nathan Wagman again. She opens it, her whole body bracing as though she's preparing for a bumpy landing in an airplane.

I guess that's my cue to leave.

"Good night, Mom."

"Good night, sweetie!" she calls without looking up from her laptop. "Thanks for the s'mores. They were perfect."

I shuffle back to the door to the sound of Mom's typing. It's not until I reach the hallway that I remember the phone still gripped in my hand and the picture I took of her screen.

"Mom?" I poke my head back into the room.

"Mmm?" she says distractedly.

"Ask to meet with his mother."

The frantic tapping on the keys halts and she turns to look at me. "What?"

"Nathan Wagman," I say. "I think it would be a good idea if you met with his mother."

Mom looks confused, probably wondering if the milk I just drank was bad and has gone to my head. "Why?"

"Because . . ." I glance down at the grayed-out apps on my screen and then back up at Mom, flashing her the most confident smile I can muster. "Just trust me."

LOST IN A MEADOW

DARCY IS WAITING for me by my locker on Monday morning. "So?" she says, her face brightening when she sees me. "How was the game? Horrible? Brutal? Despicable? Hold on, let me get my thesaurus app out." I giggle while she taps on her phone and then adds, "Unbearable? Dreadful?" She squints at the screen. "Beastly? Now, *that's* a good word. I have to remember that one."

"Actually," I say, scooting past her to dial my combination, "it wasn't that bad."

"Oh?" Darcy says, leaning against the locker next to mine. She studies me closely before her face snaps into a look of sudden comprehension. "Ohhhhh!" she repeats, this time elongating the word. "Soooo, what's his name?"

I bat her away. "No. Not like that. I just mean, it wasn't as bad as I thought it would be."

"So you didn't meet a boy?"

I empty my backpack and hang it on the hook. "No, I went with my neighbor. He's—"

"*He?*"

I laugh. "Yes, he's a boy, but it's not like that. I mean, he's not *that* kind of boy."

"Cute with first-kiss potential?"

I snort at the thought. "Definitely not."

"Definitely not cute or definitely not first-kiss potential?"

And just like that, the fluttery feeling in my stomach is back. Why does it keep doing that? And now my cheeks feel hot too. The thought of kissing Grant is . . . is . . . well, it's just not a thought I think I should be having. "The second one," I say decisively.

"But he *is* cute?" Darcy confirms.

Today is an Even Day, so I grab my stuff for Social Studies. "Yeah. I guess you could say he's cute."

"OMG, you have to text him! Right now!" Darcy grabs my phone from the back pocket of my jeans and starts to tap at the screen. A moment later, her lips tug into a frown. "Why are all your apps grayed out?"

Seeing my phone in Darcy's hand makes me panic a little, and I quickly take it back from her before she has a chance to see the iSpeak Boy app. "My mom did that. And I'm not texting him."

"Why not?"

"Well, for one, I don't think he texts. I'm not even sure he *has* a phone. But also . . . he's . . . my neighbor."

"So?"

"So I've known him since I was a kid. We used to play freeze tag."

Darcy lifts her eyebrows teasingly. "So now you can play *tongue* tag."

"What? Ew! No!" I stop and study her. "Wait, have you done that? Did you kiss Dev?"

Her expression crumples in an instant. "No. And I don't want to talk about Dev."

I close my locker and face her. "Oh no. What happened?"

She blows out a breath. "I don't know. He's acting weird again."

My heart starts to beat faster as I think about the secret Grant told me this weekend. About Dev being in therapy three times a week because of his parents' divorce. "What do you mean by weird?"

Darcy chews on her fingernail. I can tell she's anxious about this. "It's that same stupid stuff again. We'll be texting back and forth, and everything seems great, and then poof! He'll just disappear and won't text me for a whole day. And then when he finally does text me back, it's like he's a different person. He's all cold and moody, like he doesn't like me anymore. I think maybe . . ." Her voice trails off, and for a moment she looks like she might cry. "I think . . . he likes someone else."

"No!" I say, way too forcefully, because it causes Darcy to flinch and a few people to turn and look at us. I quickly lower my voice. "No, I know it's not that."

"What do you think it is, then?" Darcy asks, and her eyes are so wide and hopeful, it breaks my heart a little. I can tell she's waiting for me to use my superpower and tell her exactly what's going on with Dev. But I can't do that. I can't betray him (or Grant). I pinkie swore!

"I think . . . ," I begin hesitantly. The first-block bell rings, and I glance anxiously down the hall and then back at Darcy. She's still staring expectantly at me. "I think he's probably just busy," I lie. "I mean, you know how hard Weymouth Academy is. They get way more homework than we do. I'm sure that's all it is."

Darcy nods, but I can tell she's not convinced. "Yeah, maybe."

"Don't worry! It'll be fine," I assure her, and when she still doesn't look convinced, I say, "Hey, do you want to hang out at my house after school today?"

This seems to do the trick. Darcy's usual bounciness returns, and her cloudy expression clears. "Yeah! That sounds fun! I can help you pick out your outfit for the dance this weekend. You're going, right?"

"Of course I'm going!"

Darcy giggles. "Okay. I'll see you at lunch, then."

We part ways and I sprint down the hallway. Ms. Baldwin's Social Studies classroom is on the other side of school, near Harper's locker, so it's always a marathon to get there. It's not until I'm steps from the door that I realize I was so distracted by my conversation with Darcy, I left my pencil case in my locker. And we're supposed to have a quiz today.

I groan and glance back in the direction I came, then at the clock on the wall. I have two minutes before the final bell rings. I'll never make it back to my locker in time. Normally, I would just borrow a pen from Harper's locker. It's right down the hall and I know her combination. But now things are all weird between us and she basically told me to leave her alone. Does that apply to her locker as well?

The clock ticks forward one minute and I realize I'm

out of options. I dash to Harper's locker, dial the combination, and yank open the door.

Harper keeps a small cup of pens and pencils on the bottom shelf. I'm careful to select a black one—Ms. Baldwin has a weird prejudice against blue pens—and start to close the door. But something catches my eye and I stop. Slowly, I ease Harper's locker back open and stare incredulously at the painting hanging on the inside of the door.

That definitely wasn't there the last time I looked inside Harper's locker.

The painting is *gorgeous*. It's a blurry picture of a meadow with sprinklings of white flowers, a partially collapsed three-rail fence in the foreground, and the hazy outline of green trees in the distance. The sky looks like it's just finished raining. Dark gray storm clouds are parting, making way for a bluer, brighter, happier color.

Harper must have painted this in her Art class. It's good. *Really* good. Like it belongs in a museum or something. And when I look at it, I immediately feel that strange stabbing sensation I felt last week, when I watched her sit down in her new Art classroom and take out her sketch pad. When I saw how happy it made her to be there, instead of in Computer Science with me.

But also, the longer I stare at the painting, the more I start to feel something else. A kind of peacefulness. It settles over me. Almost like I'm *in* that meadow right now, lying on that grass, surrounded by those flowers, waiting for the rain to pass and the blue skies to return.

For a moment, I get so lost in the painting, I forget where I am and where I'm supposed to be.

That is, until the bell rings, pulling me back into the hallway. Back into reality.

I'm late!

But for some reason, I can't bring myself to close the locker door. I can't bring myself to leave that meadow. It feels like saying goodbye, and I'm not ready to say goodbye.

I pull out my phone and, grateful that Mom's phone curfew doesn't block the camera app, snap a picture of the painting and then slam the locker door. I'm going to have to run. I'm going to have to beg Ms. Baldwin to forgive me. I'm going to have to pray she's in a good mood this morning and doesn't give me a tardy.

But the moment I turn around, ready to sprint the ten feet to my classroom, I see her.

Harper is standing right there, watching me with suspicion in her eyes.

I fumble for something to say, but it's like my tongue is tied in knots. After nearly five years of friendship, hours of conversation, hundreds of late-night sleepovers, thousands of text messages back and forth, I suddenly can't come up with a single thing to say to Harper Song.

Except . . .

"Uh, hi," I stammer. "You're late."

She holds up a pink slip from the office with the messy signature of Ms. Watts.

"Uh, hi," I stammer. "What are you doing here?"

She holds up the little wooden owl that I recognize as Ms. Hendrickson's hall pass. "I forgot my copy of *A Midsummer Night's Dream*."

Her words are like ice. They cut right through me, leaving me cold and shivering.

"Oh," I reply, unsure what else to say.

"What were you doing in my locker?"

I turn back to the locker door and make a startled face. Like I've just woken from sleepwalking and have no idea how I got here. "Oh." I let out a nervous chuckle. "Sorry. I just forgot a pen and we have a quiz and I didn't want to go all the way—"

"You were doing it again, weren't you?" Harper asks, and I've never heard her tone so accusatory before. Like she's confronting a criminal. Not her best friend. Or, I guess, *ex*–best friend.

"Doing what?"

"*Scheming.*"

"What?" I don't have to pretend to be confused, because I'm genuinely one hundred percent baffled.

She points at the locker door. "Are you trying to ruin this for me too?"

"Ruin what?" I try for a light laugh. "Harper, I honestly have no idea what you're—"

"You always do this!" she cries, and I can hear that the anger is still fresh in her voice. She hasn't forgiven me. Not even close. "You're always *interfering*. You're always coming up with complicated plans and stupid schemes!"

Plans? Schemes? What is she talking about? I was just borrowing a pen.

"You can't just let me like someone without getting involved!" she says, throwing up her hands.

I blink, certain I misheard her. "Wait. So you *do* like someone? But you told me—"

"I told you to leave me alone. And stop trying to meddle with my life."

I feel flustered. She's not listening to me. She's got this all wrong. "Harper, I swear, I was just trying to—"

But again, she won't let me finish. "That's your problem, Emmy. You try *too* hard. You get too obsessed. You can't just let things be. Let things happen. You have to be in control of everything!"

What is she talking about? Let *what* happen? I'm so lost.

"But I won't let you meddle with this," she goes on, and for some reason, she motions toward her closed locker door again.

I take a deep breath. "I wasn't trying to meddle with anything. I promise. I was just borrowing a pen." I watch her reaction carefully. Her gaze darts between me and the locker door, considering. She looks like she might be starting to believe me. Her face softens. Her shoulders fall away from her ears. The anger starts to fade from her eyes. And for a second, I see the old Harper. My best friend.

And I'm so desperate to cling to her.

"So," I say playfully, trying for a smile. "Who's the new boy? Is it someone I know? Is it Cole Campbell?"

Instantly, I know it was the wrong thing to say. Like

a curtain being drawn across a stage, the lightness in Harper's expression is gone and the anger is back.

She scoffs and shakes her head, like she can't believe what she's hearing. "Why would I tell you who I like?" she asks, and once again, I feel the chill of her words like ice down my spine. "You'll only mess it up."

The pain is sharp. And deep. "Harper . . . ," I start to say, but my voice is broken, and I can't finish.

It doesn't matter, though, because Harper is not waiting around to hear the rest anyway. She forgets all about her copy of *A Midsummer Night's Dream* and pushes past me, past her locker, storming down the hallway and taking any chance of a blue sky with her.

"I **CANNOT** *WAIT* for this dance!" Darcy does a little skip as she emerges from my closet, carrying an armful of clothes. She dumps them on the bed with a dramatic sigh and begins to riffle through her selections. "Did you see they already started putting up posters for it in the hallways? I'm so excited! Our first middle school dance. My sister is in high school and she says middle school dances are totally lame and no one dances with each other and it's really boring. But I don't know. I feel like ours will be different. Especially after the boy expert has worked her magic on half the school! What do you think of this dress with these shoes? Or would you rather do skirt and top? Emmy, are you even listening to me?"

I blink and focus on Darcy, who is holding a black chiffon cap-sleeve dress in one hand and a pair of glittery wedge heels in the other. "Oh yeah. That looks good," I say absentmindedly before my gaze floats back to the wall and settles on Harper's drawing. I haven't been able to stop staring at it since Darcy and I got here.

The entire walk home from school today, Darcy couldn't stop talking about the dance this weekend.

Then, the moment we got to my house, she made a beeline for my closet to search for outfits and I nearly collapsed on the bed, weighed down by the haunting memory of Harper's words in the hallway this morning. They haven't stopped echoing in my head all day.

"I don't know." Darcy studies the dress with a frown. "This is a little fancy. I wonder if it'll look like you're trying too hard. We need to find that perfect balance between effortless and drop-dead gorgeous."

Normally, I would get excited talking about this kind of stuff. Normally, I'd be the one doing most of the talking. It was only a few weeks ago that I was in Harper's room, picking out clothes for her to wear to the carnival while she sketched the very drawing that's now hanging on my wall. Now that feels like light-years ago.

How can an entire friendship fall apart so fast?

How can a crack spread that quickly?

Unless the crack was there long ago, and I just didn't see it.

Darcy holds up a green-and-white belted dress. "Now, *this* one feels much more like 'I don't really care what I look like, I just found this in the back of my closet.' And it will totally coordinate with what I'm wearing. All I can say is, Dev better not show up in jeans and a T-shirt. Why are boys so clueless about clothes? Do you think I should text him and maybe subtly suggest some outfits to him so we don't end up looking ridiculous together? Emmy?"

Darcy snaps her fingers in front of my face, and once again, I pull my attention away from the drawing and try to focus on her. "Sorry," I mumble.

"What's up with you?" she asks.

I shake my head. "Nothing," I lie. "Just school stuff."

"I can't believe I forgot to tell you!" Darcy plops down excitedly on the bed, her previous question forgotten. "Guess who else is going to the dance *together*?"

"Who?"

"Archie and Delia!" She does a little bounce.

"Really?" I ask, trying to sound as excited as she is. But for some reason, I just can't get there.

"Yes! Delia told Isla this morning that she took your advice and casually mentioned her dragon backpack from fifth grade to Archie, and everything just kind of whirlwinded after that. I mean, *dragon backpack?* Where did you even come up with that? How did you know those were the magic words?"

I shrug. "I don't know. Just a hunch."

"Right, right." Darcy gives me a cryptic wink. "Your *hunches*. Well, anyway, he asked her to the dance last night. And now they're going together!"

"That's great," I say, but it comes out way flatter than I intended.

"All thanks to you!" Darcy playfully bumps my shoulder. "My sister says that when she was in middle school, no one went to the dance 'together.'" She makes air quotes around the word. "But apparently, that's just because they didn't have a boy *expert* on the job."

I laugh weakly. "Yeah."

"That's three couples who are going to the dance together because of you." Darcy starts to count on her fingers. "Alexis and Garrett. They totally hit it off at the

Shakespeare play last weekend, by the way. Let's just say Puck worked his magic on *them*. Now there's Delia and Archie. And—hopefully—me and Dev."

"Hopefully?" I ask.

She rolls her eyes. "He still hasn't texted me back from lunch. I'm thinking about sending him like a zillion texts in a row. You know, just bombard him until he writes back."

"No, don't do that," I rush to say.

I don't need a magic app to know that's a very bad idea. Dev is dealing with some really serious stuff right now. The last thing he needs is to be overloaded by text messages.

"He's probably just busy," I tell her for the hundredth time. "I would give him some space."

Darcy sighs. "Okay, you're the expert. But I still think there's something weird going on with him."

"I'm sure it's nothing," I lie again.

She shrugs and goes back to the tally on her fingers. "Oh, and I also heard that Vivi Lee and Micah Lowenstein are getting together to play video games this afternoon." She raises an eyebrow. "They could be number four. And I saw Tyler Watkins talking to Logan Lansing's little sister in the hallway today." She crosses her fingers tightly. "Maybe five?"

"Wow. Five," I say, once again trying to find the enthusiasm that I know I would have felt a week ago. But it's like the well has dried up. And after what happened today at Harper's locker, it all just feels like too much.

The boys.

The matches.

Being the Love Coordinator.

Although I would never admit this to Mom, I was actually grateful for the silence of my phone today. With the iSpeak Boy app locked out, there was no constant buzzing in my pocket, alerting me to every single thing every boy around me was thinking. It was a nice break.

It gets exhausting, knowing that much.

"Emmy? Are you listening?" Darcy asks impatiently, and I realize I've gone back to staring at Harper's drawing again. "What are you even looking at?"

Darcy scoots over on the bed and angles herself so she can follow my eyeline. I can tell the moment she spots the picture, because her face kind of scrunches up like she's just been asked to solve an unsolvable math problem. "What is that? Why is it all blurry? Did one of your little brothers draw that?" Darcy's eyes light up. "Wait a minute. Did neighbor boy draw that for you?" Her lips curve into a playful smile. "Is that like some kind of modern-art expression of his secret childhood crush on you?"

"What? No!"

But she's barely listening. She scrambles over to the drawing to study it closer. "Ah, yes, now I can see it." She traces the blurry Cupid figure with her finger, like she's a tour guide at a museum, showing off a classic piece of art to a group of students. "Here's neighbor boy. The shape of him is fuzzy because his feelings are all confused and muddled." She moves on to one of the smudged heart-shaped balloons. "And here's his heart bursting with love for you!"

"Stop!" I don't even realize how sharp the word is until I see Darcy flinch. "Sorry," I mumble again.

"Are you okay?" Darcy asks, and she sounds more concerned than offended.

I stand up and snatch the picture from the wall. I want to tell her to stop teasing me about Grant. I want to tell her that not everything is about boys. I want to tell her that, no, I'm not okay. I lost my best friend today.

But when I look up at her and see the genuine worry on her face, I immediately feel bad. She only came over because I invited her. And she's only talking about boys because that's what we normally talk about. We bonded over boys. Something Harper and I never really did.

Now I wonder if Harper even *liked* talking about that kind of stuff, or if she was just playing along and pretending to be interested because I was. Sometimes, when I would go on and on about some cute boy in our school, I felt like she was barely even listening.

But Darcy *is* listening.

She's been listening since the beginning.

Is it possible that Darcy and I just have more in common than Harper and I ever did? Is it possible that *we're* the better match?

I swallow and glance down at the drawing in my hand. My gaze travels slowly over the blurry Cupid and the smudged balloons, the hazy letters spelling out the words "Love Coordinator," and finally, to Harper's signature in the corner. Barely legible. Barely even there anymore.

"It's nothing," I say quietly, opening a random drawer in my desk and stuffing the drawing inside. "You're right. One of my brothers drew it."

Darcy seems to accept this answer as the truth, because she stands up and goes back to her pile of clothes, sorting through the hangers until she finds a cardigan to go with the dress she picked out. "So is that how you understand boys so well? Because you grew up with brothers?"

I bark out a laugh, and this time, it actually does feel genuine. "My brothers are *eight*. And they don't even speak the same language as me. Literally. I definitely didn't learn anything from them."

"What's your secret, then?"

"There's no secret," I say automatically, because that's the lie I've been repeating for the past week. It feels like second nature now. "I just get these . . ."

"Hunches, right," Darcy says, and for some reason, I *know* she doesn't believe me. She leans over the bed to poke me in the shoulder. "Come on. There has to be more to it than *that*. Practically half the school is falling in love because of you. You gotta tell me how you do it!"

I drop my gaze to my phone, lying on the bed beside me. The clock reads 3:58, which means in two minutes, my apps will be unlocked and iSpeak Boy will be working again.

I haven't told a single soul the truth since I saw that first translation pop onto the screen. All this time, I've kept it a secret. *My* secret. But a gloomy cloud seems to settle over me as I realize that the only person I would have told—the only person I ever could have trusted with it—doesn't want to know any of my secrets anymore. Because she doesn't even want to be my friend anymore.

But this person—this girl standing in front of me with her wide, curious eyes and giddy smile—she does.

Maybe I just need to accept the fact that Harper has moved on. She transferred out of our only class together. She has a lunch table full of new friends now. She even has a new crush. Someone she won't even tell me about.

I watch the clock on my phone click over to 3:59. And I know that it's time. Time to share my secrets with someone new. Time to replace this empty spot in my heart. Time to move on too.

Which is why I take a deep breath and say, "Well, you're probably not going to believe it, but . . ."

STOP! THIEF!

DARCY DOESN'T SAY anything for a whole minute after I've finished talking. Finally, after what feels like a lifetime, she speaks. Actually, it's more like a squeal.

"ARE YOU SERIOUS?!"

"Yes. Totally serious. That Enchanted Lagoon at the carnival must have really been enchanted or something because once my phone turned back on again, this app was just . . . there."

"And it works on *any* boy?" she asks.

"Well . . ." I falter, my gaze drifting to my bedroom window. Grant's curtains are shut. "Technically, yes."

"O.M.GEEEEE!!!!" Darcy screams. "This is amazing! This is life changing! This is like the secrets to the universe!"

I giggle because that's pretty much the same reaction I had.

"That's how you've been getting inside *all* those boys' heads?" Darcy confirms, still clearly unable to bring herself to believe it.

"Mmm-hmm," I say before my tone turns stern. "But,

Darcy, you can't tell *anyone* about this. You have to swear. This has to be our secret."

Darcy drags her finger across her heart in an X. "Oh, of course. I swear. I mean, imagine if this fell into the wrong hands?"

"Exactly," I say, breathing a sigh of relief. "It could be disastrous."

Darcy does a giddy little hop on the bed. "So what else have you found? I mean, what's the most shocking thing you've discovered about a boy in our class?"

"Hmm." I take a moment to think about that. There's *so* much to choose from! "Well, Mitchell Valentine farts all the time and blames other people."

"No!" Darcy squeals with laughter.

"Ian Burke can never remember if he's changed his underwear or not."

"Gross!"

"Jeremy Mason always forgets his own locker combination. Oh, and Tyler Watkins stuffs his shoes with socks so he can look taller."

"Get out!"

"And oh my gosh, the hair!"

"What about the hair?" Darcy leans forward, hanging on my every word.

"Boys are *obsessed* with their hair. And bras."

"Bras?" Her brow furrows.

"Yup. Ob-sessed. And they're all paranoid about getting pimples."

"Really?"

I nod. "Liam Cruz uses more-expensive face wash than any girl in our school."

Darcy is laughing so hard, she falls onto her back, holding her stomach and rolling from side to side. I laugh too, because for starters, laughter is contagious. And also because it *is* really funny.

I was pretty nervous about telling Darcy the truth, but now I admit, it's nice to have someone to finally talk to. It wasn't until a few minutes ago that I realized how lonely it's been keeping this to myself.

"What else?" Darcy prompts once she's gotten her giggles under control.

"Well . . . ," I say, thinking.

"What about that new kid, Robby Martinez?" Darcy asks, sitting up. "The app *has* to have revealed some freaky stuff about him. He's *so* weird." Darcy scrunches up her nose, and I feel a sting of insult on Robby's behalf.

"He's not that weird," I tell her. "He's just . . . quiet."

"Yeah, but what's with that dirty old notebook he carries around?"

I think back to the amazing drawings Robby showed me during detention. Drawings of people the way they were afraid to be seen, but that somehow he saw.

"What is he writing in there?" Darcy asks. "Angry poetry or something?"

I don't like the way this conversation is going, so I quickly steer it in a new direction. "Who knows?" I say with a shrug. "But I did find out that Jackson Harris is a huge Berrin James fan."

Darcy snorts. "Who isn't?"

"Right?" I say. "What's the deal with those 'Magnolia Street' lyrics?"

"There's no *deal*," Darcy says authoritatively. "The song is about Kelsey Kapur. The proof is in the line 'thieves in the night.' Because he stole her from Maddox King."

My mouth falls open. "That's what I said!"

I let out a deep, contented sigh. This feels good. Sitting in my room, talking about boys and Berrin James. This feels right. And I don't think I've laughed this hard since the night of the carnival.

I scoop up my phone and click to the music app. "Want me to put on the song and we can dissect every line?" I ask.

Darcy twists her mouth to the side. "Maybe later. I have a better idea."

"What?"

In one quick motion, she swipes the phone from my hand. "Let's find someone to use the app on!"

My face falls into a slight frown. "I don't know. There's no one around but my brothers, and they're kind of—"

"What about neighbor boy?" Darcy asks.

"Grant?" Once again, my gaze slides to the window and I feel a Tummy Tornado brewing. For some reason, I don't like the idea of Darcy using the app on Grant. It feels . . . wrong somehow. I mean, I know it hasn't worked on him in the past, but what if today is the day it does? And what if the app reveals something private that he doesn't want anyone to know?

"I don't think that's a good idea," I finally say with a shake of my head.

"Oh." Darcy looks crestfallen. "But I want to see it in action!"

I eye the phone still clutched in Darcy's hand. I'm not sure why, but it's starting to make me nervous seeing her with it. "How about tomorrow at school?" I suggest as I casually extend my hand toward the phone.

Darcy stares down at it, and for a moment, I get this flash of panic that she's not going to give it back. Which is stupid, I know, because a second later she says, "Yeah, okay," and hands the phone over to me.

"How about a snack?" I say, just as my stomach lets out a hangry growl. Darcy and I both giggle.

We scurry down the stairs into the kitchen, and I set my phone on the counter before heading into the pantry to seek out something that hasn't been sitting around for the past twenty years. "Let's see," I call as I take inventory. "There's cereal. *Always.* Some cheddar cracker thingies. A bag of popcorn that doesn't look *too* stale. Ooh! How about some peanut butter pretzels?"

I emerge from the pantry, holding my prize-find above my head, but my arm automatically falls back to my side when I notice the kitchen is empty.

"Darcy?" I call, peering around. I wander into the living room, where my brothers are watching TV to see if she plopped down on the couch or something, but Isaac and Ben are the only ones in there.

"Have you seen my friend Darcy?" I ask them.

"Nack-o," says Ben.

"Darcy!" I call again, heading down the hall to the bathroom. The door is open, and the room is empty.

Where did she go?

It isn't until I arrive back in the kitchen that I notice something else is missing too.

My phone.

It's no longer on the counter.

My stomach swoops and my head instinctively turns toward the front door.

No.

She wouldn't. Would she?

I dart to the window and peer out at our front lawn. I don't see anything unusual, but then, a second later, I hear it.

The faint *Pop! Ping! Pop! Ping!*

The Tummy Tornado revs up, turning into a full-on storm. I don't have to see inside Grant's garage to know who's there. Who's making the *Pop!* to his *Ping!*

Yanking open the front door, I sprint across the front lawn. I can already hear the voices as I get closer to Grant's house.

"How was your session today?" Grant is asking in a casual tone.

"Fine," Dev replies dismissively.

"What's it like? What do you talk about?" Grant asks. I can tell he's trying to get Dev to open up, like he told me he's been doing.

But Dev just says, "I don't know . . . stupid stuff."

"So do you think they're helpful?" Grant asks.

There's a pause before Dev replies, "No, I think they're lame. The whole thing is lame."

Staying out of sight, I scan the front lawn for signs of Darcy and my phone. It's the slight rustle of leaves that eventually gives her away. My gaze darts to the hedges that separate our yard from Grant's. The perfect spot to eavesdrop. Hidden from view, but still close enough for the microphone to pick up the sound.

The panic is choking me as I dart toward her. I never should have told Darcy about the app! I never should have left my phone out of my sight after telling her!

I dive into the hedges. Branches scrape painfully at my face and arms, but finally I reach for her and snatch the phone out of her grip.

"What are you doing?" I practically shout.

"Shhh!" she whispers irritably to me. "They'll hear us."

"Darcy," I seethe. "You can't just . . . you can't just steal my phone and eavesdrop on anyone you want. Some things are private."

"Why not?" she asks, shooting me an accusing look. "*You* did."

"Yes, but I . . . but I . . ." No matter how hard I try, I can't seem to finish that sentence. I can't seem to come up with any logical argument that works.

But Darcy doesn't seem interested in anything *I* have to say. Her face lights up as she points at the phone. "Anyway, it worked! It wasn't about me at all!"

My heart starts to pound. "What do you mean?" I ask warily.

"Dev!" she says, like it's obvious. "He doesn't like anyone else! That's not why he's been acting so weird lately. Look!" She points again at the phone, but I'm afraid to look. Afraid of what might be staring back at me.

My gaze slowly drops to the screen and all the blood drains from my face.

Because there, on full display for anyone to see—including Darcy—is Dev's secret.

MAFIA MOM

"EMMY, IS EVERYTHING okay?" Mom asks the next morning. "You've barely touched your breakfast."

I stare at my bowl of cereal, which has now turned soggy.

"Are you feeling all right?" Mom asks when I don't answer.

I shrug. Because there's really no response that feels right. I don't know what I'm feeling. Frustration. Confusion. Helplessness. Guilt. They're all like mismatched ingredients in a mixer inside me, making what is sure to be the worst-tasting cake in the world.

"Is everything okay with school?" she asks. "Is it Harper again? A boy?"

I know she'll continue to keep guessing until I tell her. So I just say, "Yeah, it's school. But it's no big deal. Just a test I'm worried about."

I can't tell her. Because if I do, then I'll have to tell her everything: Elliot Phillips, the carnival, the magic app on my phone, my fight with Harper, Darcy, Grant, Dev. It'll take a lifetime to explain all of that. And I'm just not sure I can relive it all.

Especially not yesterday. I haven't been able to get it out of my head.

Darcy's mom came to pick her up shortly after she stole my phone and used it to spy on Dev. And the weird thing is, Darcy didn't even seem bothered by the fact that she'd just pried into Dev's life. She only seemed relieved that he didn't like another girl. Like that was all she really cared about. Meanwhile, I felt horrible. And still do.

That was Dev's secret. Dev's private, personal business. But Darcy just barged right in without asking. Like she had every right to know. But she didn't. She didn't have *any* right to know.

I made Darcy swear not to tell anyone else, especially not Dev. And she promised she wouldn't. But I don't know. I just have a bad feeling about this. I feel prickly all over. Like the weird mix of emotions inside me is making me itch.

"You'll do fine!" Mom comes around the back of my chair at the kitchen table and hooks her arm around my chest, hugging me from behind. "You're the smartest person I know."

I roll my eyes at Mom's obvious exaggeration, but I admit it does make me feel a little better. "If that's true, then you've been hanging out with a bunch of dummies."

Mom suddenly lights up. "Oh, speaking of dummies! I forgot to tell you. You were right."

"About what?"

She pulls out a chair and sits down, taking a bite of

my soggy cereal. "Aboh Nah-tah Wah-mah," she mumbles with her mouth full.

"Oh great, now my *mom* is speaking alien too."

Mom chuckles, nearly spitting out the chewed cereal. Finally, she swallows, wipes her mouth, and says, "Sorry. I said, you were right about Nathan Wagman."

For a moment, I'm confused. What is she talking about? But then she adds, "I had lunch with his *mother* yesterday."

I glance down at my phone sitting on the table next to my cereal bowl and it all comes back to me. The email he sent her on Saturday night that I translated in the app!

"Oh?" I say.

Mom takes another bite of my cereal. This time, however, she makes sure to chew and swallow *before* answering. "Yup. Turns out this whole time his *mother* has been the reason for all of the drama. *She's* been the one who's been changing his mind. I keep picking out stuff he and his wife love, but then he makes the mistake of asking his mother's opinion and she apparently hates my taste in everything."

"Oh my gosh!" I say, sounding shocked, even though I already knew. It was in Nathan Wagman's email. Or rather, in his *head* as he wrote the email. "So what did you say at lunch?"

"Well," Mom says after taking a sip of my orange juice to wash down the cereal. "I told her that her *son* hired me. Not her. And that she's completely stressing him out with all her interference. Then I reminded her that this is *their* house and *they* are the ones who are going to live in it, so she needs to back off."

My jaw drops. "You said that?"

Mom nods. "I did. I don't know what came over me. I felt like I was in the Mafia or something! It was just all that frustration of returned couches and reinstalled tile and pulled-up carpet and months of back-and-forth, it all just came bubbling to the surface."

"And what did she say?"

"She was a little shocked." Mom giggles at the memory. "I don't think she's used to being spoken to that way. But eventually, she agreed to butt out."

"So you're not dropping the Nagmans anymore?"

Mom shakes her head. "Nope. In fact, Nathan emailed me this morning to apologize for being so difficult lately. He said, and I quote, 'Let's wrap this thing up already. It's gone on too long.' We have a meeting today to settle on some *final* choices. So, fingers crossed, we might have to stop calling them the Nagmans."

She crosses her fingers, and I cross mine as well. I can't stop staring in wonderment at my mom. She really *is* amazing.

"What?" Mom asks self-consciously, touching her hair. "Why are you looking at me like that?"

"I'm just . . . ," I say, a smile tugging at my cheeks. "I'm just proud that you're my mom."

Mom's eyes get misty as she beams back at me. "Right back atcha, kiddo. But hey, it was a team effort. You're the one who gave me the tip about the mother in the first place. How did you know? What possibly made you think that his mom was involved?"

I shrug and take a bite of my cereal. At this point, it's more like cold oatmeal. "Just a hunch, I guess."

FINDING MAGNOLIA STREET

WHEN I SEE Darcy waiting for me at my locker before school, I get a kind of cringey feeling. I don't *really* want to talk to her, but I know it's unavoidable. Besides, she's not completely to blame for what happened yesterday. I'm the one who told her about the app in the first place.

"Hey!" she says in her usual bouncy greeting. "Good morning!"

"Hi." I try to sound just as bouncy, but it doesn't quite work.

"So, I didn't get much sleep last night," Darcy says, her voice taking on a more serious tone.

I pause in the middle of dialing in my combination. "Why not?"

She scuffs one of her shoes across the floor. "I just couldn't stop thinking about yesterday. It's crazy what the app revealed about Dev, right?"

I swear I detect a hint of remorse in her voice and my hopes lift. Finally, she's come to her senses and realized that what she did was wrong.

"Yeah," I say, relieved. "I've been thinking about it all night too."

"You have?" Darcy asks.

I yank open my locker and reach inside for my Computer Science notebook. "Totally."

"So who do *you* want to use it on next?"

My arm falls back down to my side. "What?"

"The app," she whispers, leaning in. Her eyes are sparkling. "I was thinking we should totally use it on a few teachers. You know, maybe get some dirt on them that could come in handy if our grades start slipping. Oh, and Ryan Cho! He's so mean to everyone. He's got to have some juicy secrets. If we find a good one we can spread it all over the school. Instant payback. And there's this eighth-grade boy on my bus who's been acting really weird. I need to find out what's going on there. Also, this matchmaking thing? I don't think we should continue to do that for free. Girls would pay good money for this kind of information."

An icy chill creeps down my spine. "You want to *charge* people to find out what boys are thinking about them?"

"Yes!" Darcy says with excitement. "I mean, this app is a miracle. We're sitting on a gold mine!"

I feel my locker start to suck me in. Every time she says the word "we," my heart squeezes. She's not *sorry*. She's not *remorseful*. She just wants more.

"Darcy, I don't think we should—" But I'm cut off by the warning bell.

Darcy bounces on her toes again, looking like someone told her she just won the lottery. "We'll talk more at lunch, okay?"

And then she's gone.

I spend the rest of the day in a daze. I feel like I'm sleep-walking. I'm here. My eyes are open. But I can't see anything that's happening in front of me.

Even in Computer Science, when Mr. Weston announces that we'll be starting to build our very own websites, it's like I can't even hear him.

"Em-dash," he says, waving a hand in front of my face. "Everything okay?"

I blink and try to focus on the screen in front of me. Everyone has already started working on their HTML coding assignment. "Yeah," I mutter blankly.

"It was fun seeing you and your family at Lickety Split," Mr. Weston says.

"Yeah," I say again. He probably could have just come right out and said, "Your mom is one hot babe," and I think I'd still be too distracted to feel annoyed.

In Language Arts, Ms. Hendrickson reads aloud from act 3 of *A Midsummer Night's Dream*. The class all laughs when she gets to the part about Puck turning Bottom into a donkey and then tricking Titania, the fairy queen, into falling in love with him. But I can barely crack a smile.

At lunch, Darcy and I sit alone at a table, and I hardly even hear her as she chatters on about all her ideas for the app. I can't absorb a single one of them, but I know for certain that I cannot let Darcy get her hands on my phone ever again.

At one point, my gaze drifts across the cafeteria, and for just a fleeting moment, my vision clears, and I can focus on Harper, sitting at her new table with her new friends. But then Darcy taps my tray to get my attention and everything goes fuzzy again.

No one is home when I get back from school. I drag myself up to my room and collapse on my bed. I watch the clock on my phone, counting down the minutes until four o'clock. Then, once my apps are unlocked, I do the one thing that has always managed to cheer me up in the past, no matter what.

A few seconds later, Berrin James's voice drifts through my wireless speaker, filling my room with music. The phone is set to shuffle, and the song that has come on is "Every Heartbeat." It was always Harper's and my favorite. We would put it on before any big event to pump ourselves up. But the last time I heard it was right before we left for the carnival and the memory of that is still too painful, so I skip to the next one. This song doesn't make me feel much better, though.

A familiar piano riff floats into the air, soft and delicate. The drums kick in next, a slow, purposeful beat. Then Berrin sings,

> You said, "Meet me on the corner of
> Magnolia Street and Yesterday."
> Back when we were thieves in the night,
> Before Tomorrow stole you away.
> Pink-scribbled hearts on the sidewalk

All cracked and faded to dust.
Gold-painted stars on the ceiling,
But it was never enough.

It's the last song Harper and I ever listened to together. The song we argued about in the car, the one
everyone in the world seems to be arguing about. But
now the lyrics seem to hit me harder than they did before. Like Berrin James is writing about *me*. About my
scribbled hearts that have cracked and faded to dust.
About the tomorrow that stole Harper away from me.

I stand and walk over to my desk. Pulling out the
top drawer, my gaze lands directly on Harper's drawing.
The blurry lines of my Cupid arrows. The smeared colors of my heart-shaped balloons. The smudged edges of
Harper's signature.

And I remember . . .
All the ways you'd say my name
All the things I couldn't say
Was there any way we could have stayed?

My mind suddenly rushes back to that interview I
watched on the Xoom! channel last week. What was it
that Berrin said when the interviewer asked him about
the meaning of the song? Something about his lyrics
being the way he processes what's going on in his life?

As Berrin launches into the chorus, belting the lyrics that have left the whole world stumped, adrenaline
shoots through me. I turn my head toward the speaker.

Now I've walked every block
And I've roamed every road.
I've wandered in circles to find my way home
To Magnolia Street.
Headlights so dim
And memories so blue
I've lost every road that might lead me back to you
On Magnolia Street.
On Magnolia Street.

I nearly forgot that Berrin James writes all his own songs. These words flooding through my speaker are his words. Which means . . .

I dive back to my bed and scoop up the phone. The second verse starts as I fumble to get to the app, my heart pounding, my head swimming with possibilities. I'll be the only one in the *world* who knows who the song is really about. I'll be the only one on earth besides Berrin himself, who knows his secret.

You said, "I'll race you to the end,"
As we took off through the night.
Back then, everything was sweeter
with Magnolia Street in sight.

His secret.

Now I remember exactly what he said in that interview.

"Sometimes the lyrics become a little too personal and you just . . . want to keep some secrets for yourself."

I freeze. My finger hovers over the iSpeak Boy icon. But I just can't do it. I can't press it. Even if Berrin James is a celebrity who I'll never meet in my life, it's still not my secret. And I don't have the right to know.

The chorus comes to an end and I glance down at Harper's drawing once again. In that moment, I realize it doesn't matter what the lyrics really mean. What Berrin was really trying to say.

Maybe the world will never know who the song is about. Maybe no one will ever find the real Magnolia Street on a map. But I know where it is. It's right here. In this room. On this water-crinkled paper smeared with color. In the cafeteria at school. In front of my locker. It's everywhere Harper used to be. It's every space she left behind since tomorrow stole her away.

Plink!

I startle out of my thoughts and turn to the window just as the pencil bounces off the glass. But there's something less innocent about the noise. It sounds much more like a demanding *bang* than a harmless little *plink*.

And when I open my window, I find a very angry boy glaring at me from the next house.

"How could you do that, Emmy?!"

VIOLENT STORMS AHEAD

"I TRUSTED YOU!" Grant bellows before I can say a single word. "What I told you about Dev and his parents was a secret. You knew that. And you broke it anyway. You betrayed me *and* him. You pinkie swore!"

I've never seen Grant this worked up before. He's normally so cool and collected.

"Grant," I try to explain. "I swear I didn't—"

But he doesn't let me finish. "You told Darcy, didn't you? The one person I specifically told you *not* to tell. And then she talked to Dev about it and now Dev is furious and won't even talk to me!"

"What?" I reach up with one hand and squeeze my temples. I feel like my head is going to explode. This is such a mess. Darcy talked to Dev about the divorce? She told him that she knew? I told her not to do that!

"Grant," I try again. "I'm so sorry. It was an accident."

He snorts. "An accident? How do you *accidentally* spill someone else's biggest secret?"

"Well . . . ," I begin, staring down at the phone still clutched in my hand, but I'm not sure what to say next. Should I just tell him the truth? Show him the app?

Tell him *my* secret? Darcy already knows, so what's one more person?

"You know what I think?" Grant says before I can make a decision. "I think this is all because of your little matchmaking schemes."

My nose crinkles. "Huh?"

"I warned you not to get involved in other people's lives. I told you someone would get hurt. I think Dev was acting weird and Darcy was getting worried, so you told her his secret to make sure your precious love match didn't fall apart."

"What?" I repeat, shocked. "No, that's not at all how it happened."

But clearly Grant doesn't believe me. "What you did was low, Emmy. Selfish and low."

My throat suddenly feels tight, and my eyes sting like I might cry. I swallow hard and try to speak, but no words come out. Grant and I have fought across these two windows for years. But it's always been teasing and fun. It's never actually been hurtful. And he's never said anything like *that* before.

"Grant . . ." I finally find my voice, but it's too late. The door to Grant's bedroom opens and Ms. Knight walks in.

"Grant?" She sees me through the window and waves. "Oh, hi, Emmy!"

I sniffle and dab at my eyes with the heels of my hands. "Hi, Ms. Knight." I pray she can't hear the crack in my voice.

"What's up, Mom?" Grant asks, and I can hear him

trying to sound normal. But Ms. Knight seems to sense something is wrong. Her gaze bounces between me with my teary eyes and Grant with traces of anger still left in his voice.

"Everything okay?" she asks.

Grant clears his throat. "Yes. Emmy and I were just talking."

Ms. Knight looks to me for confirmation and I force myself to nod.

"Okay," she says, still not sounding convinced. She turns back to Grant. "Well, Harper is here. She's downstairs in the living room."

Suddenly, the world beneath my feet tilts and I feel like I might fall right off the edge of it. Did she just say *Harper*?

"Okay, thanks," Grant says. "I'll be right there."

Ms. Knight ducks out the door and Grant turns back to the window. I'm fully expecting a very lengthy explanation, but instead he just gives me another harsh look and says flatly, "I gotta go. Bye, Emmy."

The window closes in my face, followed by the swish of the curtain. And I'm left to stare speechless and stunned at the side of Grant's house.

Harper?

I'm absolutely certain I must have misunderstood. Or Ms. Knight is talking about some other Harper. Because why would Harper *Song*, my ex–best friend, be coming over to Grant's house? They hardly know each other. I mean, sure, they've met plenty of times over the years, with Harper being my best friend and Grant being my neighbor. But they've never, like, *hung* out. Alone. Together.

Have they?

And then, through the narrow gap in Grant's curtains, I see her.

Harper.

My Harper.

Grant is showing her into his room. I lean out the window, trying to see through the small opening in the drapes. It looks like they're sitting down on the futon in the corner. Grant is setting up his laptop, like they're getting ready to watch something together.

The world is no longer tilted, it's now completely upside down. My mind is spinning. The Tummy Tornado is swirling at max speed. Whatever the ratings are for tornados, this has got to be the highest. I'm talking buildings destroyed. Houses swept away. Century-old trees reduced to nothing but a pile of leaves and twigs.

What are they doing? Watching a movie? Is this, like, a *date*?

Bile instantly rises up in my throat. Grant and Harper can't be on a date. They can't be together. They're . . . totally wrong for each other!

He's . . . *you know.*

And she's . . . *you know.*

They're just . . . *different.*

It's a horrible match!

Grant sets his laptop down just out of sight. I can't

see the screen through this gap in the curtains. I need a better angle. I need to move farther to the left. Pocketing my phone, I shove half of my body out of the window, until the bottom of the frame is pushing painfully against my stomach. But I still can't see the laptop.

Maybe they're watching one of Grant's lame documentaries. Maybe he's just helping her with something for school. It could be totally innocent.

Then again, it could not be.

Another wave of nausea hits me and I think I'm going to be sick. I need to see that screen. I need to figure out what is going on in there! But the stupid curtain is in the way.

I peer out from my window and my gaze falls on the section of roof just below my bedroom, where the dining room bumps out from the rest of the house. If I shimmy to the end of it, I'll have the perfect line of sight into Grant's room. The roof is only a little slanted, but I can definitely still balance on it. I just need to get a peek at that screen, I tell myself. And then I'll come right back inside.

Ever so carefully, with the delicacy and precision of a cat, I swing one leg over the windowsill and rest it on the nearest roof tile. I press down with my foot, testing my weight. It holds. I swing the other foot out and slide onto my butt.

I did it!

This isn't bad at all, I think as I gaze out from my new perch. I could sit out here all day. The view is actually pretty nice.

Staying on my butt, I shimmy to the left a few inches, until I can just make out the edge of Grant's laptop through the gap in the curtains. He has propped it up on a small table next to his easel.

And that's when I notice something strange. Not on the laptop screen. But on the easel.

The painting Grant has been working on for the past few weeks is gone.

Where did it go? Did he finish it?

My thoughts continue to swirl as fuzzy slivers of memory dance at the corners of my mind.

Patches of gray and green, dotted with white flowers. Stormy clouds chased by blue skies.

Grant told me he was trying to paint something that looked purposefully blurry.

With sudden inspiration, I lean back and dig into my pocket for my phone. As soon as it's out, I click on the photos app. I swipe left until I'm staring, once again, at that peaceful meadow. The one I saw hanging up in Harper's locker.

I swore, when I first saw it, that Harper must have painted it. But now, when I look closer, when I zoom all the way in on the bottom left, I see what I failed to see before.

No signature.

Harper always signs her name on her artwork. She's been doing it for as long as I've known her.

But this painting is not signed.

Which means she isn't the one who painted it.

My breathing grows shallow. I grip onto a roof tile

for support as more jagged pieces fall into place. Things Harper said to me at her locker yesterday are buzzing around my head like flies.

"Are you trying to ruin this for me too?"

"You can't just let me like someone without getting involved!"

"That's your problem, Emmy. You try too hard. You get too obsessed. You can't just let things be. Let things happen. You have to be in control of everything!"

"Why would I tell you who I like? You'll only mess it up."

Is that what she was talking about? Does Harper like Grant? Does Grant like her back?

I don't know why, but for some reason the idea of Harper and Grant together makes my chest tighten. And my whole body ache. Like I'm coming down with the flu.

I sit on the roof and glare down at the picture on my phone. An idea is gradually forming in my mind. An idea that could put an end to all of my anxiety. Or make it a thousand times worse.

My brain tells me not to do it. My heart agrees. But my fingers move on their own. Within seconds, the iSpeak Boy app is open. I click on the camera icon from the options list and select the picture of the painting.

Then I click TRANSLATE.

The little wheel starts to spin, matching the tornado still churning in my stomach. I don't even know if this is going to work. I've never used the app on a painting before. Does it only translate words? Or does it also translate—

The thought cuts off as the wheel stops spinning and the screen splits in half. On the top is the picture I just uploaded. And on the bottom:

I love you.

And that's when my foot slips out from under me, and I slide right off the roof.

FLYING HOMEWORK

THE EMERGENCY ROOM of Highbury General Hospital is packed. Thankfully, one of the doctors here is Mom's former client (she helped her remodel her kitchen) and we get right in.

X-rays are taken. Doctors prod and poke at my right arm before proclaiming that it's cracked in three places. It'll heal, but I'll have to wear a cast for the next six weeks.

I don't cry. From the moment I hit the pavement below my bedroom to the moment the nurse finishes wrapping the cast, I don't shed a single tear. I think I'm still too much in shock. I can feel the pain throbbing from my arm. It's like nothing I've ever experienced before. But it doesn't compare to the memory of what I saw on that screen. What I witnessed through that window.

Grant and Harper.

Harper and Grant.

My two ex–best friends. Together. Matched. Like some kind of "we used to like Emmy" club.

It doesn't make any sense. It makes the opposite of sense.

"Are you sure I can't get you anything?" Mom asks

for the third time. We're sitting in one of the patient rooms, waiting for my cast to set.

I shake my head, saying nothing. I'm not sure I've muttered more than a few words since we got here, except "no" when the nurse asked if I was in a lot of pain, "yes" when he then asked if I was comfortable, and "blue" when he asked what color cast I wanted.

"Okay," Mom says after a deep breath. "I'm going to go find the doctor and ask her how much longer we have to stay."

I nod and Mom reluctantly stands up. She hesitates at the door, like she's not sure she can actually leave. I think she's a little anxious now about letting me out of her sight. And I know she's feeling guilty that this all happened when I was alone at the house. Thankfully, though, her car pulled up just as I was tumbling off the roof. Right after I hit the ground, she came running. She stashed the twins with Ms. Knight next door and drove me straight to the emergency room.

I'm sure as soon as all this is over, I'll be getting a very long lecture about climbing onto roofs. And I guarantee it'll be added to the list of things I'm not allowed to do when she's not home, if she ever allows me to stay home alone again. I think I might have lost that privilege until college.

"She'll be here in a few minutes to check on you," Mom says, reappearing in the doorway. She lowers back down into her chair. "In the meantime, I have some questions for you." Her voice is calm, on the verge of playful, but also stern.

I take a deep breath and wait for the inquisition to begin.

"Let's start with why you were on the roof."

I've actually been practicing this answer for the past hour, knowing it would eventually come up. "I had my window open," I begin steadily, like an actress delivering a well-rehearsed script. "To let in some fresh air. And some of my homework blew onto the roof. So I climbed out there to get it. Then I slipped and fell."

I hate lying to Mom. And I feel like I've been doing it a lot lately. But the truth is just too much right now. Too much for her to hear and too much for me to relive.

I can't very well tell her that my neighbor is in love with my best friend, and for some reason, every time I think about it, it sends my heart into a sickening gallop.

"Uh-huh," Mom says. I can tell she's trying to figure out whether or not to believe me. "Do we need to put up a screen in your window? You've never had one because I know you like talking to Grant, but if this is going to be an ongoing problem? Homework mysteriously flying out the window . . ." Her voice trails off, and that's when I *know* for sure that she doesn't believe me.

She knows something is up. She could probably tell from my strange behavior over the past few days. Long stretches of silence and lost appetites. Hanging out with the boy next door after claiming to despise him. I definitely haven't been acting like myself lately. But thankfully, because my mom is awesome, she doesn't press the issue. She just says, "So, do you want me to put up a screen?"

We both know she's not asking if I want to avoid more homework flying out the window. She's asking if I want to avoid something else. Something that she's clearly caught on to. Even if I haven't fully caught on to it myself.

I swallow, imagining one of Grant's pencils flying across the small space between our houses and then bouncing off the screen instead of hitting my window. I imagine what life would be like if his friendly little *plink*s were silenced for good.

It hurts to even think about. But what if Harper keeps coming over? What if they keep hanging out? What if they go on to date for years, all through high school, and then eventually get married? Would I still be able to talk to Grant?

Not the way I used to, that's for sure.

My conversations with Grant are . . . well, I can't put my finger on what they are. They're not about the same silly things we used to talk about as kids. Stuffed rabbits and dinosaurs and which part of the lawn was marked as a safe zone. And they're not about the kind of things that Harper and I talk about. They're different. There's something unique about them. I guess I never really noticed it before. Not until I started to think about it being gone.

And I have a feeling that with Harper added to the picture, it would definitely be gone.

"Maybe that's a good idea," I say quietly to Mom. "To put up a screen."

2.5 SECONDS

AFTER THE DOCTOR comes to check on my cast and gives me the go-ahead to leave, Mom disappears into the hallway to sign some papers. The moment she's out the door again, I remove my phone from my pocket and swipe on the screen. It turns on without complaint or hesitation. It's almost funny, really. How my arm is cracked in three places but my phone, which was in my hand at the time of the fall, survived without a scratch.

It's almost impossible to navigate around the screen with this cast holding my fingers in place. I'm sure that wasn't Mom's first thought when they said I would need a cast, but I know she'll appreciate it as an extra bonus.

I have one missed call and one voice mail. At first, I don't recognize the number. Or the area code. I'm about to delete the message, assuming it's just some telemarketer trying to sell me life insurance, but something stops me.

The number *does* feel somewhat familiar. Like I've seen it before.

I scroll through my call list and freeze when I see the

same number marked as an outgoing call. I dialed it. On Friday night.

A gasp erupts in my throat as the memory shoves its way back in my mind.

It's that woman who answered when I called the number I found in Dad's file!

My gaze darts to the doorway and I listen for footsteps or Mom's voice in the hall. The coast is clear.

Grasping the phone in my good hand, I steer my shaky, casted fingers to the screen and click on the voice mail. The moment the woman's familiar, accented voice pours through the speaker, I stop breathing.

"Hello. This is Edith. You wanted to know about a Henry Simmons. I still say the guy's a bum, and you should steer clear, but that's not my business. Anyway, I found his number. I had it written on the back of one of the unpaid phone bills the guy left me with. The bum. Here it is."

As she recites the number, I press the phone harder against my ear, focusing all my attention on those ten digits. I don't need to write them down. I don't even need to relisten to the message. I'm pretty sure I'll remember that number for the rest of my life.

When the voice mail comes to an end, I quickly click on the keypad and punch in the numbers one by one. I work slowly and carefully, making sure not to miss a single digit. A single step. I don't want any mistakes.

My heart is beating hard but steady. I can hear it echoing in my ears. The Tummy Tornado has reduced to a low, humming whirl. Gentle breezes and rustling leaves.

For eight years, I've been waiting for this moment. For this chance. The opportunity to talk to my dad. To ask him why he left. To get the *real* answer. Not the bogus one I've been given all my life.

"He didn't give a reason, Emmy. He just left."

I know that's not the truth. It can't be. The laws of nature—of the *universe*—wouldn't allow it. There's always an answer. There's always a reason. For everything. For every star and every planet. For every orbit of the earth around the sun. For every season and every day. For every step anyone ever takes. There's always an explanation behind it.

You just have to keep looking until you find it.

Until it's right in front of you.

A series of numbers waiting to be dialed.

A call waiting to be made.

A question waiting to be asked.

I can feel it burning in the back of my throat. I swallow hard and click call.

If I thought the last pause was long, it's nothing compared to the next two point five seconds. I swear an entire lifetime goes by outside the doors of my hospital room. Doctors and nurses come and go. Patients are cut open and stitched back together. Hearts and livers are replaced. Broken limbs are set and cast. Babies are born. Loved ones celebrate the healed and mourn the lost.

It all happens in the span of those two point five seconds. The time it takes for my phone to connect and the voice on the other line to say, "I'm sorry. This number is no longer in service."

ALL THE BROKEN THINGS

"**YUCK. I HATE** hospitals," Mom says with a shiver once we're back in the car. "Let's get home and get some s'mores in the microwave ASAP."

I struggle to fasten my seat belt with my one good hand and Mom reaches over to help. The moment the buckle clicks into place, I burst into tears.

They're not the quiet, polite, sniffling kind of tears you shed during the sad parts of movies. They're full-on, open-the-floodgates, body-wrenching sobs.

Mom's eyes widen. "Emmy! What happened? Is it your arm? Is it hurting? Should I go back in and ask for some more pain medicine?"

I shake my head. I try to tell her that it's not the broken arm that's hurting. It's the broken heart. And there is no medicine for that. There's no magic pill that's going to explain why my father left us. I thought there was. I thought the answer was right here on my phone. But I can't use the app on someone who clearly doesn't want to be found.

I try to say all this, but the only thing that comes out are more tears.

Mom puts an arm around my shoulders and squeezes. "What's happening? Emmy, talk to me. Tell me what's going on."

"I tried . . . ," I say, my voice cracking on every syllable. Every letter. "To find him. I . . . wanted . . . to know . . ."

"Find who?" Mom asks, wiping my cheeks. "Wanted to know what? Slow down. Take a deep breath. You're okay."

I do as she says. I breathe in and breathe out, again and again, until finally, *finally*, the shudders start to soften, and my chest stops hurting and the sobs settle to quiet sniffles.

"Good," Mom encourages me. "Now tell me."

I look at her through blurry tears. Her face is so open. Her eyes so kind. Her smile so warm. I instantly feel guilty for even telling her this. For even wanting more than just her. But I'm done hiding things from Mom. That strategy is what got me here: sitting in the parking lot outside the emergency room, with cracks in my arm *and* my heart.

I inhale one more deep breath before I steadily hold her gaze and say, "Dad. I was trying to find Dad. I thought if I could find him, if I could just talk to him, I could understand why he left."

I search for the hurt on her face. The betrayal. I search for a hint that I've let her down. That finding my dad is the same thing as rejecting her. But I don't see any of that.

Mom's eyes soften. And she lets out a heavy breath

that sounds a lot like the one I've been holding for eight years.

Then she nods. Over and over.

Like she gets it.

Like she understands.

Like maybe she's been on the same quest.

"And you couldn't find him," she says knowingly.

"I found a phone number in your office," I tell her. "I thought it was his. It used to be his. But the woman on the other end said he didn't live there anymore. She gave me a new number, but it was disconnected. It was a dead end."

Mom nods again. "Your father's been changing his phone number for years. It's how he avoids whoever is currently looking for him. I knew eventually that person would be you."

"I'm sorry," I say, the tears instantly welling up again. "I just wanted an explanation. I didn't want him back, I just wanted to understand why—"The words are choked by more sobs.

"I know, sweetie." Mom reaches out and strokes my hair. "I know. I used to want that too."

I let out a small hiccup and look up at her. "You don't want that anymore? You don't want to know the reason he left?"

To my utter shock and disbelief, Mom shakes her head. "It's not about not *wanting* to know. It's about accepting the fact that I never will."

"Huh?" I say, and Mom chuckles.

"You and I are so similar. I see myself in you a little more every day. We both want to think that we have even a sliver of control over what's going on around us. We both want to believe that the universe makes sense. Or that it *can* make sense if we just try hard enough."

"That's your problem, Emmy. You try too hard."

My head falls into a nod. That's exactly what I've been trying to do. With Harper and Elliot and Darcy and Dev and all of them. I've been trying to make it all make sense. I tried so hard that eventually, it stopped making sense at all.

"Your dad left without an explanation," Mom goes on, turning her gaze out the windshield. "He just said, 'I can't do this,' and then he was gone. I tried to track him down too. I tried to get an answer out of him. But I never did."

I stare at her. She's still a little blurry from the tears, but she slowly starts to come into focus. "And you're okay with that?"

Mom smiles and turns back to me. "I wasn't at first, no. But I've come to learn that some things in life you will never understand. No matter how hard you try. And knowing *that* is like a whole other level of under-standing."

I'm not sure I'm completely following what she's saying, but I'm also not sure it matters. Because I actually do feel a little bit better. Mom's words are not an instant cure, by any means. But they take a small bit of the sting away.

Like medicine is supposed to do.

VOICES FROM ANOTHER DIMENSION

IT'S ALMOST DINNERTIME when Mom and I get home. She goes next door to pick up the twins from the Knights and I go straight to my room. I can tell this cast is going to take some getting used to. The doctor said that because I'm right-handed, I'll have to learn how to use my left for a while. I never noticed how many simple things I used to take for granted. Easy things like opening doors and brushing my teeth and getting undressed. Without the use of my right hand, they all become chores.

Even scrolling through my phone is difficult. My left thumb can't quite figure out which way to swipe. My left index finger isn't used to clicking apps. And texting? Forget it. I'll just have to rely on the text-to-speech feature that never works.

Mom must have felt bad for me, because she removed my phone curfew and unlocked all my apps. I guess she figured with my broken arm, I'm going to need some good distractions. And I do. I feel fidgety and antsy, and my arm is already starting to itch under my cast.

But for some reason, I can't find a single thing on my phone that I want to do or watch or play. I used to open my phone and feel like the world was at my fingertips. The sky was the limit. I could do anything! My apps used to glitter and glow. But now they all seem kind of blah and boring, like they're still grayed out. Even my favorites seem to have lost their shine. I open YouTube only to close it a moment later, despite the fact that there are about a hundred new videos posted from my favorite channels. I open SnipPic only to find it's filled with pictures of people having much more fun and living much better lives than I am. I open my messaging app, but the only texts in there are from more girls at my school begging me to help them with their boy problems, plus a few from Darcy with more ideas on how to get the most out of my magic app.

It all just makes me feel . . . I don't know . . . sort of restless.

I try to start a new game with Aurélie, my French game-pal, who I've totally neglected recently. But as soon as I roll the dice and my little Scottie dog lands on the Electric Company, my chest starts to squeeze again. Harper always bought the utilities. She called them her "secret weapon." And I'll probably never play another game of Monopoly with her again.

I'll never do anything with her again.

We'll never listen to a new Berrin James song together. Or make chocolate chip cookies and watch movies. I'll never raid her closet to help her choose the perfect outfit for some big event. She'll never draw me another picture. I'll never find her waiting for me at my locker in the morning. We'll never sit in her room talking about boys or apps or homework or teachers or Shakespeare or lame dad jokes.

With a heavy heart, I click on the Photos app. I have an album set up with all the pictures and videos Harper and I have taken together on this phone. It feels like a lifetime of memories, even though I've only had the phone for a couple of months.

I scroll all the way back to the beginning. To the first video I ever took. I remember because it was the second week of school and I'd finally convinced Mom to get me this phone. The fastest, most expensive model on the market, which I simply had to have. I desperately wanted to try out the fancy, high-res camera, so Harper and I set up the phone in the corner of my room and put on a fashion show.

I press PLAY on the video and watch through misty, tear-filled eyes as Harper and I strut back and forth across my room like we're supermodels on a runway in Paris. Berrin James is playing on the speaker, and we've set up a row of stuffed animals on the bed as our "audience." We only make it across the room twice before we both crack up and collapse on the bed in fits of giggles.

We'll never film another silly video again. I'll never again hear that laugh I love so much.

I drop the phone on the bed and roll onto my side, sobbing into my pillow until my stomach hurts and my eyes are dry and my pillowcase is soaking wet.

I can't lose Harper. I can't lose my best friend. But what else can I do? I've tried to get her back. I tried to find the start of the problem and fix the crack, but I only ended up making the crack worse. I made everything worse.

I'm just like Puck in *A Midsummer Night's Dream*, a merry, restless wanderer who tries to make people fall in love but just ends up filling the world with chaos.

Somewhere in the distance, the sound of muffled voices pull me out of my stupor. I sit up and glance around the room, but there's no one there. I'm all alone.

The voices continue. Soft murmurings interrupted by titters of laughter. I stand up and listen carefully, trying to make out what's being said. But the words are all distorted.

Who is that? Who's talking?

Is it coming from another dimension? Another world?

I walk slowly around my room, listening at the door, the window, the closet, before finally tracking the sound back to my bed. Digging around in my comforter, I find my phone and stare at it incredulously. The screen is black, but the voices are still talking. Did I butt dial someone?

"He's pretty cute. But what's going on with his hair?"

"I know! It looks like it might come alive at any moment and eat someone."

Instantly, I recognize the voices. It's me and Harper. I peer closer at the screen, zooming in. And that's when I realize that it's not dark. It's just pressed up against the carpet. It must have fallen during our fashion show and we forgot to turn it off. The video is still playing. The voices *are* coming from another dimension. One where Harper and I are still friends.

"What about Mr. Weston?" Harper asks, and my voice on the phone squeals.

"Eww. He's a teacher!"

"I know. I mean, just as a person. He's cool, right?"

"Totally cool," I hear myself reply. "I can tell Computer Science is going to be my favorite class this year. I'm so glad you transferred out of Art to be in it with me."

There's a pause on the recording before Harper says, "Yeah, me too."

I'm not sure how I didn't hear her hesitation back then, but I definitely hear it now. She didn't want to be in that class. She never wanted to be in that class. She transferred into it because of me.

"What about Garrett Cole?" I ask Harper. "He's in my Language Arts class. He's a football player, but he's kind of cute."

"I guess," Harper says with very little enthusiasm. "You know who's *really* cute, though?"

"Who?"

"That new boy Robby Martinez."

"You mean, the weirdo who doesn't talk to anyone?" I cringe at my own words. They're almost exactly what Darcy said about him.

"Maybe he's not weird," Harper says. "Maybe he's just shy."

"He's weird," the me on the video says definitively. "He scribbles in that ratty old notebook all day long."

"Maybe he's writing a novel! Like an epic historical tragedy about World War One or something."

Video Me snorts. "I highly doubt that. And he's *not* cute."

"You don't think so?" Harper asks, and I immediately hear the hurt in her voice. How did I not notice that either? How was I so oblivious?

"OMG!" Video Me says with sudden enthusiasm. "I can't believe I forgot to tell you. I downloaded this cool horoscope app that matches you up with your soul mate based on your birthday."

"Really?" Harper asks, sounding skeptical.

"Yes! And I put in your birthday and the birthdays of a few of the boys in our class, and guess who it matched you with!"

"Who?"

Video Me does a dramatic pause, and my stomach instinctively clenches. I can picture myself staring at Harper with wide eyes and a determined smile, trying to build the suspense for as long as possible, like I always do. But now the buildup is only making the tightness in my stomach worse. Because I know what happens next. I know which two little words are going to come out of my mouth. Because they're the two little words that sent my entire life spiraling out of control.

"Elliot Phillips!"

And there it is.

The beginning.

The crack.

Not Elliot himself. Not even the horoscope app that matched him with Harper. But *me*.

"Elliot?" Harper repeats dubiously.

"Yes! You two would be perfect together. You're the same height. You both love to run the mile. You both have nice hair—I mean, I *assume* his hair is nice under all that gel. You're both really smart. And he's *super* cute!"

"You think?" Harper asks.

"Totally!" Video Me says. "And I saw him looking at you during assembly today."

"Really?" Harper asks, and in that instant, I can hear the switch. The moment Harper went from skeptical to intrigued. The moment I started to *convince* her.

She was right. What Harper said in the hallway last week was right. I did talk her into liking Elliot. I did interfere. I completely shut down her spark of a crush on Robby and steered her straight toward heartbreak.

And to think, if I had just let her continue to like Robby, none of this would have happened. Elliot wouldn't have rejected her at the carnival. We wouldn't have drifted apart. We wouldn't have had those terrible fights in the hallway. She wouldn't have said those hurtful things to me.

And she wouldn't have . . .

My head turns instinctively toward the window. It almost feels like there's a magical force drawing my gaze outside, across the narrow gap between houses and into Grant's room. The curtains are open again, and I see him standing in front of his easel with his painting smock on, working on some new masterpiece.

I press STOP on the video and swipe over to the iSpeak Boy app. The last thing I translated is still on the screen. The thing that sent me tumbling off the edge of the roof. I stare, once again, at the picture of the painting that was hanging up in Harper's locker, and the words inscribed below like an engraving. Like fate written in permanent ink. And I'm the one holding the pen.

I love you.

And suddenly, I know what I have to do. The crack might be too deep to repair. It might be too late for me and Harper. I might never be able to fix what I've done. But there is one thing I *can* do.

I can let her be.

I take one last look at the painting—that beautiful green meadow with stormy skies and the promise of a blue horizon—and then I close the iSpeak Boy app and delete it from my phone.

PLAN B

THE NEXT MORNING, I walk to school with a whole new plan. This one is different, though. I'm determined for it to be different. Because I can't keep creating disasters wherever I go.

The problem, I've realized, is that all my other plans were too complicated. Too many layers. Too much preparation. Too many phases. Too many apps to download and people to manipulate. Which means there were way too many things that could go wrong. And usually *did*.

That's why my new plan is *super* simple.

There's only one phase. One layer. One thing to do.

". . . then the whole bottle blew up in his face! It was the funniest thing ever!"

As I approach school, I spot Kyle Bates and some of his friends gathered in a circle near the flagpole, talking and laughing. I would have preferred to start with an easier group, maybe even a one-on-one, but that's not how the plan works.

So I take a deep breath, hitch up the straps of my backpack, and dive in.

"Not as funny as when the cake exploded in the

oven!" Cole Campbell is saying as I push my way into the circle.

"Hey, guys, what are you talking about?"

All four boys turn and look at me like I've just crash-landed from another planet.

"Let me guess: 'Dude-Possible'?" I say when no one speaks.

More stares. A few mouths drop open; others stay sealed shut like they're secured with glue.

I feel my Tummy Tornado start to swirl and I instinctively reach for my phone in my pocket. But I stop myself, remembering that the app is gone. My phone can't help me now.

I take another deep breath and tell the Tummy Tornado to settle down. They're just boys. They're just people. They have brains and hearts and lungs and spleens just like anyone else.

"So," I continue, trying my best to sound interested. "Like, what is the deal with that channel? Why do you guys like it so much?"

Kyle looks to Cole, who looks to Lewis, who looks to Mitchell, like they're all trying to decide who's going to respond first, but still no one does.

So I keep going. "I mean, do they *just* blow things up, or do they do other stuff too?"

"They do other stuff," Kyle says, and everyone else turns to him in disbelief. Like he's betrayed his country.

"Like what?" I say.

"They throw things," Cole says quietly, refusing to look me in the eye. I can't say I blame him after I followed him into the boys' bathroom last week. That was a low point for sure.

"Throw things?" I repeat, trying to understand. "What kind of things?"

"One time," Mitchell Valentine says eagerly, "Dude Nathan threw a golf ball through a second-story window and it landed right in his girlfriend's empty coffee cup and she was, like, 'Dude, why is there a golf ball in my coffee cup?' "

"No way!" I say in disbelief that, surprisingly, I don't have to fake.

"Way," Kyle says with a nod.

"How did they do that? Is it for real? Or is it, like, movie editing?"

"It's for real," Cole says. "They do it, like, a thousand times before they get it right, and then they only post the good one."

"Yeah, but they always include some of the outtakes in one of their 'Epic Fail' videos," Mitchell informs me.

I let out a sigh. "I had my own epic fail last night."

"What happened?" Lewis asks.

I pull up the sleeve of my coat to reveal the blue cast underneath. I expect them all to gasp and fawn over it, the way a bunch of girls would. But instead, they all lean in closer and say, "Cool!" almost in unison, which makes me crack up.

"Did you fall off the roof or something?" Kyle asks with a snort.

"Actually, I did."

And it's like I've just told them I was a celebrity in

disguise. Their faces light up, and all eyes are on me. Even Cole manages to look up.

"How did that happen?" Kyle asks.

"Oh, it's a long story," I begin, delighted that I've managed to capture their attention. "But basically, I climbed out onto the roof to get something and I slipped."

"Did you break it?" Cole asks as Mitchell says, "Did it hurt?" and Lewis says, "Did you get to ride in an ambulance?" and Kyle asks, "How many stories did you fall?"

I chuckle. Who knew boys were so fascinated by injuries. I'm about to start answering their questions when a deep voice booms from behind me, "Emerie Woods, what have I told you about using your phone on school—"

I turn around and hold up my empty hands. "No phone, Mr. Langley. See?"

The Gargoyle scours me as though he's searching for a hidden device. When he can't find one, his face clouds over in confusion.

"We were just talking," I tell him.

"Talking?" he repeats skeptically as his eyes travel from me to each of the boys and then back to me.

"Yup," I say cheerfully. "Just talking."

"Emmy was telling us how she broke her arm," Cole says, and I point to my cast as proof.

I can see Mr. Langley's tongue jabbing at the inside of his cheek, like he's trying to figure out another way he can bust us. But there's nothing written in the P-PUP or any of the other school policies that prohibits us from talking to each other outside of class.

"Uh-huh," Mr. Langley finally says with a grunt before moving on to find someone else to give detention to.

The warning bell rings, and we all share a look of commiseration before turning to head into the building. As I bound up the steps, Kyle hurries to catch up with me.

"I can send you that 'Dude-Possible' video if you want. The one with the golf ball."

I flash him a genuine smile. "That would be great! Thanks!"

My plan is working already.

NEW THEORIES AND OLD FRIENDS

BY THE END of the day, my head is bursting with knowledge. Some of it fascinating, some of it not so fascinating.

For instance, I learned that Archie Evans's obsession with dragons started when he was five and his grandpa bought him a guidebook to mythical creatures. I learned that once you get Matt Clemens talking about ham radios, it's hard to shut him up. I learned that ham radios have nothing to do with pork. They're actually these cool devices that allow you to communicate with people all around the world (without the use of a phone!). I learned that the video game Leo, Victor, and Micah are all obsessed with is called "Ring of Darkness" and it actually has a pretty interesting storyline. I learned that the reason Jeremy Mason is always forgetting his locker combination is because his brain often mixes up numbers and letters. I learned that Eric Garcia's favorite breed of dog is the Cavalier King Charles spaniel and that his family might be getting one for Christmas this year.

All of this I learned just from striking up conversations. It turns out boys aren't that big of a mystery once you get them talking.

But probably the most enlightening of all is what I learned from Jackson Harris, who I sat with today at lunch. He's been working on a theory about the "Magnolia Street" lyrics that completely blows my mind.

"Did you know," Jackson told me as we opened our drinks, "that Berrin James grew up on a street called Louisiana Avenue? And do you know what the state flower of Louisiana is?"

"A magnolia?" I asked, dumbfounded.

"Yup. I think he swapped out the name of the street to protect who the song is about."

"And who do you think it's about?"

Jackson took a sip of his juice and leaned in closer. "Do you remember a few years ago, during an interview with Summer Crush, all the members were asked about their own childhood crushes, and Berrin said he used to be in love with a girl who lived next door to him growing up, but it ended very badly?"

"'Pink-scribbled hearts on the sidewalk,'" I whispered, a chill spreading over me.

"'Back when we were thieves in the night,'" Jackson added with a glimmer in his eyes.

"'I'll race you to the end'!"

Jackson nodded. "Exactly. The lyrics are talking about things he did as a *kid*. Like scribbling on sidewalks, racing through streets, stealing cookies from the pantry."

The chill continued to spread as I recited the beginning of the chorus: "'I've wandered in circles, to find my way home.'"

And then, in unison, we finished the lyric, " 'To Magnolia Street.' "

"Oh my gosh!" I squealed, causing a few people to glance over at us. "You did it! You cracked it!"

Jackson chuckled, looking bashful. "It's just a theory."

"It's the best theory I've heard. Even better than Liza Wu's!"

"You watch 'Crushin' on the Crush'?" Jackson asked, immediately perking up. And then we spent the rest of lunch rehashing all of our favorite videos.

Now, as I close my locker door, I'm feeling pretty good about how today went. But I also know it's only the beginning. And that's the thing about my new plan: it's less of a plan and more of just a way of life.

I loop my left arm through one backpack strap and reach for the other. But the cast makes it difficult, and I can't quite snatch it with my fingers. Just when I'm starting to think I should have put my right arm through first, the strap slips effortlessly onto my shoulder, like someone pushed it up for me.

I snap my head up and jolt in surprise when I see Harper standing there, her own backpack on her shoulders, her expression unreadable.

"Thanks," I say quietly, because despite all the talking I've done today, I still don't know quite what to say to her.

"I heard about your arm," she says, gesturing to my cast, which has been signed by half of the school. That's the best thing about having a cast, I've discovered— everyone wants to sign it. "Does it hurt?"

I shrug. I want to tell her that it doesn't hurt nearly as much as standing in this hallway with my lungs full of trapped air and my throat full of words I'm too afraid to say to her. I want to tell her that the cracks in my bones are nothing compared to the ones I caused in our friendship. But somehow all that comes out is "A little. Not too bad."

"There's a rumor going around that you fell off the roof."

I nod. "Unfortunately, that's true."

"What?" she says, and I'm relieved to see genuine concern on her face. She still cares. That's got to count for something, right?

"Yeah, it was stupid," I say with a chuckle. "I shouldn't have been out there."

I hold tightly to her gaze and try to convey a million things with my mind. How sorry I am. How I'm trying to do better. How I hope someday she'll give me another chance.

But she doesn't seem to get any of that. Because she just hitches up her backpack straps and says, "Okay, well, I better go catch my bus."

I watch her turn away, and it feels like someone has released all the air from my lungs. I deflate like a popped balloon. A slashed tire. A bouncy house that's being packed up and put away at the end of a party. And it feels like everything I did today—every bit of progress that I made—has been for nothing. It's been released right out with the air.

Harper and I have always had our own way of

communicating. Like a secret language. We put on Berrin James to pump each other up. We send funny GIFs to make each other smile. We squeeze each other's hands when we're nervous.

I've always been able to read her like an open book, but lately that book has been closed to me and I feel lost. Like a traveler without a guide. A visitor to a foreign land. I instinctively reach for my phone, but once again I stop myself. Because there's no app to tell you how to make up with your best friend.

But suddenly, I know I can't just let her walk away.

"Harper! Wait!"

I sprint down the hallway and jump in front of her, forcing her to stop. "You were right," I begin breathlessly. "About all of it. I convinced you to like Elliot. I talked you into it. Because of something a stupid app said. And I'm the reason you transferred out of Art at the beginning of the school year. I never should have asked you to do that. It was selfish. I just couldn't imagine not having a single class with you this semester. But I guess the joke's on me. Because now I have *nothing* with you. And it hurts so bad." The tears are starting to flow freely down my face. I know I'm technically in the middle of the hallway and I'm breaking middle school rule number one—no one sees you cry—but I don't care. "I miss you, Harper. Every day. I miss your drawings and your laugh. I miss that look you give me when I'm explaining one of my crazy schemes. But I'm done with those. I swear. I'm done interfering. I'm done meddling. I'm just done."

I sniffle and wipe my cheeks with the back of my

hand. For a long time, Harper says nothing. She just stares at me, her own eyes glistening a little. And I'm suddenly terrified that she's going to walk away again. That nothing I just said mattered at all.

"I know about your new crush," I say quickly, desperate to fill the silence and keep her from leaving. "I saw you with . . ." But I can't even bring myself to say his name. "Your, um, new boy."

"You saw us?" Harper asks, her eyebrows rising.

I nod. "And I saw the painting he did for you. It's really good. And really sweet. I admit the whole thing took me by surprise. I wasn't expecting it. But I swear, I just want you to be happy." I bite my lip. "*Are* you happy?"

Harper doesn't even have to answer. I can see it in her eyes. The way they suddenly sparkle. I can see it in the soft pink glow of her cheeks. But she nods anyway. "Yeah, actually, we're going to the dance together this weekend. Well, we're not technically *going* together, because I live too far away for his mom to pick me up, so we're going to meet here instead. But you know . . ."

I feel a stab in my chest at the thought of Grant and Harper slow dancing—his hands on her waist, her head resting on his shoulder—but I quickly push it away and force myself to smile. "That's great! That'll be so much fun."

She nods. "I hope so. Are you going?"

I shrug. "I don't know."

"You have to go!" Harper says. "It's our first middle school dance. You've been so excited about it!"

"I know, I just . . ." But my voice trails off and I drop my gaze to the floor. I *was* excited. But now, the thought of standing on the sidelines, alone, watching all the couples *I* matched giggle and flirt and hold hands, it might just be too much.

"You should come," Harper says, and there's an insistence in her voice that catches me off guard. When I glance back up at her, I notice the hint of a smile on her face. "I think you'd regret not going."

I hear the rumble of an engine outside, and Harper looks on in panic as, one by one, buses start to pull away from the curb. "I gotta go!" She starts to turn away again, but this time stops all on her own. "What were you doing on the roof, by the way?"

My cheeks warm with embarrassment and I snort out a nervous laugh. "It was . . . nothing. I was just . . . trying to find something I'd lost."

Her eyes flick to mine, and for a second, I wonder if she knows the truth. If she knows what I was really chasing out on that roof.

"And?" she asks. "Did you find it?"

I swallow hard. Because it's a good question. A question I'm still not sure I know the answer to.

"Not yet," I finally say, my throat tight, tears threatening to spill out again. "I'm afraid it might be gone for good."

Harper holds my gaze for a long moment before reaching down and giving my hand a squeeze. "Maybe not for good."

THE PERFECT AMOUNT OF SWEET

INSTEAD OF ORDERING in from one of my apps, Mom suggests we all go out for dinner. After sharing a large veggie supreme pizza, we drive to Lickety Split and storm the shop like pirates ready to plunder and pillage. After everything that's happened in the past few weeks, I don't even cringe when I see Frankie working behind the counter. I guess the days of feeling embarrassed because you mistakenly thought a cute boy was asking you out are over. That version of me feels like another lifetime. I have so many more important things to deal with now.

The boys order chocolate-vanilla swirls with chocolate sprinkles, and Mom and I decide to be adventurous and choose the flavor of the day, key lime pie. Once Frankie hands over the cups, we find a table in the back and sit down.

"What do you think that flavor means?" Ben asks Mom as she takes her first bite.

"What?" Mom asks, confused.

"Mr. Weston's family tradition," Ben reminds her. "Fro-yo fortune-telling."

A smile sneaks onto Mom's face at the mention of

his name. "Oh, right. I don't know. Maybe that we're all going to visit Florida soon?"

"Huh?" Isaac asks.

"Key limes are from Florida."

I snort. "Mom, you're terrible at this game."

"Well, what do *you* think it means?" she fires back at me with a chuckle.

I take my first bite, concentrating hard on the flavor. It's creamy and citrusy and delicious. It might be my new favorite. The perfect balance of tartness and sugar. Just when you think it's too sour, the sweet comes to chase it away. "I think it means the best is yet to come," I decide.

Mom holds up her cup and taps it against mine. "Cheers to that."

As we eat our fro-yo, I think back to the last time we were here. When we ran into Mr. Weston and he made everyone laugh with his lame jokes and strange family traditions. I think about how the twins looked at him, like he was the coolest person they'd ever met. The same way I've been looking at him every day since school started. I think about how they never once felt the need to speak to him in a language he couldn't understand. But mostly, I think about the way he looked at Mom. Like he could keep looking at her for a long time.

And then I think, *Mom could do a lot worse.*

"Mr. Weston is a good guy," I say, focusing hard on scooping up yogurt with my left hand.

"We like him," Isaac declares officially, like he's a CEO making an announcement at a press conference.

"Yeah," Mom agrees. "He's very nice."

When I peer up at her, that same smile is back on her face. I wonder if she even knows she's doing it.

"I think you should go out with him," I say.

The twins drop their spoons into their cups in perfect unison. Mom nearly chokes on her yogurt. "Excuse me?"

"Mr. Weston," I say. "He's nice. And funny. I mean, his jokes are kind of cheesy, but that's forgivable because they're like lame dad jokes. You should go on a date with him."

"Yes!" Isaac squeals.

"Yes! Yes! Yes!" Ben joins in.

Mom laughs and stares at all of us like we're aliens. "You guys, he hasn't even asked me out."

I flash Mom a mischievous grin before digging my spoon back into my cup. "Then I guess you'll just have to ask him."

THE PENCIL GARDEN

I NEVER THOUGHT I'd be getting ready for my first middle school dance alone. Harper and I talked about this moment for years. We were going to do each other's hair and help each other pick out clothes and then have a slumber party afterward so we could rehash every detail of the night.

But now I'm standing in front of the mirror on Saturday night staring at my own reflection, with no one beside me. Not Harper. Not even Darcy. She hasn't said much to me since I told her I deleted the app. I'm starting to wonder who she was really friends with: me or the boy expert.

I've decided to go with a casual look. I'm wearing a pair of cropped black jeans, a gray zip-up hoodie that hides most of my cast, and white-and-black-checkered sneakers with no socks. My hair is hanging long and straight down my back. I thought about dressing up, going all out with frills and ruffles and a complicated side braid, but the moment I put on the first dress choice, I just felt silly.

Besides, I don't plan on staying long. Harper is right,

though—I do think I'd regret not going. I'm just going to go, see what it's like, maybe eat some snacks, and then leave. I'm not sure how long I'll be able to watch Harper and Grant together on the dance floor before my heart squeezes right out of my chest.

Stepping away from the mirror, I peer out the window into Grant's room. The curtains are open and the lights are on, but I don't see Grant. He must already have left. Then, a second later, his head pops up like he was bending down to pick something up, and I see that he's wearing his painting smock.

He turns toward his easel and starts to drag his brush across the canvas.

I check the time on my phone.

It's already seven-thirty and the dance starts at eight. He better hurry. Harper said they were meeting up at school. I wonder if he got so absorbed in his painting that he lost track of time. She's not going to be happy if he's late.

Rummaging through my desk drawer, I find a pencil and clutch it awkwardly between my fingers. It's been a long time since I've done this, and I've never tried to do it with my left hand. I shove open the window and take aim, grateful that Mom hasn't yet gotten around to putting up the screen.

The first try predictably fails: the pencil hits the side of the house and bounces off. I watch it fall down onto the grass between our two houses, and suddenly I remember what we used to call that narrow strip.

"The Pencil Garden," I whisper, a warm, fuzzy feeling spreading through my limbs.

We named it that when we were kids because of how many of the pencils landed eraser side up, like little wooden weeds growing out of the ground.

Back then, everything was sweeter
with Magnolia Street in sight.

No, I scold myself silently. *He likes Harper. He's with Harper. It's too late.*

Swallowing the lump in my throat, I search for another pencil in my desk and chuck it at Grant's window with all my strength.

This one is a direct hit. In fact, I think it might have cracked the window. But it works. Grant puts down his brush and walks over. He examines the place where the pencil hit the glass before opening the window with a scowl.

"That was a bit hard, don't you think?"

"What are you doing?" I blurt out. I didn't plan on sounding so rude, but I can't help myself. Something about Grant just puts me in a sour mood.

Grant looks taken aback. He glances behind him with confusion. "I'm . . . painting."

"It's seven-*thirty*," I tell him with a meaningful look.

Grant stares back at me and I wait for the light-bulb to go off over his head. For him to shout, "Crud! You're right," and then take off for his bathroom. But he doesn't. He just gives me a blank look in response, which instantly infuriates me.

I haven't forgotten what he said about middle school dances. That he thinks they sound awkward and awful. I remember he said, and I quote, "There are *so* many things I'd rather be doing with my time."

I glance suspiciously between him and his easel, and suddenly I understand what's going on here.

He doesn't even care! He's probably just going to paint right up to the last minute and then rip off his smock and go. He's probably not even going to change his clothes! He's going to go to the dance in those old, paint-stained shoes of his and not even think twice about it.

"Don't mess this up, Grant," I say in a warning tone.

"Okay," Grant replies slowly, but that vacant expression never goes away.

"Emmy!" Mom calls from the hallway. "You ready to go?"

"Yeah!" I shout before turning back to Grant. "Look," I say sternly. "I know this thing might not matter to you. Because you're homeschooled and don't care about our 'lame normal-school stuff.'" I make air quotes around the words like I'm impersonating him. "But this matters to *her.* She's been talking about this night for years. *We've* been talking about this night for years. I can guarantee you that *she's* not just going to roll up in the same clothes she wore all day. You need to take this seriously. You need to walk into that closet and find something to wear that's worthy of her." I pause and take a deep breath. "She's my best friend. And I won't let you break her heart."

Grant continues to stare at me, and I hope I've gotten through to him. He opens his mouth to say something, but I don't even want to hear it. I shove the window shut and close the curtains in his face.

A DANCE TO REMEMBER

THE GYM OF Highbury Middle School has been completely transformed. The moment I walk through the doors, it's like I've been transported to a tropical island. There are papier-mâché palm trees lining the walls, cardboard clouds and suns hanging from the ceiling, and, in the corner, a giant surfboard stands upright in a sandbox. People are gathered around it taking selfies.

Music is playing, and the place is packed with seventh graders dressed up and dressed down. I see jeans and dresses, suit jackets and T-shirts, tennis shoes and high heels. Some people are mingling on the sidelines, some are huddled around the food table, and others are dancing in the middle of the gym, under one gigantic sun that kind of looks like a yellow disco ball. It's even more beautiful and magical than I thought it would be. And it's not at all *lame*. I wonder if it's the work of Brianna Brown's mother again.

I keep my eyes peeled for Harper. I know Grant can't possibly be here yet. I check the time on my phone and let out a frustrated snort. If he's not here in fifteen minutes, I'm walking straight to his house and giving him another earful.

It's strange being here alone. Not because I ever expected to come with someone, but because of how many people are here with someone *because* of me. Or, more accurately, because of the app.

As I move through the room, I spot Alexis and Garrett slow dancing. Her head is resting on his shoulder, and he has this relaxed, easy smile on his face that makes me smile a little too. Micah and Vivi are standing by the snack table, and from the looks of it, he's saying something funny, because she's got her head thrown back in laughter. Archie and Delia are sitting on the bleachers, nestled close together, while he shows her something on his phone. Tyler Watkins and Chelsea Costas are also on the dance floor, and I notice she's wearing flats and he's wearing shoes with just the slightest bit of heel, making them the exact same height.

As I watch all the happy couples, I wonder if any of them would have gotten together *without* the app. Without the Love Coordinator stepping in to help.

I guess I'll never know. But I'd like to think so. I'd like to think that destiny has a way of working itself out. I suppose I have to think that way. Otherwise, how am I ever going to get over the fact that I lost my chance with the one boy I might have liked because I was too eager to get involved?

The slow song ends, and a fast one comes on. I continue to make my way through the gym, keeping a lookout for Harper, but I still don't see her. I do, however, spot

Elliot Phillips. He's dancing with Aggie Hawkins, the girl he wanted to try to run into at the movie theater. When he glances over at me, I don't turn away and pretend I didn't see him, like I've been doing for the past few weeks. Instead, I smile, and he smiles back. I guess the whole misunderstanding at the carnival is now officially behind us.

I'm just completing my second loop around the gym when I spot two people walking through the doors hand in hand. My heart lurches to a stop at the sight of them. She looks beautiful in a pink-and-purple-sequined flapper dress with a matching bejeweled headband. He's dressed in dark jeans, a white button-down shirt, and a blue bow tie, with his hair slicked back. I almost giggle. I've never seen him all "done up." He's much cuter than I ever noticed.

I had a feeling this moment might come, and I knew exactly what I'd have to do if it did.

I take a deep, encouraging breath, and walk toward them.

"Hi," she says, slightly confused, like she's not sure what I'm doing here.

"Hi," I say back, keeping my voice steady. Then I turn to him. Because he's the reason I walked over here. He's a wrong that I have yet to right, and it's been eating away at me every day.

"Dev," I begin after another breath. "I need to talk to you." My gaze flicks to Darcy, who returns it with a chilly look. "In private."

"Okay," he says, but I can tell he's reluctant. He's obviously still angry with me, and I don't blame him.

Darcy spots Alexis and Garrett, who have stopped dancing and are now at the drinks table, and strides off to join them.

I turn to Dev, whose eyes anxiously follow Darcy. He's fidgeting with the cuffs of his shirt.

"I . . . ," I begin clumsily. "I wasn't sure if you were still coming. After . . . you know . . ." I gesture vaguely to Darcy, who's now fawning over Alexis's dress.

"It wasn't Darcy's fault," Dev says icily.

"Right." I nod, running through the speech I've been practicing in my mind for the past few days. "Look, please don't be mad at Grant," I tell him. "This wasn't his fault either. It was my fault. I deserve all the blame. I'm the reason Darcy knows your secret."

"But Grant told *you* first," Dev fires back, and I can see traces of the same anger he must have thrown at Grant when he found out.

"I know," I say quickly, "but he only told me because he was worried about you. He wanted so badly to help you, to be there for you. He was just . . . you know . . ." I wheel my good hand around in a circle. "Venting to me."

Dev snorts. "Well, it wasn't his secret to vent."

I sigh. I've officially run out of rehearsed speech. I have no planned words left. I'm not sure I have any *un*rehearsed words left either. But I can't just leave it there. I can't let Grant take the fall for my mistake. "You're right," I say in exasperation. "But he only told me because he trusted me. Because I swore he *could* trust me. And he believed me." I close my eyes for just a moment, but it's enough. Enough to conjure all sorts of memories: Rabbits and dinosaurs. Chalk drawings on the sidewalk. Pencils sticking straight out from the grass like they grew that way.

And as soon as my eyes open again, the words come.

"We've been friends since we were three years old," I tell Dev. "We grew up together. We went trick-or-treating together every year. We even had matching costumes. We played hopscotch and freeze tag and Marco Polo. We camped out in his backyard and played pirates in my front yard. I knew the names of every stuffed animal he owned, which one was for sleeping and which one was for when he was sick and which one was for long car trips. We were inseparable."

I feel tears glistening in my eyes, but I blink them away and keep going.

"But then, somewhere along the way, we just grew apart. We grew *up*. We weren't kids anymore. And I guess, deep down, I believed that that meant we couldn't be friends anymore either. He's a boy and I'm a girl, and it just wouldn't work. But that day, when he told me about"—I lower my voice—"your parents . . . I think we both saw a glimpse of what we used to have. For a brief moment, our old friendship was back, and I know that's the only reason he told me. Because for that brief moment, I was the girl he used to know. The girl he could trust with any secret."

I drop my gaze as something heavy settles over me. It drags me down, making me feel like I might sink right through the gymnasium floor. "But he was wrong," I whisper, "I wasn't that girl. I had become someone else.

Someone I didn't even recognize. And that's the girl who betrayed you. Not Grant."

When I peer back up at Dev, he has this pensive, far-off look on his face, like he's absorbing everything I said, processing it all. Either that or he's trying to remember whether he finished all his algebra homework.

I don't know. I can't read his mind.

Dev glances over at Darcy, who's now tossing us worried looks. He breathes out a sigh, and I desperately want to know what it means. Is it a sigh of forgiveness? A sigh of rejection? A sigh of "I'm sorry, Emmy. That's just not good enough"?

Unfortunately, I'll have to add that to the growing list of things that I don't know. Things that I *can't* know. That I'll just have to wait and see how they turn out. Because Dev flashes me one more regretful look and says, "I should go," before turning and heading toward Darcy.

I stand alone near the door, watching him sidle up to the drinks table and put his arm around Darcy's shoulders. I never thought those two would make it. With all the drama of the past few weeks, I thought they'd be over before the dance ever arrived. Maybe they'll live happily ever after. Or maybe they'll break up next week.

Either way, I'm not getting involved.

I lean against one of the papier-mâché palm trees and cast my gaze across the gym. The current song comes to an end and a new song begins. Within three notes, everyone breaks out in screams and charges the dance floor. It's a Japanese pop song that became popular this summer because the girl in the video does a dance that makes her look like she's swimming. No one knows what the lyrics mean but *everyone* knows the dance. I'm so distracted watching hundreds of my classmates front- and backstroke across the gym, I don't even notice the two people who have just walked through the door.

That is until Harper taps me on the shoulder and I turn around to see her standing before me, wearing an adorable coral-colored, flutter-strap crochet dress that must be brand-new because I've never seen it in her closet before. Her hair is done up in a tight ballerina bun that sits on top of her head and her cheeks look like they've been sprinkled with fairy dust because they're actually sparkling.

But despite how gorgeous she looks, it's not her who I can't stop staring at. It's the boy standing next to her. He's dressed in his usual jeans and T-shirt but now he's wearing a cool black-and-white-striped blazer over it and his dark hair is still wet from the shower. I'm so stunned to see him, I can barely even speak his name. *"Robby?"*

CLOSING THE GAP

I CONTINUE TO stare as Robby lifts his hand and gives me a silent wave.

"Have you two met?" Harper asks, seemingly oblivious to the shock radiating off me in waves. "Emmy, this is Robby Martinez. Robby, this is . . ." She pauses, like she's trying to figure out what to call me. My friend? My best friend? My former friend? Some girl who I used to know before she completely humiliated me at a school carnival and I'll never forgive for the rest of my life?

Finally, she just finishes with "Emmy."

"Yeah," I say quickly. "We've met. In detention, actually."

Robby nods, looking embarrassed.

"You were in detention?" Harper shrieks, and I honestly don't know if she's talking to me or Robby because I'm not looking at her. I'm still staring at Robby, my mind churning.

"Wait a minute," I say, pointing between Harper and the dark-haired boy standing next to her. "You and him are . . . This is the boy who . . . When did you . . ." Finally, I get so frustrated with my inability to finish a sentence,

I just huff and say to Robby, "*You* painted that picture in her locker?"

Harper's brow furrows. "Who else would have painted it?" She turns to give Robby an adoring look. "Although he was too embarrassed to give it to me himself, so he had Cole Campbell slip it into my locker."

Cole Campbell? That's what he was doing lurking around Harper's locker?

"B-b-but . . . ," I stammer, once again unable to form a complete sentence. "I thought that . . . and Grant was . . . and you were . . ."

Even though I'm not making one bit of sense, Harper still seems to catch at least a smidgen of my confusion. "Grant has been *amazing*. Robby invited me to go to this art museum with him, but I was super nervous because I don't know much about analyzing paintings and stuff and I didn't want to come off like a total airhead, so Grant offered to show me a documentary about how to look at art in museums."

"WHAT?" The word is so loud and so forceful, a few people still doing the swimming dance peer over at us in concern.

"I went to his house," Harper says, clearly just as confused by my reaction. "To watch the documentary."

"So he didn't . . . he doesn't . . ."

This time, however, I don't need to finish the sentence aloud, because I've already finished it in my mind.

"Emmy, are you okay?" Harper asks. "You look a little—"

But I'll never know what I look like, because I don't

wait for her to finish. "I gotta go!" I shout as I'm already halfway out the door.

"Good luck!" someone calls after me. It's not until I'm racing down the hallway of the school that I realize the voice belonged to Robby.

My legs are on fire. My lungs burn. But I keep running. Faster and faster, until the wind is whipping through my hair and slapping against my cheeks. It's a good thing I wore sneakers and jeans, instead of the dress-and-wedge-heel combo that Darcy picked out for me.

The whole way back to my street, the last week of my life is flashing before my eyes. Every sight, sound, and thought playing in high-speed reverse, until I get all the way back to the football game. Our walk home. Grant's voice is echoing in my ears like speakers turned up too loud.

"Have you ever used your boy expertise to find out if someone likes you?"

"Really? You figured out that a boy likes you?"

"So you never even thought about liking him back?"

"You and Harper are really close. I wouldn't want anything to come between that."

Oh my gosh! We *were* having two different conversations that day. I was talking about Elliot and he thought I was talking about *him*.

My chest squeezes tighter and I run even faster.

This is all such a mess! How could I have been so wrong . . . *again*? Will I ever get this right?

I round the corner. My bare feet are aching inside my

sneakers. I think I've picked up about seven blisters on the way home, one for every block.

By the time I get to Grant's house, I'm doubled over, gasping for air. But I muster one final ounce of strength as I reach out, ring the doorbell, and run.

Winded and panting, I watch from nearby as the door opens and Grant peers out curiously at his empty front porch. I wait, trying to call to him with my eyes, trying to pull his attention toward me with my mind, trying to summon our nine-year connection. It has to count for something, right?

I don't know if it's my mind, or fate, or just the sound of my labored breathing that does it, but eventually Grant turns, peers out into the night, and sees me standing in the small triangular-shaped patch of grass between our two driveways.

International waters.

The safe zone.

Where no one can be tagged. No one can win. No one can lose. And all disagreements, big or small, cease to exist. It's the place where two warring countries are forced to get along.

With a puzzled expression, Grant calls out something to his parents before closing the door behind him and walking toward me. I see the uncertainty in his gait. He's not sure what this is about, but he knows something is up. He has to, after I yelled at him from my window earlier, lecturing him about not breaking Harper's heart. Jeez, he must have been so confused!

But I don't give him a chance to speak. I don't want any more distractions or misunderstandings or delays. As soon as he steps onto the grass, I say, "Do you want to go to the dance with me?"

Grant startles and flashes me what has to be *the* most baffled look I've ever seen on his face. "What?"

"I know, I know, you think it sounds awkward and awful, but I'm hoping that if you go with me, you might change your mind." I pause long enough to catch my breath. "Because even though there are so many other things you'd rather be doing with your time, there's nothing else I would rather be doing with mine."

In the faint glow of the streetlamps, I catch the ghost of a smile on Grant's face. But it quickly morphs back into confusion. "Isn't the dance tonight?"

I nod. "Yeah, it's happening right now. Seven blocks from here."

This only seems to bewilder him more. He glances in the direction of the school, like he can see it from here, and then back at me and the thin layer of sweat on my forehead. "Did you just *run* from there?"

"Yes," I say, feeling my confidence slip. He clearly thinks I'm insane. What if he hasn't forgiven me for what I did to Dev? What if he never forgives me? What if that one mistake has erased all the things he was feeling before?

"Look, I was wrong," I say, finally getting my breathing under control. "*Again*. About everything. I thought you . . ." I shake my head. "It doesn't matter what I thought. The point is, I'm so sorry for what I did. You were right. It was low and selfish. It's no secret that I haven't been a very good friend. To you or to anyone."

"Friend," Grant repeats the word with a curious kind of inflection.

"Yes," I say hurriedly. "I've been a bad friend. And I want to make it up to you. So will you *please* go to the dance with me?"

"So you want to go as friends?" Grant asks, and I don't need a magic app to recognize the disappointment in his voice.

It instantly fills me with hope.

With giddiness.

With all the confidence that I felt slip away just a moment ago.

It makes me believe that maybe I haven't completely lost my chance.

My heart starts to pound, and I *know* it has nothing to do with running seven blocks. I swallow and shake my head again. "No."

"No?" he confirms.

"No," I say again, this time much more assertively.

Grant raises an eyebrow and gives me that know-it-all smirk that used to drive me crazy. And I guess it still does, except this time, it's sort of a good kind of crazy. "So then what do you want to go as?"

I roll my eyes and feel my cheeks warm. "Are you going to make me say it? Aloud?"

He crosses his arms over his chest. "Yeah, I think I am. I mean, I can't read your mind. I'm certainly no girl expert."

"Doesn't that assume all girls are the same?" I retort playfully.

"Oh, I know they're not," Grant says. "They're all mysterious in very different ways. Which is why I want to make sure there are no *gaps*."

"Gaps?" I repeat with the same skepticism he showed me when I first used that word a few weeks ago, standing on this very patch of grass.

"Yes, gaps. Between what you say and what you mean."

He's so totally mocking me right now. But I don't care. We've been playing games since we were three years old. I know how to handle Grant Knight.

"Gaps are bad," I tell him in all seriousness.

"Very bad," he agrees.

"Gaps can be problematic."

"Which is why," Grant says knowledgably, "I think it's best if we always say exactly what we mean and leave nothing open for interpretation, because—"

But I don't let him finish. I take one step toward him and press my lips to his, closing the gap for good.

ALL GOOD

"I DEFINITELY LIKE the red ones better," I tell Mom as she balances on one foot and then the other to show me her two shoe options. But honestly, it doesn't matter what she wears. She always looks beautiful.

"Are you sure?" Mom asks, and I immediately detect the anxiousness in her voice. "Maybe I should try on the jeans again. Is this dress too dressy? I mean, I don't even know where we're going. What if he shows up in sweatpants and a baseball cap?"

"He won't," I say decisively, and nearly giggle aloud at the image of Mr. Weston wearing a baseball cap. Or sweatpants, for that matter. "This is a man who wears vests and ties to school every day."

Mom surrenders with a sigh. "I can't believe I'm taking dating advice from my twelve-year-old *daughter*."

I shrug. "I can't believe I'm giving dating advice to my *mother*."

We both laugh, and Mom rummages through her jewelry box for a pair of earrings.

It's been a few weeks since the middle school dance, and I'd like to say that things have gone back to normal, but that's simply not true. It feels like everything has changed around here. Mom's going on a date with Mr. Weston, and she has a brand-new client who, thankfully, is super easy to please and loves all of her ideas. The boys hardly ever use their alien language anymore now that I taught Mom how to understand it. And the doctor says my arm is healing so well, I can get my cast off in two weeks! A week early! I'm definitely looking forward to using my right hand again.

"Okay, the twins are at a friend's house," Mom says as she fastens the backs of her earrings. "I'll have my phone with me, and the ringer turned on all night. Are you sure you're going to be okay?"

"If you're asking if I'm going to fall off the roof again, then no."

Mom gives me her "That's not funny" look.

"Mom," I whine. "I'll be fine. We're just going to eat dinner and watch a movie. There will be no roof climbing whatsoever. Don't worry."

"And you can order food from your phone?" Mom confirms.

"Yup. My phone curfew starts in ten minutes. I'll do it before then."

As much as I complained about the phone curfew at first, I actually kind of appreciate it now. It was me who asked Mom to turn it back on. I think she might have been right. I *do* need some limits when it comes to my phone. I mean, don't get me wrong; I still love *all* my apps. I just don't need to be using them *all* the time.

"Ugh. I feel weird," Mom says, clutching her stomach.

"Is it a kind of swirling sensation?" I ask, sounding like a doctor treating a patient. "Like something is spinning round and round in your stomach?"

"Yeah!" Mom says, looking impressed. "How did you know?"

"That's a Tummy Tornado," I say expertly. "It must be hereditary. Don't worry. It'll pass. It's probably just an EF-1. No permanent damage. Maybe a few broken windows."

Mom looks at me like I'm speaking a foreign language. "Huh?"

I laugh. "Just take deep breaths!"

She inhales deeply and her shoulders relax. "This is my first date in fourteen years," she tells me. "What if I've forgotten how to . . . you know, *talk* to men."

"He's just a person, Mom."

She takes another breath. "Right. You're right."

The doorbell rings, and Mom and I both turn to each other. I'm excited. She looks like she's going to be sick.

"I'll get it!" I shout as I bound down the steps.

I swing open the door, fully expecting to see my Computer Science teacher standing on our front porch, but it's Harper instead. She waves goodbye to her mom, who's waiting at the curb, and steps inside.

"How's she doing?" Harper immediately asks, glancing upstairs.

"She's nervous."

"She'll be fine!" Harper says.

"That's what I keep telling her."

"So when are we going over to Grant's?" she asks.

"I told him we'd come over around six."

"Perfect. I told Robby to come around then too. What is this documentary Grant is showing us?"

I scrunch up my nose. "I think it's about snails?"

"Snails?" Harper repeats in disgust.

"I'm trying to have an open mind," I tell her.

The four of us have started a regular movie night. It's super fun. We order food and eat popcorn and trade off who gets to choose the movie. It's been cool getting to know Robby more. He's really sweet, and it turns out he actually does talk. It just takes him a while to open up. It's like he wants to make sure he can trust you before he lets you in. Knowing how middle school can go, I don't think it's a terrible strategy.

"Oh, I almost forgot," Harper says, reaching into her bag. She pulls out her sketch pad, rips off the top sheet, and hands it to me. "This is for you. I did it in class today. It's to replace the other one."

I turn it over and immediately gasp. It's stunning. Even better than her Cupid one. In this drawing, Harper has depicted me as a cartoon rabbit with bunny ears, a fluffy tail, and hearts where my eyes should be. The heart eyes are staring across the page at a little, smiling Tyrannosaurus rex. And at the bottom of the drawing, next to her signature, Harper has written:

Emerie Woods: In Love

I giggle and pull Harper into a hug. "Thank you! I love it!"

The doorbell rings a second time, and I glance eagerly at Harper. "It's him," I whisper.

Harper gives me a giddy smile as I turn and swing the door open once again. This time, it *is* my Computer Science teacher. He's dressed in dark jeans and a collared shirt with the sleeves rolled up, and he smells of some kind of piney aftershave. I thought maybe it would be weird to see Mr. Weston standing on my front porch, but it's not. Because outside of school, I've realized, he doesn't really look like Mr. Weston. He just looks like a guy. A very *nervous* guy.

"Emmy!" he says, using my real name for the first time since I've known him. "Hi! How are you?" There's a definite tremor to his voice, which kind of warms my heart.

"Good," I say. "How are you?"

"Oh, you know . . ." He chuckles and runs his hands through his already-tousled hair. "Feeling like I might throw up, but otherwise good."

I fight back a groan. Honestly, what's wrong with adults? They really need to chill out.

"Oh, hi, Harper!" he says, noticing her for the first time. "I haven't seen you in a while. How's Art?"

"It's great! I *really* love it."

"Well, we miss you in class, but I'm glad you found your place."

I turn and give Harper a smile. "Me too."

"Hi, Jim." We all turn to see my mother descending the stairs, but from the way Mr. Weston is staring at her, his eyes all goggly and his mouth open, you would think she was *floating* down them.

He seems to forget how to speak for a moment, because the next word out of his mouth is not really a word. "Hu-hu-hi," he stammers, which I think translates to "Hi." But I can't be sure. I don't speak Man.

"So." Mom turns to me with her eyebrows raised. "Everything's good? You're good? It's all good?"

I roll my eyes. "Yup, we're . . . *good*. We're going to order some food, make some popcorn, and then head over to Grant's. His parents are both home."

She takes a deep breath. "Okay. Well, call me if you need me. I won't be out too late." She gives me a kiss on the forehead before following Mr. Weston out the door.

"So," Harper says as soon as they're gone. "You're really okay with this?"

"With what?"

"Your mom," she says, and I notice she's studying me, searching my face for cracks. "Dating your *teacher*."

I let my gaze drift out the window, watching as Mr. Weston walks Mom to his car, and I'm filled with a warm, fuzzy sensation.

"Yeah," I say, turning to smile at Harper. "I think they make a good match."

ACKNOWLEDGMENTS

Thank you again to my wonderful editors, Wendy Loggia and Alison Romig; my agent, Jim McCarthy; the talented Simini Blocker for the most adorable cover ever; and all the wonderful people at Delacorte Press/Random House Books for Young Readers.

Thank you to Joanne, who will always be my coauthor, even if her name is not on the book, and to my family, especially Charlie, who is the only boy for me.

And as always, thank you to my readers. I'm so happy the universe matched us together.